"Let's start that scheme of yours."

Nonoa Miyamae

The girl at the top of the school pecking order. She's got a strong fashion sense and inherited her natural blond hair from her American grandmother. She's like a magnet who attracts those around her, regardless of gender. But there's something behind her facade of being the most popular girl at school…

"You took a bite, so now you better clench your jaw and not let go."

"Want a reset?"

Chisaki Sarashina

The current student council vice president. Also known as one of the two most beautiful second-years at Seirei Academy and nicknamed Donna. She supports her boyfriend, Touya, in the student council with her overwhelming physical strength. A superhero in the form of a high school girl—her only fault being that she's a bit too hot-blooded.

Masachika Kuze

Alisa's running mate for the election and the former vice president of the student council in middle school. While he took the last name Kuze after his parents' divorce, he grew up as a child prodigy, carrying the hopes of the Suou family.

Contents

Не падай духом⋯⋯♥

Alya
Sometimes Hides Her
Feelings in
Russian

3

Sunsunsun
Illustration by **Momoco**

YEN
ON
New York

3

Translation by Matthew Rutsohn
Cover art by Momoco

This book is a work of fiction. Names, characters, places, and incidents are the product of the author's imagination or are used fictitiously. Any resemblance to actual events, locales, or persons, living or dead, is coincidental.

TOKIDOKI BOSOTTO ROSHIAGO DE DERERU TONARI NO ARYA SAN Vol.3
©Sunsunsun, Momoco 2021
First published in Japan in 2021 by KADOKAWA CORPORATION, Tokyo.
English translation rights arranged with KADOKAWA CORPORATION, Tokyo, through TUTTLE-MORI AGENCY, INC., Tokyo.

English translation © 2023 by Yen Press, LLC

Yen On
150 West 30th Street, 19th Floor
New York, NY 10001

Visit us at yenpress.com • facebook.com/yenpress • twitter.com/yenpress • yenpress.tumblr.com
instagram.com/yenpress

First Yen On Edition: May 2023
Edited by Yen On Editorial: Leilah Labossiere
Designed by Yen Press Design: Liz Parlett

Yen On is an imprint of Yen Press, LLC.
The Yen On name and logo are trademarks of Yen Press, LLC.

Library of Congress Cataloging-in-Publication Data
Names: Sunsunsun, author. | Momoco, illustrator. | Rutsohn, Matthew, translator.
Title: Alya sometimes hides her feelings in Russian / Sunsunsun ; illustration by Momoco ; translation by Matthew Rutsohn.
Other titles: Tokidoki bosotto roshiago de dereru tonari no Arya san. English
Description: First Yen On edition. | New York, NY : Yen On, 2022–
Identifiers: LCCN 2022029973 | ISBN 9781975347840 (v. 1 ; trade paperback) |
    ISBN 9781975347864 (v. 2 ; trade paperback) | ISBN 9781975367572 (v. 3 ; trade paperback)
Subjects: CYAC: Language and languages—Fiction. | Friendship—Fiction. | Schools—Fiction. |
    LCGFT: Humorous fiction. | School fiction. | Light novels.
Classification: LCC PZ7.1.S8676 Ar 2022 | DDC [Fic]—dc23
LC record available at https://lccn.loc.gov/2022029973

ISBNs: 978-1-9753-6757-2 (paperback)
        978-1-9753-6758-9 (ebook)

10 9 8 7 6 5 4 3 2

TPA

Printed in South Korea

PROLOGUE **Suou**

In the reputedly upscale residential part of town, where large homes lined the streets on each side, stood a certain mansion. It was a Western-style house with a manicured garden and a rich history expressed by its classical architecture. This historic mansion dated back hundreds of years and drew attention even among all the other luxurious houses in the neighborhood, but it was simply known as home to the Suou family.

Three members of the family were having dinner at a long rectangular table. The atmosphere was serene and elegant. The head of the household, Gensei Suou, sat at the head of the table with his back to the fireplace. Although he was sixty-nine years old, his body was still strong, showing absolutely no signs of his age, and he had the perfect posture of a distinguished individual. The wrinkles creasing his face made him look not only dignified but also somehow unconquerable. They were like the rings in the trunk of a large tree that had weathered devastating storms over the years. Sitting across from Gensei were his daughter, Yumi, and his granddaughter, Yuki. With the exceptions of height and figure, Yuki bore a striking resemblance to her mother. In fact, looking at Yumi was like seeing Yuki in the future. While Yuki had her mother's nose, mouth, and profile, they didn't have the same eyes. Unlike her daughter's, Yumi's eyes seemed to permanently droop, and she had a mole under the right one. That and her melancholic expression made her seem timid—the complete opposite of her father, Gensei.

"I heard you had a student assembly the other day," stated Gensei slowly in the middle of their meal. "Furthermore, I heard Masachika and the young lady from Taniyama Heavy Industries participated?"

"Yes. However, to be clear, my brother was Alisa Kujou's assistant."

Yuki explained only so there would be no misunderstandings, but she knew that Ayano, who was standing behind her, had already given him a detailed rundown. Gensei, however, snorted haughtily, as if he didn't care in the least—which was entirely in character for him.

"I thought she would put up more of a fight, since I remember her being your last standing rival in middle school, but…she ran out mid-debate? Tsk."

"I am sure she had her reasons."

"Hmph! The reason doesn't matter. The issue is that she made Masachika look like a good candidate for student council president."

He downed his wine in disgust, then placed the empty glass back onto the table. Ayano's grandmother, who stood behind him, immediately poured him another glass. After she finished pouring, Gensei turned his penetrating gaze on Yuki.

"Listen. I don't care who you are up against. Losing isn't an option. You *are* going to become the president of the student council, no matter what."

"Yes, Grandfather. I will."

"While you may not be as talented as Masachika, you understand your obligations as someone born with a gift like yours… unlike Masachika, who took the talent and environment he was blessed with and threw it all away," spat Gensei bitterly. Yumi lowered her gaze.

"Are you listening? The world isn't fair. Wealth, family, appearance, talent… You are either born with it or you are not. Yuki, you were born with it all, and that is why you have to give back to the world. That is the responsibility of those who have privilege."

Gensei Suou's absolute set of values, like this one about responsibility, had been carved into Yuki's and Masachika's minds ever since they were children.

"It is a sin to be born with ability yet let it go to waste. Those with a gift are obligated to use it for the sake of society. That is why, no matter what happens, you must not lose to someone who abandoned their obligations. Do you understand, Yuki?"

Her grandfather's harsh words toward her brother—who she loved more than anything in the world—tore at her heart, but she did not express even a hint of pain. She replied with a graceful smile and nod:

"Yes, Grandfather."

"Yuki."

"...? Yes, Mother?"

Yuki was on her way back to her room after dinner when her mother stopped her, which was quite out of the ordinary, so she turned around curiously.

"Is something the matter?" Yuki asked.

"..."

But Yumi continued to stare at the floor in silence. It seemed she was having trouble getting the words out. She eventually fought through it and quietly asked:

"Are you and Masachika...getting along?"

"Yes, of course," Yuki replied with a smile.

"...Oh." Her mother nodded, looking away.

"Uh... Is there something wrong? Did you want to talk about him?"

"Oh, no. It's nothing… You still have Chinese class tonight, right?"

"Yes. Online, though."

"Oh, okay… Have fun."

"I will."

After bowing gracefully, Yuki returned to her room with Ayano by her side, Yumi watching her every step of the way.

"Phew…"

Yuki sighed softly once she closed the door to her room.

"…Ayano," she called to the girl behind her without turning around.

"Yes, Lady Yuki?"

"I need you to be my body pillow for a minute."

"As you wish."

Most people would have thought they had misheard what she said, but Ayano promptly agreed and lay down on the bed as though she were used to it. Yuki then silently crawled on top of her, wrapped her arms around the other girl, and buried her face in Ayano's bosom. Yuki rolled side to side while holding Ayano tight, rubbing her face in circles on Ayano's breasts. Ayano simply allowed Yuki to have her way with her, neither embracing Yuki nor rubbing her head. She knew it would hurt her master's pride, so she didn't say a word and committed to being a body pillow. A few minutes had passed when Yuki suddenly lifted her head, kneeled up on the bed, and exhaled with deep satisfaction.

"I'm back and better than ever!"

"Was that enough?"

"Yep. Thanks. Boobs really are incredible, aren't they?" praised Yuki with passion as she got off the bed and headed over to her computer.

"Allow me to brush your hair."

"Oh, thanks."

Ayano began fixing Yuki's hair, which had become disheveled from rolling around in the bed so much. Each stroke was gentle and loving, and Ayano's eyes were filled with unlimited affection.

"You don't have to make it look perfect, though, okay? They'll only be able to see me from the shoulders up. More importantly, do you think you could get me something to drink?"

"Very well. Would you like some coffee?" ,

"Sure. I've got to stay up late tonight anyway so I can watch *Brain Hazard* and *Dream*. *Brain Hazard*'s supposed to be especially good tonight. Heh-heh-heh… I'm not letting you get any sleep tonight, brother. ♪"

Yuki smirked with unmistakable amusement in anticipation of their late-night anime discussion, a nightly custom whenever something good was on. Ayano, meanwhile, silently exited the bedroom, exhaling a relieved sigh in her mind as her master returned to normal.

CHAPTER 1

Two rom-coms in one.

"Yo, Kuze! That debate last week was incredible!"

"I heard you took down Taniyama. I'm impressed. I wish I hadn't had cram school so I could have gone."

It was the following Monday after the debate. Masachika was welcomed with genuine curiosity and praise the moment he stepped inside the classroom.

"That's too bad, man. You should have been there. Seriously."

"Yeah, it was intense. I've honestly never seen a more exciting debate in my life."

The debate had apparently been the talk of the class before Masachika had even gotten there. He'd heard a few students gushing about the event on his way to the classroom as well. That was simply a testament to how exciting the student conference the week before had been.

"To tell the truth, I thought the debate was over the moment I heard Taniyama's argument."

"Yeah, and the fact that you two didn't have any questions for her after her argument made me even more confident that she'd already won."

"Hey, what was your strategy for that debate anyway?"

"Come on, guys. At least let me put my bag down first."

With a pacifying grin, he put out a hand to hold his overly enthusiastic classmates back while he headed over to his desk.

You guys could just ask the main speaker over there if you're so curious...

He thought this as he looked over at said main speaker—Alisa Kujou. Though she had been the star of the debate, nobody was gathering around her. The sight made it painfully clear how unapproachable she seemed to fellow students.

It's not like I don't see where they're coming from, but she's going to be running for student council president, so this isn't going to work.

How was she going to gain support from her peers and win if her own classmates wouldn't talk to her? That's why Masachika decided to proactively drag Alisa into the conversation.

"Morning, Alya."

"Good morning," she replied, lifting her head and taking her nose out of her textbook, which she always had open before class. She was reviewing before the day's lesson as if the gossiping going on had nothing to do with her.

She probably doesn't know how to react to all these people talking about her...but her behavior's making it hard for anyone to approach her, too.

In his mind, Masachika smiled a bit evily at his socially inept partner.

"They want to hear about the debate you put on last week!" he exclaimed, gesturing with his eyes to their classmates behind him.

"Huh?"

Despite her bewilderment, he set down his bag, turned around to face their classmates, who seemed just as confused as Alisa, and raised a hand to excuse himself.

"All right, guys. If you have any questions, Alya here will answer them in my place...because I've got a game to play, and it's not gonna play itself."

""""Seriously?!"""" shouted the class half jokingly while Masachika whipped out his phone with a serious expression. Nevertheless, he stared at his phone screen and shamelessly launched an app.

"I'm counting on you, Alya."

"W-wait. I—"

The troubled star of the debate and her classmates observed one another from either side of Masachika. As the students exchanged glances, wondering who would be the first to talk, Masachika discreetly glanced at Hikaru, who was sitting in front of him, and his friend immediately knew what Masachika was trying to communicate.

"So, Alisa, I was wondering about your speech. Did you come up with that all by yourself? Or did Masachika help?" asked Hikaru with a slightly embarrassed smile.

"Huh? Oh... I created the speech. Kuze did give me some advice, though."

"Oh, wow. I was surprised, to be honest. I had no idea you were going to be that good at debating."

"Th-thanks...?"

The other students started chiming in as well—thanks to Hikaru initiating conversation—until eventually everyone was speaking their mind as though their curiosity had overcome their anxiety.

"Was not asking any questions during the Q and A session part of your strategy?"

"Yes, it was something we had planned before the debate."

"Then, was Masachika suddenly taking over during the second half of the debate part of your strategy, too?"

"That actually took me by surprise as well..."

Although unaccustomed to this type of interaction, Alisa did her best to answer the questions while Masachika nodded to himself, content with how she was handling things as he gazed at his random loot box reward for the day. Alisa was the center of attention in

Class B for once…but everything suddenly changed the moment a certain male student opened his mouth.

"Too bad about what happened, though, right? Like, Taniyama just ran away before the debate even finished. It was a pretty disappointing ending to a good show. Know what I mean?"

Perhaps he was trying to butter Alisa up but was overly excited by the chance to finally speak with such a beautiful girl. Other guys began to get in on it as well, until they were all basically putting Alisa on a pedestal and absolutely trashing Sayaka.

"Yeah, for real. Challenging someone to a debate, then running off like that? Pathetic."

"Yeah, that was pitiful. She ran away the moment things started to get hard."

"Alisa won the debate the moment the Q and A started. Sayaka used to seem unbeatable, but she gave up the moment someone actually stood up to her."

Maybe they were all waiting for Alisa to say, "Yeah, she was all bark and no bite," but Alisa's reaction told a different story.

"…"

Her lips were pressed firmly together, and her brow was furrowed. She was clearly displeased, and her classmates were taken aback, at a loss for words to continue the conversation. In the midst of that awkward silence, Alisa stood up from her seat.

"Kuze. Come on."

"Hmm? All right."

Masachika slipped his phone into his pocket and got out of his chair, then acted as if he had just remembered something.

"Ohhh, right. We have student council business we need to take care of still. Sorry, guys. Looks like we'll pick this back up later."

He briefly apologized to his classmates before swiftly following

Alisa out of the room. He kept up with her brisk pace until they arrived at the student council room.

"So? What happened back there?"

But Alisa didn't respond, her brow still pinched together. He had a good idea why she was upset, though.

"You didn't like them talking bad about Sayaka like that, huh?"

"…Of course not. She—"

"She challenged us to a debate, but she ran away before it was over. They didn't say anything that wasn't true."

"But still…!"

Alisa seemed to have raised her voice unintentionally, but she didn't continue that sentence. Instead, she gritted her teeth in frustration.

Masachika sighed as she stayed silent, struggling to put her feelings into words. He understood how she felt, and that was exactly why he'd sighed. She was far too socially inept.

"We now know what was going through Sayaka's mind when she challenged us, and we know why she ran away during the debate. So I can understand how frustrated you must feel when people who don't know the details just focus on how she took off."

"…" Alisa listened in silence.

"But to be honest, we don't need to feel guilty for fighting fair and square, and we shouldn't have to feel bad no matter what Sayaka says. Am I wrong?"

"…I know, but we didn't actually win. The debate essentially ended in a no contest, right?" Alisa argued.

Winning the way they had wasn't enough for her. Because she knew that Sayaka had reacted to Alisa teaming up with Masachika. They were the root cause of her rage, and Alisa didn't want to admit that she'd won simply due to her opponent forfeiting. Her pride wouldn't allow that.

"So what are you going to do? Hypothetically speaking, of course. What would you do if everyone suddenly decided that the debate was a no contest and didn't count? Sayaka would be able to redeem herself, but...our victory would be all for nothing. Praising and glorifying the loser would end up cheapening the victor's win as well."

"..." Alisa fell silent again.

"More importantly, we don't even know if Sayaka would want that. Receiving pity and charity from the person who beat her could crush what little pride she has left. Plus, it was her partner, Nonoa, who admitted defeat."

"...I know that."

But Alisa's frustration didn't ease, no matter how reasonable Masachika may have sounded. She probably realized this, but that still didn't mean she was happy about it. If they were logical about this, their best choice of action would be to pretend not to notice. They should accept the victory Nonoa gave them and nonchalantly act like winners. That was how Masachika felt, and Alisa, too, likely believed this to be the right decision. However, he didn't call her stubborn or push her away. He just watched over her.

She's really beautiful... Almost blindingly so.

Masachika could have continued trying to convince her to get over it if their only goal was to win the election, but there was something more important to him than the election: protecting Alisa's brilliant glow. He wanted her to be satisfied with how she became the student council president. That was why...

"Anyway, if we were to act rationally, that would be our best option, but...it doesn't really matter."

"Huh?"

"What matters is what you want to do. Come on. Quit trying to smother your feelings. Stop with that huffy expression and spit it out. Tell me everything on your mind."

Alisa pouted after suddenly being teased like that.

"What do I want to do? I want to help Taniyama. But that's—"

"All right. Then let's help her," Masachika said with a shrug.

"Huh?"

She was caught off guard by how easily he agreed to help, and her expression filled with disbelief.

"...Are you sure? I mean, you said it yourself. She might not even want our help. I'd be doing this for me. Besides, this might make the effort you put into the debate all for nothing..."

"That's fine. Better to go into the closing ceremony with no regrets than to drag this baggage along with us," he replied casually, and Alisa began to look a bit guilty.

"I'm sorry for this. I know it's probably aggravating."

"Don't worry about it. I told you, right? I'll be there for you."

I will be by your side to support you. Alisa suddenly remembered what Masachika had promised her.

"Kuze..."

Something welled up inside her heart as she stood before Masachika, who was bashfully avoiding her eyes and scratching his head. Alisa clasped her hands in front of her chest, wondering what this sensation was. Some overwhelming emotion glowed in her eyes, and that deep, burning passion he saw...was not the only thing on his mind right then because he'd just realized something else. When he'd shyly averted his gaze, he'd noticed something by the window at the back of the student council room. Lurking under the student council president's desk...were two shadows.

Someone's there.

They appeared to be the shadows of the president and the vice president of the student council. In fact, it was less of a maybe and more of a sure thing. It was the most famous lovey-dovey couple in the entire school. The massive president, Touya, and the tall vice president, Chisaki, were crammed under the desk and smushed together as much as two people could be.

What are they doing? What is this, some kind of romantic comedy?

Masachika caught his breath and shuddered because it was like the pot calling the kettle black.

Is this what I think it is? They were in their own little rom-com world when we came in, which made them panic and hide. Then they were like, "Wait. What are we hiding for?" If you're going to do the trope, then at least hide in a locker, not under a desk!

He could vividly imagine the exchange that would follow:

Chisaki would say, "Hey! Where do you think you're touching me?!"

And Touya would respond, "Ouch! I didn't mean to! It's cramped under this desk!"

And if things kept going in accordance with said trope, they were soon going to be so close that they could feel each other's breathing and hearts racing, sweat dripping from their hot, firm bodies until their hormones couldn't take it anymore.

Huh. It looks like the main event was happening over there. Then I guess it's my job to wait until the moment is right and leave as if I didn't see a thing. I guess you could say I'm the guy who has to set the stage for the main show. A stage prop, if you will.

Masachika's dirty nerd brain led him to this conclusion, so he turned to face Alisa once more…and instinctively leaned back when he saw the girl's pure, angelic face.

Huh?! What's going on over here now?! A-am I in the middle of a romantic comedy, too?! Tsk! Dammit! How could I not have noticed?! This isn't just a scene where two people hide in a tight space, bringing both their bodies and hearts closer together! This is a scene where they are watching a romantic comedy play out for them as well! And they're loving every moment of it! We are stage props to get those two closer and tools with the sole purpose of making things even more exciting for them!!

Even as Masachika's 2D-addled mind ran wild, Alisa slowly closed the distance between them...with fire in her eyes and her hands folded on her chest.

Yeah, this isn't good. What exactly about this isn't good? Everything. Anyway, it's just...not good. Ack! It looks like I have no choice but to change the direction this is heading!!

The unbearable sense of danger forced Masachika to switch genres, a forbidden technique he swore never to use again. He switched gears from romantic comedy...to serious drama.

"How long do you two plan on hiding, Mr. President and Ms. Vice President of the student council?"

The moment Masachika muttered that line, which could be found on any top ten list of Lines Otaku Want to Say at Least Once in Their Lives, Alisa's face was overcome with bewilderment. At the same time, loud thuds sounded from under the president's desk.

Oof. One of them must have hit their head.

With no sympathy, Masachika watched Touya emerge from under the desk and stand awkwardly, followed by Chisaki, whose gaze wandered the room.

"Sorry... We accidentally waited too long to come out, until it would have been embarrassing if we did."

"Yeah, we were looking for something we dropped when we suddenly heard you two having a serious conversation, so we didn't want to interrupt..."

Chisaki was ad-libbing a painfully unconvincing excuse, but Masachika wasn't in the mood to call her out, and Alisa wasn't in the right mindset to say anything.

"Hmm... All right, then. How about we both pretend like we didn't see or hear anything and call it a day?"

"Y-yeah, good idea. Let's do that."

"Great. Come on, Alya. Let's go."

After they'd all calmly come to an agreement, Masachika grabbed

Alisa and exited the student council room. But right as he closed the door and sighed deeply…his eyes met Alisa's, and she immediately stepped back and looked away.

"I, uh… Like…"

She spoke nervously, mumbling and tripping over her words, then swiftly turned on her heel as though to escape her emotional stress.

"I…! I have something I need to do…!"

And she took off running, which was unusual for her. Meanwhile, Masachika looked up at the hallway ceiling and groaned, turning his head.

"Maybe I should put my ear to the door and eavesdrop? According to the tropes, the door should suddenly open, and someone will say, 'H-how long have you been there?!' But I feel like Chisaki would be able to sense my presence almost immediately…," muttered Masachika as he glanced over his shoulder at the student council room. Giving the scenario such serious consideration truly marked him as the epitome of an otaku… But perhaps he was only doing this so he didn't have to face reality.

"Oh my god! Check this out. It's the newest bag from Faimel, and it's so totally cute."

"That *is* cute! ♪ I want one, too, but I doubt I'll be able to snag one this month."

"Faimel? I know someone who can get you one. You're gonna have to give me a shout-out online, though."

"Seriously? You're the best!"

"Hold up. She barely has six thousand followers. Not much of a shout-out if you ask me."

"Oh my god! That's rich coming from someone who doesn't even have a thousand followers."

It was lunch. Alisa had been exuding vibes that said, "Don't even think about talking to me, let alone look at me," ever since what happened that morning, so Masachika decided to visit Class D alone to solve their issue...but he froze the moment he saw the girl he wanted to talk to. Given her surname, he figured she would have been assigned a seat near the window to the hallway, so he wouldn't even have to step foot into the room...but his plan proved to be far too optimistic.

Dammit! Their conversation...! They're way too cool for me! I can't. I can't get any closer!

There was Nonoa Miyamae, one of his and Alisa's opponents from the debate the other day, and she was surrounded by four other students: two boys and two girls. It didn't help that they were clearly at the top of the school pecking order, either. In addition to being good-looking, they were dressed fashionably, albeit borderline against school rules. Nevertheless, they expressed no signs of guilt and were brimming with confidence. The way they dressed essentially gave off an aura that kept away those ranked in the middle or lower castes.

"Hey, Nonoa. What do you think of this?"

"Hmm?"

Meanwhile, Nonoa—the center of attention—hardly contributed to her followers' conversation and seemed a bit bored, with her eyes half-closed and glued to the phone screen.

"This is Faimel's newest bag. Isn't it adorable?"

"Oh, that? Hmm... I used one during my last photo shoot, but I wasn't really feeling it."

"Oh my god. Really? I guess I don't want one anymore, then."

"Wait. Seriously?"

"Seriously. If Nonoa's seen the real thing and didn't like it, then that's all I need to know."

"Anyway, Nonoa, what are you doing next Sunday? I'm having a party at my house. Wanna come? My cousin is a huge fan of yours."

"This Sunday? But we have a test on Monday."

They were lower than followers—they were worshippers. They tried everything they could to get Nonoa's attention, but she was blowing each and every one of them off while she fiddled with her phone. It was like a group of retainers or jesters trying to please their queen.

"Then we can study for the test together on Sunday, too. Come on. Please?"

"Mmm..."

"Oh, come on. Nonoa, you've been so cold lately," one of the girls said, pouting. That was when Nonoa, who had expressed absolutely no interest in their conversation up until now, suddenly placed her phone down, stood up, and wrapped her arms around the girl with a radiant smile.

"Oh my gosh. I was totally just messing with you. A party? This Sunday? I'm *so* there."

"Really? Yesss!"

"Really. But..."

After letting go of the girl, Nonoa slowly turned to Masachika, then leaned out the window to the hallway.

"Kuzeee, what's up?"

"H-hey. It's, uh... Yeah."

"Can't talk here?"

"I'd rather not if that's okay..."

"Sure," Nonoa agreed easily without even asking why.

"I'll be right back, guys," she assured her followers.

"Oh, okay."

"I'll fill you in on the details later, then."

"See ya."

"Have fun."

Her followers shot Masachika glances, each with a different emotion, as if to say, "If Nonoa's not here, then what's the point?" before they all got up and left.

They really do worship her. She has her own freakin' entourage...

Masachika watched in something between disgust and interest until Nonoa stepped out of the classroom, idly fidgeting with her hair and saying:

"So where do you wanna go? Wanna look for an empty classroom or something?"

"Yeah, sure... Interesting hairstyle you have today, by the way."

Masachika smiled awkwardly after seeing Nonoa up close. She almost always did her hair in the morning based on how she felt that day, but today was something else...to say the least. She had braids of all shapes and sizes randomly scattered about with ribbons for seemingly no particular rhyme or reason. And yet it didn't look bad at all. It was impressive that she was able to pull it off.

"Oh, this? I let Shuna and Mia do my hair today, and this is how it turned out. Oh, hey. I almost forgot to take a picture for the gram."

She promptly whipped out her phone, raised it high in the air, and took a selfie as if she had done it thousands of times. Masachika felt a smidgen of admiration at how she could pose perfectly at the drop of a hat and how bold she was to use her phone in the hallway, despite it being against school rules.

"Hmm. Perfect."

"Uh-huh... Anyway, come on."

"A'ight."

After stepping into an empty room, Nonoa crossed her arms with her usual unmotivated expression, then leaned against the wall.

"So? If you're gonna ask me out, I'm totally cool with that, but... that's not what you wanted to talk about, is it?"

"Nope… Wait. You'd be cool with that?" asked Masachika reflexively, unable to let that slip by.

"I mean, I'm not seeing anyone right now. And I don't *dislike* you," replied Nonoa, twirling her hair around her finger and tilting her head.

"Wait, wait, wait. You should definitely go out with someone you like, not someone you don't dislike."

"What? I would have never had a single boyfriend in my life if I did that."

"Aaand I think I've found your problem."

"Not my fault I don't know what it means to 'fall in love,'" Nonoa said with a shrug as if it wasn't a big deal, which made Masachika frown in discomfort.

"I'm not trying to push my opinion of love on you or anything, but don't sell yourself short. You don't have to get with every guy who begs."

Nonoa's half-closed eyes opened wide for the first time that day, and her lips curled somewhat gleefully.

"Ha-ha! Saya said the same thing to me. Her advice came with a slap, too, though."

"Seriously? She didn't strike me as the kind of person who would slap her best friend."

"Yeah, she's… Yeah."

Her smile faded into a half smirk, and her eyes wandered the room.

"I'm not even gonna guess what you did," he muttered with a sigh as though he wasn't really expecting her to explain what she meant any further.

"Like, you know? It was a long time ago, and she had this boyfriend. And, like, she caught us making out in the classroom. And we were at, like, second base."

"The hell?! Seriously?"

"Ha-ha! You must think less of me now, huh?"

Masachika's eyes widened. He was taken aback by what he'd heard for more than one reason. As Nonoa arched an eyebrow and smiled in a self-deprecating manner, Masachika gulped before replying in a trembling voice:

"That sounds just like how the protagonist usually meets the heroine in *yuri* comics!"

"…This is actually one of the things I like about you, Kuze."

"That could have been the first chapter's two-page spread *in color*. The prudish class president finds some flirty guy and a delinquent girl in the classroom. She regards them with contempt, but she can't look away for some reason…"

"Yooo. Reality to Kuze. Come iiin, Kuze."

"O-oh… Ahem!"

Nonoa sighed softly.

"Anyway, I was kidding about going out with you…and I haven't been fooling around with any guys ever since Saya scolded me, either," she half-heartedly confessed, twirling her hair around her finger.

"'Fooling around'? You're a freshman in high school this year, you know."

"Yeah, yeah… So? What do you want?"

She stared at him with half-lidded eyes once again, and his expression instantly changed.

"Oh… Uh… It's about Sayaka."

"Ohhh. She's not here today. When something gets her down, it gets her way down… Anyway, what about her?"

"You hear the things they're saying about her around school, right? About how she challenged us to a debate but ran away before it even ended. I was wondering if there was anything we could do to stop all this gossiping."

"Oh? I didn't know you were the kind of guy who cared about stuff like that."

Puzzled, she quirked her head to the side.

"My partner cares," he said, shrugging.

"Ohhh. Now it makes sense." Nonoa nodded before she looked up at the ceiling with both disgust and admiration.

"Heh... Aren't you sweet?" she added.

"I'm not doing this to be nice. I'm serious about this—about a lot of things."

"What you're doing is still nice." She grinned faintly, but her smile became more self-deprecating.

"And? Why are you telling me all this? I'm your enemy, you know?"

"'Enemy,' huh?"

"Don't tell me you didn't notice I had a few plants in the audience to stir things up."

"Yeah, I know. Konda from Class A, Nagano from Class C, Satou and Kunieda from Class D, and Kinjou from Class F, right?"

Her eyes widened in astonishment, but her grin grew.

"...Seriously? You found every one of my plants from the stage in that dark auditorium?"

"I was actually only about seventy percent sure until I saw your reaction just now."

"So you tricked me into admitting it. You got me. Looks like you had a backup plan ready just in case, huh?"

She smiled and gazed up at him from under her eyelashes, but Masachika just shrugged, maintaining his silence, so Nonoa decided to speculate on her own.

"Well, the faculty has become pretty sensitive when it comes to cheating, ever since all the bribing and threats during that election a few years back, so if word got out that a few plants influenced the results of the debate, and if their actual names were leaked, too, then the school would have to get involved, seeing as how big of a deal the student council is... And the worse the situation got, the worse we would look, which would end up making you two look even better. Plus, if there were any doubts of wrongdoing, the subject of debate wouldn't be considered anymore. You could have won by default that way... You're sick. I like that."

"...There aren't any rules that say you can't run for student council president even if you lose at the debate, and I didn't want to hurt your reputations if I didn't have to."

"But you would have if you had to, huh? Scary stuff. I'm really glad we didn't win."

But it was obvious she wasn't actually scared, and Masachika's gaze was piercing.

"You're far scarier if you ask me. Asking your buddies to be plants? Sounds like a good way to lose all your friends."

"Hmm? Oh, people are welcome to come and go as they please. And honestly, I'm, like, not really attached to any of my friends other than Saya, so it doesn't matter to me if they end up not wanting to be friends anymore anyway."

It wasn't what you would expect from someone so popular— basically the school's queen bee. Her indifferent expression didn't help, either. Masachika, however, wasn't surprised in the least.

"Can I ask you something?" he asked.

"Hmm?"

"When you say you aren't attached to friends other than Sayaka, does that also mean she's the only person you're close to? Why? I thought you didn't get people like her who internalize their harsher side."

"The fact that I don't get it is why I'm interested in her and want to hang out with her."

"If you say so," he replied, tilting his head in curiosity. Nonoa suddenly brought her face close to his, then smiled suspiciously.

"You know how I feel, Kuze. You know what it feels like to be attracted to someone with a sparkle—someone who has something you don't."

But there wasn't a hint of humor in her eyes as she stared into his. It was as if she saw right through him, making Masachika fall silent. She chuckled at his reaction, then took a step back and raised her voice.

"Anyway! Now that you've shown me something amusing, let's start that scheme of yours. I'm sure we can come up with something really evil, since we both understand how it feels to be drawn to our glowing partners."

"It's nothing evil, but sure…"

With a smirk, Masachika looked at her seriously and continued:

"It's simple, really. I just want to spread a rumor about why Sayaka ran away during the debate. Something that sounds plausible."

"…You mean so it doesn't sound like she ran away once things started to get tough. Are you sure? It'd cheapen your victory."

After she raised an eyebrow skeptically, Masachika shrugged and replied:

"I know. In any case, the reason can be anything. Like she suddenly heard that something happened to her parents, maybe? …By the way, what did you two do after that? Because we wouldn't be able to use an excuse like that if you went to a café to wind down or something."

"Oh, after that? We, like, waited until Saya finished crying, then we stalled until everyone was gone so we could go home without anyone seeing us. But it's not like there were zero witnesses, so I doubt we could get away with saying she had urgent business to take care of."

"Oh… Hmm…"

What now? Masachika crossed his arms and pondered for a few moments until Nonoa suddenly spoke up with an annoyed sigh.

"Mmm… I'll figure something out."

"Wait. Are you sure?"

"I mean, she's, like, my partner. So it's my job to help her. Plus, I'm good at spreading rumors."

Then she turned on her heel, ending the conversation.

"Anyway, laters."

"Y-yeah, see you around."

After Nonoa left the classroom, Masachika stood alone helplessly and scratched his head, still baffled by the unexpected turn of events.

Huh. If this were a comic, the next scene would be me calling for one of my minions hidden in the shadows and saying, "Follow her. And don't let anyone see you."

The geeky scenario came to him after he thought about how he was chatting with one of his rival candidates and what had happened in the not-actually-empty student council room that morning. He smiled cynically at himself and decided to jokingly call out the name of his childhood friend who was kind of like a shadow.

"Ayano."

But he was immediately overcome with embarrassment.

"What am I doing?" he muttered. And he was reaching for the door to leave when—

"Yes, Master Masachika."

"Whoa?!"

He jumped, literally, at the sudden voice coming from behind him. Masachika swiftly turned around to find Ayano really standing there, and his jaw dropped.

"What are you doing here?!"

"…? I came because you summoned me," stated Ayano, tilting her head quizzically, but Masachika had already gone beyond mild confusion and had reached peak disbelief.

She's here because I summoned her?! Like a demon from a magic circle?! Can she teleport whenever I call for her? Or is this that thing ninjas can do when they clone themselves? Is one of her doppelgänger shadow things always following me around?!

His nerd brain was geeking out at max capacity when another voice suddenly called out from behind him.

"Hey, I think you're forgetting someone, bro."

He turned around only to find Yuki leaning against the wall with her arms crossed, grinning like a hard-boiled detective.

"The hell?! Seriously! What are you two doing here?!"

"Heh. We saw you trying to make contact with the enemy, Nonoa, so we hid under the teacher's desk before you came in."

Yuki approached him with a truly mischievous, fearless, and wild look in her eyes. *Under the desk? Again?* thought Masachika as he glared at her reproachfully.

"So what really happened?"

"We were pretending to have a secret rendezvous in an empty classroom when you two showed up and had a real one."

"You guys have way too much free time."

The fact that they'd been playing pretend made Masachika roll his eyes so hard he could almost see his brain. All of a sudden, the door to the classroom rattled open.

"Kuze? You in here?"

Alisa peeked hesitantly into the room, perhaps having heard him scream, but when she saw the three of them together, her expression instantly went blank.

"...Hmph."

"Alya? This isn't what you think." Masachika immediately tried to defend himself.

"What? There's nothing strange about three childhood friends playing together," Alisa said stiffly.

"Then why do you have such a scary look on your face?"

"It's just your imagination. Anyway, enjoy," she added sternly before closing the door, but right before it shut completely, she muttered with a slight pout:

"<Hmph. Didn't even bother inviting me.>"

And just like that, her peevish expression was hidden behind the door.

It wasn't like they'd been doing anything to be ashamed of, but Masachika was instantly overcome with guilt as he stood in silence.

"Bro, bro, brooo. I know that look. That's the look girls make when they prepare you lunch to pay you back for helping them at a debate and have been searching all over school for ya," claimed Yuki, mimicking a hoodlum.

"What kind of look is that?! And stop making a backstory for why she was looking for me! She wasn't even holding a lunch box!"

"The lunch boxes are probably already on the picnic blanket she laid out in the schoolyard."

"Stoppp!" shrieked Masachika.

"I bet you feel terrible now," jeered Yuki with an aggravating smirk as she placed a consoling hand on his shoulder.

"And whose fault is that?!"

Ayano watched their rapid banter from a step away with her usual empty expression, nearly about to clasp her hands together like a nun being blessed. Nevertheless, her will was as strong as steel. She wasn't going to do anything that would interrupt their exchange. She was solely going to focus on being air… But on the other hand, Ayano unfortunately also happened to look like an anime shipper watching over her favorite couple.

Nonoa was well aware that she would be classified as a psychopath by the general public if they knew the real her. Her emotions had been numbed since she was a child. Never once had she screamed tearfully in sadness or raged violently in anger. Feelings of absolute delight, enough to make her want to jump with joy, were alien to her as well. While she felt pain and pleasure, it was always so faint that she could control it before exhibiting any signs.

That was why she hadn't been able to understand Sayaka even when they were children. To Nonoa, Sayaka was a peculiar creature who was usually reasonable but who threw wild fits seemingly at random. Sayaka puzzled her, but that wasn't an issue that prevented them from being friends.

Nonoa couldn't fathom why people felt certain ways. She couldn't empathize. But that was also why she was able to objectively analyze her actions and others' reactions, allowing her to act exactly how others hoped she would. She knew what to say, what expression to make, and how to act to calm the *peculiar creature's* temper. That was what made Sayaka so easy for Nonoa to handle. Nonoa's parents had even told her to befriend Sayaka, so she figured she'd do the bare minimum to stay on Sayaka's good side. That was what she had planned on doing at least...until *that* happened.

"Stop selling yourself short and getting with every guy who asks! Have some respect for yourself!"

It was the first time someone seriously got angry at her, and it was the first time she had ever been slapped as well. The fierce words and glare had sent a vivid warmth to Nonoa's cheeks, which was a novel experience for someone who had played the "good girl" role all her life. Although no guy she had ever touched or been touched by had made her heart race, her heart had been thunderously beating against her chest then.

"How the protagonist meets the heroine in *yuri* comics, huh? He's probably not that far off," muttered Nonoa as she returned to her classroom alone. She smiled a bit while thinking about how she could help Sayaka redeem herself...but she actually already knew the moment Masachika asked for her help in that empty classroom. However, she figured he would try to stop her, which was why she ended the conversation there and left.

More importantly...there were only supposed to be four plants in the audience...

Nonoa curiously tilted her head, thinking about the fifth name Masachika had mentioned.

Kinjou from Class F, was it? He wasn't one of my plants...which, I guess, makes him someone who genuinely doesn't like Kujou?

The curiosity was there, but she was almost back at her classroom, so she decided to put it aside for the moment.

Well, I did cause a lot of trouble for Kuze and Kujou the other day, so I guess I can deal with this Kinjou kid to make it up to them.

And with that in mind, Nonoa opened the door to her classroom and returned to her seat.

"Oh, Nonoa! About time you got back."

"We were waiting forever for you! ♪ What did that kid from Class B want to talk about?"

"He just wanted to know why Saya didn't come to school today. That's all," she replied to her friends, who looked puzzled.

"Taniyama? She didn't come to school today?"

"Must be because she lost the debate, right? Is she still letting that get to her?"

"Oh, no. It's my fault she's not here, and, like, it was totally my fault she forfeited the debate."

"W-wait. What?"

"Seriously? Why didn't you tell us?!"

Their eyes glittered with curiosity.

"Like, I actually had a few plants in the audience. And Saya found out. And, like...she was pissed that I had to resort to dirty tactics to win. So she, like, forfeited," explained Nonoa as though it was no big deal.

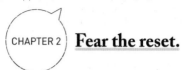

(CHAPTER 2) **Fear the reset.**

"Listen. I'm telling you the truth. I didn't even know Ayano and Yuki were there."

"Uh-huh."

"You don't believe me at all…"

"And you don't have to explain yourself to me. What's wrong with childhood friends still getting along?"

Alisa could claim it didn't bother her, but her harsh tone and temper told a different story. Even her classmates, who had no problem talking to her this morning, were now looking away, pretending as if they didn't even notice.

I guess I can't blame her, though. Who would be happy to see their partner meeting with an opposing candidate in an empty classroom? But still… Yuki is basically Alya's only friend of the same sex.

Masachika had decided that was why Alisa was in a bad mood. Alisa wasn't jealous like a girl who caught the boy she liked with another girl. That wasn't why she was in a bad mood. It had nothing to do with love. Nothing to do with love at all.

Sigh… She's going to be isolated in the classroom again at this rate…

After sighing in his mind, Masachika decided to let it go and talk about something else instead.

"Oh, right. Alya, wanna study together for the test after school?"

She looked shocked. *Study.* It was that word that clouded her expression with doubt as she replied:

"…Is that some kind of joke?"

"Wow. Rude."

He smirked at her blunt reply.

"I guess it's only natural for you to feel that way, though." He shrugged.

"But, well, there's something bothering me about the whole debate thing and Sayaka, too."

Alisa thought back to what happened the week before and fell silent. Knowing how Sayaka felt when she challenged them to the debate renewed their resolve to run for student council president and vice president.

I see… So Kuze is finally going to get serious.

While Alisa was happy her partner seemed motivated for a change, she had mixed feelings because she wasn't the spark. She kept that to herself, however, and nodded.

"Fine. We can do that."

"Oh, great… But you don't have to force yourself to study with me if you're the kind of person who can't concentrate unless you're alone," replied Masachika timidly as if there was something about Alisa's blunt response that worried him. She knitted her brow in annoyance.

"I said we can study together… We are partners, after all."

"Oh yeah… You're right. How does the student council room sound?"

"Sure."

Alisa brushed her hair back, inwardly sighing.

Hmph. I guess it is my job to help Kuze study. My partner sure is a lot of work.

She looked smug.

I guess she's in a slightly better mood now?

And with that, Masachika heaved a mental sigh of relief.

◇

After school, they made their way over to the student council room. While there were plenty of students in the library and in the classrooms at this hour, Masachika and Alisa would most likely be able to study there in peace, since usually only student council members visited the room after school.

"So let's be—...?"

Immediately after Masachika sat in his usual seat, Alisa installed herself in the spot right next to him as if it were only natural, and he froze.

Uh... Don't people usually sit across from each other when they study together?

It didn't help that she was sitting extremely close as well. If anyone saw them, they would wonder why they were using a laughably small portion of such a large desk.

"...What?"

"...Nothing."

But Masachika wasn't brave enough to say anything, and Alisa's sharp glance immediately sent his eyes back to the table in front of him.

W-well, I guess we'll be fine as long as no one sees us like this. A real couple like the student council president and vice president should be studying somewhere where they can have absolute privacy, and Masha would pretend like she didn't notice anything strange even if she stopped by. The only person who might say something would be Yuki, but she can study at home with Ayano already, so she's definitely not going to catch us like th—

"Hmm? Oh my. I apologize for not knocking. I had no idea you two were here."

Yukiiiiiiiii!! Damn you, foreshadowing! screamed Masachika in his mind. He slowly turned to look at the door, where Yuki and Ayano stood. Yuki may have appeared sorry, but he could see the mischievous glee in her eyes.

Did you think you were finally going to get a chance to be alone with her? Not on my watch.

What are you doing here?

Isn't it obvious?

No?

I came here to stop you two from playing doctor in the student council room!

We weren't playing doctor!

Yuki inclined her head, maintaining her innocent, ladylike demeanor in spite of her wild telepathic accusations.

"Are you two studying together? Do you think we could join you?"

Regardless of her reasoning, there was no way Masachika could turn Yuki away when she was acting like an innocent young lady. Although he slightly reprimanded her with his eyes, he decided to allow her to—

"<Go away.>"

Ack?!

Masachika desperately struggled to keep himself from doing a spit take the instant he heard those slightly peevish Russian words coming from behind him.

"…Alya? Yuki wants to join our study group. What do you say?"

Although mentally defeated, Masachika managed to maintain his expression as he looked to his side.

"Sure. I don't see why not." Alisa shrugged with an air of nonchalance.

"…Okay."

While maybe not in Russian, Alisa gave her consent in Japanese, so Masachika shifted his sights back on Yuki and—

"<I want to be alone with you.>"

Gwah!

Her sweet Russian hit Masachika with a mental blow that nearly knocked him off his feet. He trembled like a newborn fawn.

You little punk, being all cute like that! Stop it! You're going to make me blush and say "moeee" like some hard-core otaku.

In his imagination, he had fallen to the ground on all fours and was bashing his head into the ground, screaming in agony all the while. He wanted to look at her really bad, but he wasn't 100 percent sure his lip wasn't awkwardly twitching. All he could do now was quietly glare at his sister while doing everything he could to control the muscles in his face.

Dammit. What now? It's not like I can say no to Yuki, because if I do…it'd make it seem like I was the one who wanted to be alone with Alya! More importantly, Yuki! You heard her say she was fine with it, so why don't you just sit down and thank her?! You just want to force me to say it's okay, don't you?!

Yuki read the room perfectly and made a conscious decision to ignore it, which made her brother's disapproving stare only stronger. Nevertheless, she maintained the perfectly fake smile and inquisitive tilt to her head as though she were still waiting for an answer. Ayano was basically one with the air.

Hff…! Relax. Act cool. First things first, I'm not sure how serious she is, but either way, Alya doesn't seem to be too excited about Yuki or Ayano joining us. Personally, I'm not too fond of the idea of letting them join, either… Oh, I know. I can say something like, "We're enemies. We shouldn't get to know one another. It'll only make things harder for us down the road." I can make it sound like a joke and gently turn them down at the same time. That way—

"Oh, I almost forgot. The president and vice president lent us copies of the previous year's test problems, so if you're interested, we—"

"Welcome to our study group. Glad to have ya aboard."

Masachika quickly flipped in the face of the answer key's irresistible power.

"<Stupid jerk.>"

But Alisa's coldhearted Russian still hurt as it pierced his back.

Regardless of how they may have felt individually, the four-person study group was going well. Alisa was quietly solving physics problems in her workbook, Yuki was going over past history test problems across from her, and Ayano was by Yuki's side solving math equations. While the three of them diligently ran their pens across paper, Masachika was…

"…"

Masachika hadn't even taken out a pen but instead was silently reading over the explanations of the answers in his math workbook.

"…Hey, Kuze?"

"Hmm?"

"You've been reading the explanations for the answers for a while now. Is that honestly going to help?"

Reading how to solve the problems without actually solving them may make you think you know how to solve them, but actually solving them yourself is the only way to truly learn. Most people believed this to be the case—Alisa included. That's why she was staring at him skeptically, since he hadn't solved a single problem on his own yet. Masachika, however, shrugged as if he wasn't concerned in the least.

"No amount of thinking is going to help if you don't know how to solve something to begin with. You'd just be wasting your time. That's why I'd rather use my time to memorize how to solve every problem instead."

"Sure, but…learning theory and applying it are two different things, right? Plus, it's not like the exact same problems are going to appear on the test. I doubt you'll have enough time to solve all the problems if you don't get used to solving them yourself beforehand," warned Alisa with an entirely sound argument.

"*Giggle.* He'll be fine, Alya. This is how Masachika always studies. Right, Ayano?" Yuki chimed in with a slightly exasperated smile.

"Yes, this is how he has always studied."

Alisa looked across the table at Masachika's childhood friends, knitting her eyebrows.

"...Really?"

"Yes, he only reads his textbook and the explanations, then checks the answer key in preparation for his tests. And he never fails to get decent grades as well. Impressive, right?" Yuki said, looking like she wanted to roll her eyes. Nevertheless, Alisa still didn't seem convinced, and she pulled out an old math test from four years ago (something that had been passed down through the generations of student councils) from the pile of old tests and answers lying on the corner of the table before thrusting it in Masachika's face.

"Then answer problem number six here. You have... Let's make it twenty minutes. If you can do that, I'll leave you alone."

There were always six large problems on the math tests, and you only had two hours to finish them, so a simple calculation would come out as twenty minutes per problem, but the first two problems were usually relatively basic, while the last two were usually application problems that weren't like anything in the workbook. Therefore, solving one of those problems within twenty minutes was a difficult hurdle to overcome, and that was exactly why Masachika was reluctant to take the paper Alisa was handing him.

"Mmm... Well, I guess I could..."

"We're good? Then get started."

"H-hey, hold on. I don't have anything to write with yet."

He pulled out his notebook and pen in a panic before promptly working to solve the problem. Twenty minutes had gone by when Alisa suddenly told him his time was up, so he set down his pen and gave Alisa his notebook. The formula needed to solve the problem was written meticulously on the paper, at least in much more detail than she'd expected, making her eyebrow twitch briefly.

"The most important thing is whether you got the answer right, though," she muttered, collecting herself as she began to compare the answer key to Masachika's solution, but it wasn't long before a grim expression darkened her face. Masachika's lips slowly curled into a grin the instant he saw the change in her mood.

"Hmm? So? Did I get it right?"

"...Yes."

"Yesss! You like that?! Booyah!"

Alisa, seeming annoyed, thrust the notebook back into her gloating classmate's hands.

"...I don't care as long as you answer correctly."

"*Giggle.* I know how you feel, but you shouldn't let it bother you. Masachika is a quick study. He's not like us."

"...If you're really that smart, then I should probably be worried about why you barely pass almost every test you take."

"Huh? Oh, the reason's simple: It's because I never study!"

"That's nothing to brag about."

Alisa pierced him with a look of disgust.

"Masachika usually crams the night before the test whenever he *does* study," added Yuki, her bitter expression deepening.

"Heh. That's what you think, Yuki. Lately, I've been cramming the morning before the test," Masachika said with a smug grin.

"What is wrong with you?"

"Yes, that is irresponsible."

"Hey, I still passed all my tests. Impressive, right?"

"There's nothing praiseworthy about what you did. Wait. Don't tell me you wanted to study together because—"

Masachika promptly nodded to confirm Alisa's suspicions.

"Because I needed someone to keep me accountable, of course. I can't study alone without getting distracted."

"…At least you're aware of what kind of person you are."

"I still do not believe that is something to be proud of, though."

After Alisa and Yuki glared at him in disgust, Masachika shrugged before facing forward once more to avoid their gazes. That was when he noticed Ayano staring in bewilderment at her workbook.

"What's wrong, Ayano? Having trouble with one of the problems?"

"Oh, no. I… Actually, yes. A little."

"Let me help you."

"I appreciate the offer, but it is not worth your time."

Although her blank expression hadn't changed, Ayano was clearly refusing his help.

"Don't worry about it. What exactly is confusing you?"

"Uh…"

"Don't be so scared. I'm not going to make fun of you or anything."

"I would actually prefer if you cruelly said something like, 'How are you seriously having trouble with such an easy problem, you incompetent idiot?'"

"I'm definitely not going to be saying that."

"Oh…"

Ayano quickly drooped.

"What the…? Why do you look disappointed?" joked Masachika, slightly weirded out. Meanwhile, Alisa watched their exchange in utter confusion.

"Hey… Are you two really just childhood friends?"

"Hmm? Yeah. Why?"

"'Why'? Because it looks more like a master-subordinate relationship, just like her relationship with Yuki."

How observant is she?!

Masachika swallowed hard at her insightful comment before swiftly kicking his brain into thinking mode so he could come up with a good excuse. But before he could even say a word, Alisa continued with an urgent expression:

"Wait… Kuze. Are you and Yuki…?"

"…!"

The sudden inquiry about their relationship made Masachika's heart leap out of his chest, but what Alisa said next was something he never expected to hear in a million years.

"…e-engaged?"

"All thrusters engaged?"

"Huh?"

"It's a sci-fi series reference."

"You know it, Yuki! Yeahhh!"

Masachika and Yuki high-fived over Ayano's head as they played dumb in perfect sync. Alisa, on the other hand, didn't know how to react for a few moments. She eventually pressed her lips together tightly in irritation.

"I'm being serious, and you're just going to ignore me?"

"Oh, sorry. What you said was just so funny that it was hard to take seriously," Masachika said, brushing it off.

"What was so funny about what I said? I wasn't joking, you know."

"Think about it for a second. The only daughter of the distinguished Suou family engaged to some ordinary middle-class guy like me? How many unfortunate mistakes would it take to lead to something like that?"

"Your parents could be friends."

"This isn't a romantic comedy. Let's imagine our parents were friends. What kind of normal people would be like, 'So how about we have our kids get married?' It sounds like you've read way too many comics to me."

"…Oh, I'm the one who reads too many comics?"

Alisa frowned, somewhat surprised that she was the one being called out for imagining something that happened only in nerdy comics by someone who usually made nerdy comments because he read too many comics. Masachika smiled cheekily.

"Plus, you're missing some key points. The girl is supposed to be a beautiful, modest, traditional Japanese lady with long black hair and huge boobs! And she has to look good in a kimono! That's how the trope goes!"

"...She looks like she fits the description to me."

"Huh?"

After curiously tilting his head at Alisa's comment, Masachika looked back at Yuki once more.

Long black hair... She wears a kimono when she does flower arrangement... And she does seem modest and traditional when she's in character outside the house... Hold up.

Yuki surprisingly did fit the trope. However...

"Yeah. And those..."

"Masachika? My eyes are up here," scolded Yuki.

"Ahem. It is ill-mannered to stare like that," Ayano added.

"You disgust me," Alisa hissed contemptuously.

He accidentally acted like he would if he were just talking to Yuki at home and was met with three accusing stares because of it, forcing him to lower his head in shame.

"No, I mean, like... Anyway, we're not engaged, and we never will be. Tsk. Why are you and Takeshi always trying to pair up Yuki and me?"

"We must look like we would make a great couple." Yuki giggled and slyly glanced in Alisa's direction, making Alisa frown in annoyance.

"No... I just thought you two seemed close. That's all."

"Because we *are* really close. Right, Masachika?"

"Oh, uh... Yeah, I guess."

He may have agreed with Yuki, but his eyes were still pointed in

Alisa's direction, noticing that she was still irritably knitting her brow. Nevertheless, Yuki wouldn't be Yuki if she didn't follow that up with another attack.

"I often spend the night at his house, too."

"No, that's, uh… Yeah."

&$#%!! A cold sweat slid down Masachika's spine as the crease in Alisa's brow deepened…so he decided to retreat.

"Anyway, enough about that. Ayano, what were you having trouble with?"

"Oh… This."

Masachika ran away from his problems under the guise of helping a friend learn, but he could still feel Alisa's sharp gaze piercing the back of his head, even while he was burying his nose in Ayano's textbook. And that didn't change even after he returned to his seat once he finished helping Ayano solve her problem. Cold sweat continued to drip down his body as Alisa stared at him.

"…Alya? Everything okay?"

"…I was just wondering if you needed any help with your studies."

"No, not at the moment…"

"Okay…" Alisa nodded before shifting her gaze back to her textbooks, allowing Masachika to finally relax…

"<I want you to rely on me more.>"

It had slipped his mind. He had forgotten this Russian girl always struck the moment he let down his guard.

W-wait. Is this why she sat so close to me?

Masachika stared off into the distance, and in his mind, he saw himself vomiting blood, but the extra damage he was taking from the additional looks Alisa threw his way forced him to get his act together and say something.

"Hey, Alya? Sorry, but I'm having a little trouble with this one."

"O-oh, really?"

"Yeah, do you think you could help me?"

"Hmph. I suppose."

She may have acted as if she didn't want to do it, but she seemed somewhat happy as she swiftly brushed her hair back. Her predictable behavior and follow-up attack forced Masachika to pinch his thigh in a desperate attempt to keep his cool.

That is, until they suddenly heard a knock at the door. After the four students exchanged glances, Alisa decided to speak up on everyone's behalf.

"…? Come in."

"Good afternoon. ♪"

It was Alisa's sister, Maria, who opened the door with a bubbly smile.

"Masha? I thought you were studying for exams with your friend."

"I was, but we already finished, so I figured I could put on some tea for you all before I went home, since you're probably studying hard."

"Oh my. Thank you so much."

Yuki immediately stood up with a ladylike smile, stopped Ayano from rising as well, then went to help Maria. A few minutes went by before Maria returned with cups of tea for everyone, so they decided to take a short break.

"Oh my. What is this?" wondered Maria as she picked up one of the books on the president's desk. Printed on the cover was the sketchy title *Hypnosis for Idiots: Welcome to the Hypnotist Club.*

"Oh, Chisaki confiscated that from a student. She was probably planning on handing it over to the disciplinary committee later."

"Oh?"

After curiously flipping through the book, Maria eventually took a seat next to Alisa, then raised a finger in front of her sister's eyes.

"…What?"

"Keep your eyes on my finger. ♪ You are getting very sleepy. ♪"

"What are you doing…?"

"Um… When I clap my hands, you will find yourself in another world. A world of dreams," Maria commanded, and placed the book down.

"Ready? Three, two, one… *Clap!*"

She stared at Alisa, eyes brimming with anticipation.

"…Did it work?"

"Of course not. Why would it? Hypnosis is bogus."

"Whaaat? Hmm… Come on. Let me try it again. Just one more time."

"No. If you're going to get in the way of our studies, then go home."

"How about you hypnotize me, then?"

"No."

"Why? I want to be hypnotized! Pleeease. ♪"

Pouting, Maria rocked in her chair, but Alisa refused to engage. After glancing once more at her little sister with obvious disappointment, Maria looked past Alisa to Masachika.

"How about you, then, Kuze? Hypnotize me."

"Huh? Me?"

"You're the only one I can ask, since Alya's being mean…" Maria pouted again. With a wry smile, Masachika got out of his chair, stood by Maria's side, and picked up the book.

"Okay, then. Hmm… 'Step-by-Step Guide to Hypnosis'? Oh, this?"

He opened to the page Maria had been looking at and tried to replicate what he was reading.

"Keep your eyes on my finger. You're getting very sleepy," suggested Masachika, who was squatting and waving his index finger in front of her eyes. The change was instantaneous: Maria's excited expression and glittering eyes immediately relaxed.

"Mm…mmm…?"

Although surprised by her sudden change, he continued, since he figured she was acting.

"When I clap my hands, you will wake up in a world of dreams. Are you ready? Three, two, one…!"

Maria's head dropped the instant he clapped his hands. She wore a vacant expression like a doll as her eyes idly focused on one single point.

"Uh… What? Masha…? Masha?"

Her behavior seemed so real that Masachika began waving his hand in front of her face in a panic, but she didn't even blink.

"Hmm? Did that really hypnotize her?" wondered Yuki, blinking.

"Yeah, I seriously don't know," replied Masachika with a troubled note in his voice. But all of a sudden, Alisa lifted her head—looking really fed up—and began to shake her sister's shoulders.

"All right, that's enough already… Masha?"

But Maria didn't respond to being shaken.

"Hold on. What is going on?"

Alisa stood up with an annoyed wrinkle between her eyebrows and slipped around Maria to get a better look at her face, and she was stunned by what she found. She immediately frowned at Masachika as if she was still doubtful.

"Could you guys stop teasing me already?"

"I'm not. I'm just as surprised as you are."

"Don't lie to me. Hypnosis isn't real."

"I thought so, too, but…look at her. It says here that it works more on people who want to be hypnotized, so maybe that's what's going on?" stammered Masachika awkwardly as Alisa continued to stare at him skeptically. Masachika, however, felt he didn't deserve to be stared at like this, since he honestly didn't do anything shady.

"A-anyway, I'm going to wake her up now, okay?"

He turned back to the book to avoid Alisa's glare and looked at the part where it explained how to wake someone from hypnosis, then he squatted in front of Maria once more.

"Uh… You are going to wake up the moment I touch your shoulders, okay? Ready? Three, two…one!"

Masachika swiftly grabbed Maria's shoulders and shook her, causing her to quickly look up in astonishment. Her expression slowly went back to normal after that, and she blinked as if she had just woken up from a nap.

"Hmm…? Kuze? Go on."

"Huh?"

Maria pouted at his confused expression and pointed at the book.

"*Sigh*. It says right there that you need to wag your finger, then clap."

"Wait… Wait, wait, wait. Hold on. Do you not remember what happened?"

"Huh? When?"

Confusion filled her face.

"Wow, so that was real."

Masachika's face tensed, but there was still at least one person who wasn't convinced.

"Masha, that's enough."

"Alya? Enough what?"

"Enough—… *Sigh*… Whatever."

Alisa shook her head as if she couldn't take it anymore.

"How about you have Masachika hypnotize you and see for yourself, then?" suggested Yuki from across the table.

"Huh?"

"What?"

Yuki placed her hands together and gleefully smiled at Alisa and Masachika.

"Masha may not have been able to hypnotize you, but Masachika might be able to. At the very least, it would make you less suspicious if it works even a little."

Yuki grinned. At first glance, there didn't seem to be any ill intent hidden behind that ladylike smile, but Masachika could clearly sense the pleasure she was getting from this, and his lips couldn't help but twitch. Alisa, on the other hand, didn't catch on to Yuki's true intentions, so she returned to her seat and looked at Masachika with a disbelieving gaze.

"...Fine. Just get to it."

"S-seriously?"

"Yes. Enough playing around. Let's get this over with." Alisa snorted, still unconvinced, so he timidly approached her with a bad feeling in his gut.

"Uh... Okay, then. Watch my finger. You are getting very sleepy."

And in the blink of an eye, Alisa's skeptical gaze transformed into a vacant stare.

"You are going to wake up in a world of dreams when I clap my hands. Ready? Three, two...one!"

Masachika clapped, and Alisa's head instantly dropped. Her expression seemed dazed, eyes unfocused and unseeing like those of a dead fish. He stared at her but then continued in an almost monotone voice.

"When I touch your shoulders, you will wake up. Ready? Three, two, one!"

He grabbed Alisa's shoulders with both hands and shook her, causing Alisa to quickly lift her head and blink a few times. A few seconds went by before her dissatisfied eyes focused on Masachika.

"Why'd you stop? Hurry up and do it."

"You did the same thing! She did the exact same thing her sister did!" shouted Masachika.

"Huh? What are you talking about?"

To answer Alisa's question and frown, Yuki spoke up in a somewhat troubled tone.

"Alya, you were hypnotized."

"Huh…? No, I wasn't."

"Yes, you were. Right, Ayano?"

"Yes, it was obvious even to me that you were."

Alisa wavered, but she soon shot Masachika another piercing glare and barked:

"Sh-show me some proof! I'm not going to believe you unless you show me a video you took or something!"

"Oh, come on. Just give it a rest. It's not a big deal…"

"Yes, it is! I don't want people thinking I'm just some girl who can be easily hypnotized!"

"Who worries about that? And who cares what people think anyway?"

"Just do it again!"

"Fine. Whatever."

Masachika used the same technique on Alisa, and the result… was no surprise.

"You're kidding me, right? That was even faster than before."

He clutched his head as though he had a splitting headache, and Alisa stared blankly into the distance. Yuki was waving her hand in front of Alisa's face this time, and she had dropped her proper-young-lady act, perhaps because she knew that Alisa wouldn't remember a thing.

"Hello? Alya, you there?"

"…"

"There's no response. She's just a corpse."

"Don't say that," reprimanded Masachika weakly. Yuki smirked at him, then looked over at Maria to Alisa's side.

"So, uh… Why is Masha hypnotized, too?"

"Don't ask me."

It was as if an aftershock (?) from the spell made Maria fall asleep as well. Yuki observed the two sisters listlessly slumped in their chairs, dazed eyes staring into the distance, and gasped.

"Oh my god… We can indulge in our lewdest desires right now, and no one would ever know."

"Don't joke about that!"

"Bro, can you imagine the smut fan-fiction writers could write about this?"

"Why are you excited?"

"Why wouldn't I be? We just witnessed legit hypnosis. Tsk. Must be nice to be born with the skill 'Gained EXP × 10 (with the exception of sports involving balls).' Dirty cheater."

"I'm not a cheater."

"Show me your stats, then. I bet you've got a new skill like 'Hypnosis LV: 3.'"

"I don't have 'stats.'"

"By the way, if you get your hypnosis skill to max level, you can put the entire school under your spell and have your way with—"

"Okay, I've heard enough."

Masachika sent her a reproachful glare, wondering why she was so knowledgeable about tropes in indecent otaku media, but Yuki ignored her brother's stare and lifted her hands in a groping pose like a stereotypical creep.

"Wh-wh-wh-what do you wanna do?! Wanna squeeze their boobs first?"

"No!"

"More booby squeezing for me, then."

"What the…?! No!"

Panicked, he stopped Yuki before she could get her hands on Alisa, and his sister's face went blank. A few moments of disappointment passed until she eventually clapped her hands as if she'd had an epiphany.

"Ohhh!" she exclaimed with a pervy grin, giving Masachika a thumbs-up and a wink.

"Don't worry, bro. It's like kissing. Booby touching doesn't count since we're both girls."

"The hell are you talking about? I don't care that you're both girls. She's not even conscious."

"Mmm… I mean, maybe I could cop a feel with Masha, but Alya always has her guard up…"

"Why would you, a girl, even want to touch her boobs?"

Yuki's eyes widened at his blunt question.

"Are you stupid or something?! Girls love big boobs, too, you know! I'd bury my face is Masha's boobies every day if I could! I bet it'd feel incredible!" screamed Yuki.

"Uh-huh."

"Now, if you don't mind…"

"I do. Stop."

He roughly grabbed his sister by the scruff of her neck and jerked her back before she could dive into Maria's chest.

"Meooow! I'm not a cat!"

"I know."

She stared at her brother with displeasure as she fixed her hair.

"Hey, Ayano?"

He called out to the essentially invisible maid behind him, rolled his eyes at his sister, then continued:

"It's not a competition. Just because Yuki said she likes big boobs, it doesn't mean you have to do something about yours. Besides, this isn't the time or the place to be squeezing your breasts together or lifting them up."

Ayano looked up and meekly let go of her chest… She had been staring at her breasts and playing with them with her usual empty expression until Masachika called her out. Although Masachika scolded her, Yuki gave her a thumbs-up while grinning from ear to ear.

"Don't worry, Ayano. I love your boobs, too."

"You know you're starting to sound like a predator, right?"

"Oh, I know. I'm tryna get my hands on some sweet Russian prey."

"Alya would kill you."

"I'm kidding. The term *predator* comes from the word *predation*, which is the act of taking *booty*, so if anything, I need to get some of that—"

"Don't finish that sentence."

"Lady Yuki may prey on me as much as she would like. I welcome it, even."

"Don't encourage her just because you're weirdly into being harassed, Ayano."

"Stop manhandling me already."

Yuki was standing on her tiptoes, and she glared at her brother in protest. If this were a comic book, Masachika would be holding her in the air with one arm as she thrashed about, but of course, he was nowhere near strong enough to do that.

"*Sigh…* Anyway, I'm going to wake them up, okay?"

"Hold up. What about the video evidence?"

"Huh? …Oh, right."

It was only then that he remembered why he had put them to sleep in the first place, and he shoved his hand into his pocket.

"I guess I should at least take a picture."

But before he could take out his phone…

"And here we are with our last performance of the day! We hypnotized two beautiful young girls. ♪ What's the first thing we should make them do?!"

Masachika looked up like an idea had struck him and abruptly shouted:

"Make them act like babies!"

"Make them more open-minded and have them strip!"

"U-uh… Perhaps have them tell an embarrassing secret of some sort?"

Masachika, Yuki, and Ayano exchanged glances after each gave their suggestion, but it was Masachika who took control of the conversation and got the ball rolling.

"Being open-minded is kind of ambiguous, and just because someone's open-minded, that doesn't mean they're going to strip. I mean, that's a pretty big leap in logic there."

"Fine, but making them act like babies is still way too aggressive for their first command. We need to start slowly, then build up to that."

"Mmm…"

After silencing her brother, Yuki shifted her gaze to Ayano.

"I think your idea…wasn't bad, but it's a little weak. Plus, one of them could tell us a secret so dark that things would become awkward around them."

"I see…"

"We'd probably be better off being more specific, like asking 'How big are your boobs?' or 'How many guys have you been with?'"

"Thank you, Lady Yuki. Very informative."

"I hope you're not seriously listening to the drivel she's spouting at you."

"Anyway…! Doesn't this prove that my suggestion to make them more open-minded is the right answer? If we do that, they'd be more than willing to tell us all their most embarrassing secrets as well!"

"Okay, that's not fair! You're twisting things to get what you want!"

"Incorporating my suggestion into yours… You never cease to impress me, Lady Yuki."

"Democracy has spoken, and it looks like I won! What is the first thing we're going to make these two hypnotized girls do? We're going to make them more open-minded!"

After Yuki boastfully raised her fist into the air and grinned, she walked over to Alisa and Maria and stood in front of them.

"It's time to make you two more open-minded. ♪"

"Don't do it. Come on, don't."

"Heh-heh-heh! Alya, Masha, you two are slowly going to become very open-minded. You are going to start with throwing what was considered 'common sense' out the window and become free both mentally and physically!"

"Hold up. Have you ever heard of two people hypnotizing someone as a team like this? This is insa—"

Before Masachika could finish his fed-up rant, Alisa's and Maria's heads lifelessly drooped forward before immediately lifting back up with vacant expressions, but Yuki was clearly taken aback by their unusual demeanors.

"W-wait… Huh? Did that really work?"

"Who's the cheater with all the codes now?"

"N-no way. This can't be…"

Yuki tried to get a better look at them, her expression tense, but they instantly stood and approached Masachika.

"H-hey?! Wait! I—"

He reflexively took a step back, but they closed the distance almost instantaneously, causing him to collapse onto the sofa and…

"…Hey, Yuki."

"…"

"Why am I being consoled?"

"B-beats me."

"Hey, don't look away. This is your fault."

Maria currently had an arm wrapped around Masachika's neck and was gently rubbing his head while also rubbing Alisa's head with her other arm. Alisa seemed like she was trying to do something to Masachika, too, but it appeared Maria had already beaten her to it. Perhaps no little sister would ever be a match for her older sibling. Nevertheless, Alisa seemed irritated, as if she wanted to knock Maria's hand off her, but her eyes were narrowed like she somewhat enjoyed it as well. Perhaps this was the power of hypnosis?

I know they're supposed to be more open-minded, but they seem more straightforward instead. Masha's maternal instincts seem to have kicked in as well.

In a way, perhaps they lost not only their rationality but also their sense of shame, thought Masachika as he was slowly detached from reality.

"*Giggle!* You're such a good boy. ♪ And you're such a good girl. ♪"

Maria's expression was the epitome of pure bliss as she rubbed Masachika's head with her right hand and Alisa's with her left. Yuki (back in proper-young-lady mode), who had been watching the whole ordeal, shuddered.

"I thought it was going to be Masachika who got a harem, not Masha!"

"That's what you're surprised about?"

After shooting his sister a scornful glare, he looked up at Maria from under his eyelashes.

"Hey, uh…Masha? Do you think you could let go of me now?"

"Hmm? Nope. ♪"

"All right, then."

While it would be nice to be able to surrender himself to Maria, he wasn't in the most comfortable position right now. His head was lying on her shoulder, which sounded nice, but he was sitting much higher than her, which meant that his neck was bent pretty far down. He wanted to grab on to something for support, but Maria's leg was on one side and Alisa's was on the other. There was nowhere he could safely put his hands, and he definitely couldn't wrap his arms around the back of the sofa because Maria's body was in the way. And most importantly of all, it took almost everything he had to not think about what was happening—about *what* was touching him.

"Pardon me…"

He hesitantly moved Maria's arm out of the way to pull his head free before his muscles gave out, causing him to stagger forward…

"Ah! ♪ I'm not letting you go. ♪"

"H-hey?!"

Maria wrapped her arm around his neck once more and firmly pulled his head down. Masachika completely lost his balance. He tried in a panic to find a place to put his hands, but Maria's legs were in the way, and before he could even make a decision, he fell forward—*squish*.

A soft, squishy sensation in his hand, with something even softer touching his cheeks and nose… The smell was incredible as well. His left hand was on her thigh, and he found his head buried in her loving heart (aka titties). Put simply, he was in heaven. The fact that he had hesitated because he hadn't wanted to inappropriately touch her ended up making the situation even worse (read: better).

"I'm so sorry—?!"

He tried to get off her, but he couldn't. Pressure on the back of your neck makes it harder to move than you would think. Plus, the more he moved, the more he found himself buried in the soft, squishy, hard-to-describe sensation, which was dangerous in all kinds of ways.

"H-hey?! Help m—!"

"Ayano! Look away!"

Right as Yuki interrupted Masachika's plea with a strict order of her own, Ayano froze in her tracks before she could get a step closer to Masachika to save him.

"Now!"

Ayano swiftly turned around as if Yuki's shout pushed her away. Yuki then turned as well and gave Masachika a thumbs-up over her shoulder one last time.

"Don't worry about a thing! We won't watch! So please have enough fun for all three of us!"

"I don't need you to look away! I need you to help! Ayano, please!"

"But..."

"Ayano! I am your master! Follow my orders!"

Yuki uses "Iron Fist!" It's supereffective against Ayano's nethers! Ayano's eyes turn into hearts!

"...Yes, Lady Yuki."

"Hey?!"

After losing his lifeline, Masachika had no choice but to prepare for the worst and...

"Forgive me!"

He grabbed Maria's arm before jerking his head out of her grasp and getting off the sofa. He probably touched way more than he should have in the process, but he decided to not think about it.

Forgive me, Masha's boyfriend. I don't even know what you look like, and I still feel guilty.

After he apologized telepathically to Maria's boyfriend (who he imagined was some handsome blond dude), Maria seemed somewhat displeased. She threw both of her arms around Alisa and tightly held her.

"...I can't take this anymore."

But Alisa sternly pushed her sister away and stood up, clearly aggravated...before slowly taking off her school blazer. Masachika figured she must have been hot after all that touching, and he unconsciously began to fan his face with a hand...but it didn't stop there. As Alisa reached behind herself, Masachika curiously tilted his head because it sounded like something was being unzipped.

"It's too much..."

"What the...?!"

Right in front of Masachika...Alisa pulled down her jumper's straps. Of course, her skirt swiftly fell due to gravity. Her snow-white thighs and aqua-blue panties peeked out from under the hem of her collared shirt. Masachika's eyes nearly popped out of his skull at the risqué sight and—

"She looks like an office worker who's really good at her job but is a complete mess at home!" he couldn't help but shout.

"I know what you mean!" Yuki concurred.

"Hmm?"

"Oops."

Masachika looked back the instant he heard someone agreeing with him...and realized Yuki was holding a mirror and watching what was happening.

"So much for giving me privacy, huh?"

"Should you really be worrying about me right now? And not what's happening behind you?"

"Huh?"

He swiftly looked back to find that Alisa had already undone the ribbon at her neck and was in the process of undoing the buttons on her shirt. And if that wasn't enough, Maria had begun taking off her school blazer as well.

"Wh-what?! Hold on! Why are they taking off their clothes all of a sudden?!"

"Now that I think about it, I did say that they would slowly become more open-minded and that they were going to become free both mentally and physically..."

"You creepy little genius! Thank you!"

"You let your inner thoughts slip out again, Masachika."

And thanks to their banter, Alisa was already down to the fourth button. In no position to joke about it anymore, Masachika promptly buried his confusion and panic and desperately tried to remember the phrase to break the hypnotic spell.

"Uh... All right. You are going to wake up when I touch your shoulders! Ready? Three, two, one!" he shouted, almost shrieking. He then looked into Alisa's eyes, praying it worked...

"...?"

"What the...?! It didn't work?!"

But she continued undoing her fourth button, revealing her breathtaking snow-white cleavage and aqua-blue bra, which caused Masachika to swiftly avert his gaze.

"Yuki, tag! Your turn!"

"Huh? You want me to take the video?"

"What kind of monster are you?! I want you to wake them up somehow!"

"Oh, okay."

Masachika, heart racing, moved out of the way, still staring at the ceiling.

"Um... When I touch your shoulders, you're going to wake up. Okay? Three, two, one!"

Yuki's echoing voice was followed by a complete absence of sound. After a few seconds of awkward, painful silence, she muttered:

"Oh, crap. She isn't waking up."

"What the...?! Seriously?!"

Their despair was met with the sound of rustling clothes hitting the floor just within Masachika's sight line, making him tremble violently again.

"Seriously, what are we going to—?"

"A-Ayano! I'll hold Alya! You stop Ma—!"

"Masha? You in here? How much longer do I have to wait for you?"

All of a sudden, Masachika heard the door opening, followed by the sound of a familiar voice, but by the time he placed the voice, it was already too late. Chisaki was standing there with her eyes wide in complete astonishment.

"…Huh? What's going on?"

"O-oh! This is… Uh… We found this book on hypnosis, so we decided to try it out, but we don't know how to snap them out of it!" shouted Yuki. Chisaki shifted her gaze toward the book lying on the table…then nodded once before closing the door and marching over.

"Excuse me."

After getting Yuki to let go of Alisa's arms and stand back, Chisaki threw a perfectly angled hook at Alisa's chin in a blur of speed, then rapidly tapped the temples and cheeks of the now wobbling girl with both hands until Alisa's eyes went blank. Chisaki gently laid her schoolmate's completely limp body on the couch. The entire process took a mere three seconds. She repeated the same thing with Maria before laying her next to her sister and nodding with evident satisfaction.

"Perfect."

"Not really," chimed in Masachika, unable to keep his mouth shut. He was so worked up that he forgot to keep looking away. The corners of his lips twitched.

"So, uh… What the f—? Ahem. What exactly did you do to them?" he asked Chisaki.

"Huh? I reset them."

"Pretty sure only a mad scientist would use a word like that when referring to people!"

But right after his outcry, the Kujou sisters began to groggily groan in unison, causing him to jump.

"H-huh…? What am I doing on the sofa…?"

"Oh my… I feel like I just woke up from a deep sleep…"

"Um… Alya, Masha? I know you're still confused, but you should probably tidy yourselves up first."

"Huh?"

"Tidy...up...?"

After a few moments, sharp screams filled the student council room, and Masachika did everything in his power to look away. Soon, a hand wrapped ominously around his shoulder and forced him to turn around. It was like a wrench creaking while slowly tightening a bolt. He encountered Chisaki's beautiful face and smile. They were so close that any ordinary boy his age would instinctively avert his gaze shyly, but Masachika didn't look away...because he knew that looking away meant death.

"You weren't ogling, were you?"

"..."

This wasn't the kind of thing you could just be like, "Ogling what?" and get away with it, but it honestly didn't seem like she was going to kill him if he admitted it, either. In the end, Masachika wasn't able to say a word. He swallowed his breath as Chisaki slowly raised her right hand, bending each finger individually until her knuckles cracked.

"Want a reset?"

Masachika frantically shook his head as she tilted hers, still smiling.

"Okay, let's hear you reflect."

Masachika and Yuki headed back to the Kuze residence after the meeting instead of going somewhere else to continue studying as originally planned. Masachika took a seat on the edge of his bed and looked down at Yuki, who was sitting upright on the carpet.

Hell had broken loose. Thanks to Yuki shouting that she was the one who hypnotized them, Masachika managed to avoid being reset, but Alisa still glared at him like he was a criminal, and Maria immediately went home as if she was embarrassed as well. His head was already hurting trying to think about how he should act the next day when he saw them at school. At any rate, they decided to permanently seal that mysterious book on hypnosis, so all that was left now...was to atone for the crimes committed that day.

"Do you have anything to say for yourself, Yuki Suou, the scoundrel who sexually harassed her friends and ended up making them strip?"

"...I did no such thing."

"You're not even gonna admit it, huh?"

"Fine! I did it! I did it, dammit! You happy now?! I got carried away and made Alya and Masha get half naked! But honestly, not one of us really believed the hypnosis would work!"

"Yeah, that still doesn't mean you should lash out at others and pretend like you did nothing wrong."

Masachika gave her the stink eye, but Yuki simply looked away with a huff. After sighing deeply, he looked to his sister's side...at Ayano, who was sitting next to Yuki for some reason, even though nobody asked her to.

"Hey, uh...Ayano? You don't have to sit there. Yuki was the bad guy here, not you."

"I cannot stand when my master sits," replied Ayano without even a second of hesitation. What loyalty. She was the model maid. But there was something that still concerned Masachika...

"...My dear sister."

"Yes, my brother?"

"...Why does she look strangely happy about this?"

"Because she's a masochist," replied Yuki without missing a beat. Masachika turned his gaze up to the heavens and closed his eyes for about ten or so seconds, then slowly leaned forward and pinched the bridge of his nose. He took out his phone, launched a game, and began rolling gacha.

"Tsk. Another *Zashiki-warashi*—a useless low-level spirit."

"..."

"..."

Masachika clicked his tongue at the dud he pulled and tossed his phone onto a pillow before lightly clearing his throat. After fixing his expression, he placed his elbows on his knees and swiftly leaned forward, bringing his face closer to his sister's.

"So? Let's hear your reflection."

"You're the one trying to escape from reality," assessed Yuki calmly.

"Who wouldn't in this situation?!"

Masachika suddenly clutched his head, then covered his face with his arms as if he were taking a defensive position to protect himself from the hard-to-accept reality.

"Also, your buildup to this was way too long."

"Sorry about that. Thanks for waiting, though," apologized Masachika, meekly peeking out from the gap between his arms after getting hit by Yuki's caustic criticism.

"You're welcome."

Are they doing a bit? thought Ayano, wondering if she should speak up.

"Phew... Anyway, let's hear you reflect on your actions already."

"Hold up. Stop pretending like you didn't hear what I said."

"I heard nothing."

Masachika, staring blankly with unfocused eyes, was trying to pretend like he hadn't heard anything, so he looked to Yuki's side.

"Hey, Ayano? Quick question. Are you the M in BDSM?"

"Of course." (M = maid?)

"You heard the woman, Masachika."

"Quit iiiiiit!"

Masachika clutched his head once more, taken aback by the fact that Ayano herself admitted she was a masochist.

"I can't take it anymore! Not only is my sister abnormal, but even my childhood friend?! I trusted you!"

"The hell? You make it sound like I'm weird."

"Did you honestly believe you were normal?"

"Well, I know for certain it isn't normal to be this cute. That's for sure," Yuki said with a nod, crossing her arms with a dead serious expression.

"Don't flatter yourself."

Masachika shot his sister a disgusted glare, but Yuki simply smiled as she slyly looked back up at him.

"Be honest. I am cute, aren't I?"

She closed one eye and tapped her fist against her cheek, playing up her cuteness, but she was met with her brother's cold stare.

"Can I be honest with you?" he asked with a serious expression.

"Of course. Come at me," she replied, making a serious expression to match. A tense air reigned over the room as if he were about to confess something profound, and he gravely replied:

"To be completely honest...you're extremely cute."

"Thanks! ♪ *Boing!*"

"What are you, a koala?"

Her solemn facade disappeared in the blink of an eye, and she skillfully bounced from a sitting position on the floor to the bed, grabbing her brother with both arms and legs. In a way, she did look like a baby koala latching on to its mother, but...

"Hmm... I was thinking more like a rabbit, since I'm ready to f—"

"Shut up."

"I wub you, big bwuder."

"Stop talking like a baby."

"...That's it!" mumbled Yuki suddenly before releasing him as if she had been hit with a great idea. Smugly, she placed her left hand on her waist and her right hand on her chest.

"You win. So as my punishment, how about you hypnotize me just like we did to Alya and Masha."

"What? Your 'punishment'?"

"An eye for an eye, as they say. I can even hypnotize myself and start acting like a baby just like you wanted."

"No thanks. I know I said we should do that to them as a joke, but it was only that: a joke. Ayano, what is wrong with your master?"

"There is no way for an ordinary woman like me to understand her genius."

"Don't make it sound like there's some deep meaning to what she's doing. She's talking out of her ass, you know."

"Perhaps it only appears that way at first glance, but in actuality—"

"No. And since when did you become a stupid henchman who always positively interprets everything your master does? Next thing you know, you're gonna be going, '*Hur-hur-hur.* Yes, milord?' whenever she calls for you."

"I apologize, but what does 'milord' mean?"

"It's just a humorous way to say 'my lord.' They used to address noblemen this way...I think."

"Masachika, Yuki is a noble*woman*."

"Yeah, sure. That's— Ah. Whatever."

While Masachika was rolling his eyes at Ayano, Yuki was spreading her legs in front of him and squatting as if she were about to charge like a wild boar.

"Let's do this, bro! I'm ready to do away with my shame and revert back to an infant for you!"

"What the...?! You had shame?!"

"Of course, you little punk! *Uwooooooh!!*"

A powerful aura emanated from Yuki's body. It was like the power a warrior would release while charging their special move. She clenched her fists by her chest, roaring like a beast and slowly bending her upper body back until eventually stopping and falling silent.

"...Yuki?"

"..."

"Hey, you okay?"

"...Dear brother?"

"Gwah?!"

Yuki lifted her body back up and looked at her brother with beautiful, innocent eyes, making him clutch his chest and bend forward as if he had been shot in the heart. Yuki rushed over to his side in concern.

"What's wrong?!"

"Gwah! S-stop...! My old wound...! It's...!"

"You're hurt? Oh no! I'll call for a doctor!"

"No...! I-it's those beautiful eyes! Stop doing that!"

"Beautiful eyes? But your eyes are the same as mine."

"They aren't! Our eyes may have the same shape, but my eyes have been tainted!"

She placed a hand on her brother's lap and tilted her head inquisitively as he sat on the bed. If you coupled that with her petite body and pretty face, then threw away the rest of her, she would be as cute as an angel. However, that innocence of hers was like poison to the eyes of a boy with a deep, tainted sadness.

"Are you feeling ill?"

"H-hey, uh...Yuki? I'm sorry... So do you think you could go back to normal?"

"I have no idea what you are talking about."

"I can't! Ayano! Do something about your master!"

Unable to take it any longer, he turned to Ayano to save him, but Ayano had turned herself invisible as she took in the sacred sight.

"Hey, wait! Don't turn into air now! Get back here!"

"Masachika?"

"Stop looking at me like that! Your eyes are too pure!"

Yuki had evolved into an angel and Ayano, air. The bedroom was beyond recognition, twisted into chaos, and their original plan of studying together never came to fruition.

CHAPTER 3 | **Still not in the mood to clean.**

Silence. The apartment living room was filled with a comfortable stillness. It was hard to believe three energetic high school boys were there. Only the rain outside, the blowing breeze coming from the air conditioner, and the faint sound of pens sliding across paper could be heard. The relaxing mood along with the perfectly cool room almost made you want to fall asleep—

"It's as dry as dust in here!"

Or at least, that was how things were until a certain boy suddenly stood up and screamed, ruining the mood in the blink of an eye.

"Takeshi? You okay, man?" Masachika inquired.

"It's bad manners to slam your hands on the table, especially when you are a guest in someone else's home." Hikaru threw in a scolding.

Masachika and Hikaru looked exasperatedly at Takeshi.

"What do you want me to do? Turn off dry mode on the air conditioner?"

"I'm not talking about the air conditioner! That's not what's dry!"

"Then what are you talking about?"

"I have a good idea what he means…"

But Takeshi didn't wince under his two best friends' unenthusiastic gazes and howled:

"Why the hell do I have to spend my weekend studying with two sweaty guys?! You're supposed to invite girls to these study groups, too!"

"Yo, you're starting to sound like me," Masachika commented.

"I'm not talking about some nerdy anime fantasy of yours. I'm talking about in general!"

"Yeah, maybe if you're one of the popular guys at school, and you usually hang out with the girls in your class, which I'm pretty sure we don't."

"Oh? Did that really just come out of your mouth? Did the guy who hangs out with the two beautiful princesses of Seirei Academy really just say that?!"

"But, like… You know?"

The two beautiful princesses of Seirei Academy Takeshi was talking about were the solitary princess, Alisa, and the noble princess, Yuki. And from Takeshi's point of view, Alisa and Masachika seemed really close, since they were running together in the student council election. Plus, they sat next to each other in class. And Yuki? She was a fellow student council member and Masachika's childhood friend, as far as Takeshi knew. Although Yuki was actually Masachika's little sister. He probably looked like the luckiest guy in the world from Takeshi's perspective.

"Not only are you and Yuki close, but you're the only guy Princess Alya even talks to. And yet you claim you don't have any female friends? Apologize to all the real losers at school this instant!"

"Sorry I'm friends with two cute girls. Are you jealous? You are, aren't you?"

"You're sick!"

Takeshi glared at his smirking, trolling friend as if Masachika had killed his parents, then slammed his hands against the table once more.

"Yes, I'm jealous! So hurry up and tell them to get over here!"

"Wasn't expecting you to admit it," Masachika said as Takeshi bowed to him, hands still on the table.

"Just so we're clear, I never call them on the weekend to invite them to hang out or anything. Yuki's probably busy with her extra-curricular activities, and I don't think I've ever called Alya for something nonschool related. Plus, even if I do get them to come over here somehow, you'd be so nervous that you wouldn't be able to study."

"Yeah, I guess you're right about that...," Takeshi agreed with a sigh.

After Takeshi dropped back into his seat, he rested his elbow on the table and his chin on his palm as he begrudgingly stared at his textbooks...until he quickly lifted his head back up as if a light bulb had gone off.

"What about that girl?"

"What girl?"

"You know, the one who was with Yuki at the debate the other day."

"Oh...," Masachika mumbled lifelessly the moment he realized Takeshi was talking about Ayano, Yuki's maid and running mate.

"She didn't really stand out much, but she's actually really cute when you take a good look at her. I've never seen her around school, though. Maybe she transferred from another school?"

"Nah, she graduated from middle school at Seirei Academy."

"Wait. What? Really? Did she have some dramatic change when she started high school?"

"...Nope. She's actually been like that since middle school."

"Huh... Interesting... Wait! You make it sound like you've been friends with her since middle school, too!"

"Sorta... She's a childhood friend, too."

"What?!" shrieked Takeshi, his voice cracking a bit as he leaned forward, glaring at Masachika from only inches away from his face.

"I've had enough of your bull, man! How many cute girls are you friends with?!"

"You jelly?"

"Yes!!"

Takeshi slammed his hands against the table, looked up, and bit his lip in frustration.

"So...do you think you could introduce me to her?"

"Nope."

"Why?!"

"What kind of guy would introduce his dear childhood friend to a horny monkey like you?"

"Who are you calling a horny monkey?!"

"You. I thought I made that clear. Besides, if you want to talk to her, then why do you need me? Just talk to her."

"...?! I can't... I get nervous talking to girls I don't know."

"Ah, like an innocent little boy."

After Takeshi bashfully looked away, Masachika watched him with disgust.

"I don't see why you'd be that nervous, since you never have any trouble talking to the girls in our class."

"Come on. Talking to girls in our class is completely different from talking to a stranger in a different class. Besides..."

"'Besides'?"

"...I usually only talk to the girls in our class as a group. I never talk to them individually."

"...Oh. So you're fine addressing a group of girls all at once, but you can't talk to them one-on-one."

"Because it makes me nervous."

"And that's what makes you so pure."

Masachika and Hikaru rolled their eyes, but they also smiled as if it had warmed their hearts to learn how shy their friend was, since he usually acted flirty at school.

"*Sigh*... I bet you'd have a girlfriend or two by now if you weren't so shy."

"I agree."

"H-hey, gimme a break." Takeshi groaned.

He somehow managed to look bashful, troubled, and smug at the same time.

"I mean, you're a very positive, sociable guy, which most people like. And, well, you're not ugly, I guess... You're not the best at reading the room from time to time, but you're desperate for a girlfriend, so if you were only a bit more proactive, then I think you could actually get one."

"Yes, I agree. I think girls would find you very likable, since you're an honest, straightforward guy... You're not good at reading the room most of the time, though."

"Are you trying to compliment me or put me down?! Come on! Let me feel completely good about myself for a change! Why do you always have to add a little jab at the end?!"

"Uh... Because...well..."

"Yeah..."

After Masachika and Hikaru exchanged glances and smirks, Takeshi felt disheartened and sat back down, and for the next few minutes, he grumbled, "Look at me. I'm the guy who never knows how to read the room," to himself before eventually glaring at Masachika.

"What about you? You seem to be quite the catch, if I do say so myself. Surely you'd be able to bag yourself a girlfriend."

"Who? Me?"

"Like, I get Hikaru, since he has apparently had some unpleasant experiences in the past, but you? Don't you want a girlfriend?"

"Hmm..."

Masachika crossed his arms and thought about Takeshi's question for a few moments.

"...I'm not really interested in looking for a girlfriend."

"Why? Don't tell me you're only into anime girls?"

"It's not that. It's just...getting a girlfriend doesn't really feel realistic to me. At all."

"Why? I hate to admit it, but you could almost be a perfect superhuman if you weren't such a slacker. You don't look half bad, either. Got nothing on Hikaru, but still decent."

"Pretty sure I'm a solid six out of ten."

"I don't know about that. You'd probably fall into the 'hot guy' category with the ladies."

"Are you messing with me? I mean, I guess I have a decent body at least…"

I honestly feel like I'm average in the looks department. Of course, if you compare me with Hikaru, you could easily point out a lot of my flaws, but I feel like that's the same with most people, so it's better not to bring it up.

"I noticed you didn't deny that you are almost a perfect superhuman, though, huh?"

"…Well, I do realize that I'm *somewhat* athletically gifted and smart." Masachika shrugged at Takeshi's scornful expression. Masachika wasn't unaware of his talent, and while he added the word *somewhat,* he realized that the exceptional talent he possessed far surpassed *somewhat.* His nerdy sister jokingly said that he had the cheat skill "Gained EXP × 10 (with the exception of sports involving balls)," but that wasn't too far from the truth, either. Masachika had displayed talent in every field to the point that the employees of the Suou household used to call him a child prodigy. But even then…

"The talent I have was something I was born with. It's nothing to be proud of or brag about."

"I'm pretty sure it's definitely something you should be proud of…"

"Takeshi, let me fill you in on a little secret: There is no trope hated more than that of the cocky, overpowered protagonist who hardly had to work for what he has because he was born with it. You know those asshole protagonists who are reborn in a parallel world and given cheat skills that make them overpowered, and then they get a harem? Yeah, those guys."

"All right, I think I get it, but you never really act cocky about being OP."

"That's because I don't want to get torn apart. Easier to just be modest," replied Masachika blandly before lazily leaning back in his seat.

Besides, I can't just try to play life on easy mode using the talents my parents gave me. That would be taking life for granted. It'd be arrogant.

Using above-average intelligence and skill to get into one of the top schools in Japan with hardly any effort, joining the student council, and maintaining a decent track record was more than enough to get his foot in the door anywhere. That would be taking life for granted. It would be an insult to anyone who worked as hard as they could and took life seriously. It was no different than a protagonist in a comic book easily getting the beautiful heroine—unfair and deserving of criticism.

"'The goddess of love only smiles on those who take action for themselves,'" Masachika quoted wisely.

"What does that mean?" Hikaru inquired.

"Is that a line from a comic book or something?" Takeshi guessed.

"What? No. It's an old saying my grandpa used to love. Said it all the time. He said it meant that when it came to love, you had to be assertive if you wanted to succeed."

Incidentally, the grandpa Masachika was referring to was his grandfather on his father's side, who loved Russia. He was the man who recommended Russian movies to Masachika when he was a child and the whole reason Masachika was able to learn about Russian culture. He was a funny old man over the age of seventy who still dreamed about having two beautiful Russian girls, one on each side, serving him vodka. The only problem was that he didn't drink, so even a drop of vodka would have given him acute alcohol poisoning.

"Hmm… Well, I guess that makes sense… Hold up. What about Hikaru, then?"

"People born loved by the goddess of love herself don't count."

"It is a curse if you ask me," replied Hikaru instantly with a lifeless expression.

"Yeah, uh… I feel like the goddess of love is kind of a *yandere* with a scary style of love in your case, Hikaru," Takeshi joked tensely.

"Goddesses are often portrayed as the jealous type, after all. I bet once Hikaru becomes completely distrusting of women, the goddess is going to descend to the world and be like, 'I am the only one left now. I am the only one for you.'"

"Sounds more like a demon to me," Hikaru said tonelessly.

"True that."

"Guys, I don't care if she's an angel or a demon! I just want a woman to pursue me like that!"

Masachika and Hikaru looked amused by Takeshi's unchanging desires.

"Yeah, but I think it's dangerous to wait for someone to pursue you. Like my grandpa said, you'd be more successful if you went on the offensive yourself."

"'On the offensive,' huh? …All right! Starting now, I'm going to become a real hunter and hunt me some cuties!"

"Yeah, go get 'em," Masachika said encouragingly.

"Don't get too carried away…," Hikaru warned.

Masachika only half-heartedly encouraged Takeshi because it wasn't any of his business what his friend did… Little did he know that those irresponsible words would come back to bite him in the ass in the near future.

"…Phew."

Even after Takeshi and Hikaru went home, Masachika continued to study in his room for the next day's test, but…

"I don't feel like studying anymore…"

Even he recognized that he wasn't focusing and wouldn't be able to for much longer, either. Nothing stuck. He was just running his eyes across the words in his textbook, even though he knew it wasn't working. He couldn't absorb the information he was looking at, no matter how hard he tried. Whatever he read almost immediately faded into nothingness. In other words, he had a severe drop in efficiency.

"Oh… It's already eleven."

He had been studying for two hours or so after his bath, but it had been a complete waste of time, since he wasn't able to retain anything.

"*Brain Hazard*'s about to come on…"

Masachika started to feel anxious, since one of his favorite weekly late-night shows was about to start.

I'm wasting my time forcing myself to study when I'm not remembering any of the information. Maybe I should take a short break and resume studying after that?

He toyed with the idea, but if he were to run away to anime, he would never get back to studying. Even Masachika himself knew that.

But spending more time doing something doesn't necessarily make me better at it. I've already studied for what's essentially going to be on the test, and if I review in the morning… I mean, just considering these options is already proof enough that I can't concentrate right now…

He lazily leaned back in his chair and ran senselessly through excuses until it was time for his show to come on.

"It's starting…"

But Masachika never turned on the TV in the end. After five minutes had gone by, he faced his desk once more as if he had given up.

"*Sigh*… When did I become such a coward?"

He sighed at himself because only after waiting until the anime started was he able to finally cast aside his doubts. The old Masachika would have put forth the effort for his mother or that girl without feeling the least bit burdened. But now? It appeared he had forgotten what hard work was after all those years being spineless.

Of course, he wanted to live up to Alisa's and Sayaka's expectations. He had to become a vice president people respected, for both their sakes as well... At least, that was his goal up until a week ago.

But who cares if my grades marginally improve? I made that goal for myself, and it's not like I made a promise to anyone.

The fact that he was having these thoughts was proof he was losing motivation. This was how much he cared about it. This was the man he was.

I was doing it to make myself happy. It was for me. But, well, I guess it is ego and self-satisfaction that motivate us. Every man is his own worst enemy, as they say. Alya's amazing. It's incredible how she has been able to keep herself going for this long.

Endlessly pushing oneself to become one's ideal self and working toward an unattainable goal was not something any ordinary person could do. You could call it ambition, but it felt like a disservice to put the blinding, sparkling light that Alisa had into a single word like that.

"No ambition here, though... There's nothing I even want, really."

He wasn't interested in status or honor, money or women—there was nothing he desired. All he wanted was to continue living his relatively peaceful routine life, each day unchanging and stable. If anything, he was against gaining status or honor if it meant losing the peace he had. He didn't want to risk having any money or women disturbing his calm lifestyle, either. That was Masachika's take on life for the most part. The reason he decided to run for student council with Alisa, however, was because he felt a strange sense of urgency, like he couldn't continue living this way, and he couldn't abandon Alisa, either.

"But to do that, I have to work at least half as hard as Alya…" Masachika groaned as he sprawled across the table and rubbed his forehead on his textbook.

"I can do this… I can't let my reputation be the thing that slows Alya down…"

Masachika was currently an underachiever in the classroom, with poor behavior during class and poor grades to go along with it, but he could most likely improve his reputation if he bumped up his grades and became one of the top thirty students in his year—the ranks were posted in the hallways.

That's it. I need to be the guy who sleeps the entire time during class but gets good grades. That's what the male lead does in women's comics, after all! And it always makes them clash with the heroine!

Almost everyone would prefer to be someone born with incredible talent than be someone who worked incredibly hard to get where they were. It was kind of depressing. People who got good grades but didn't seem like they ever studied were usually praised far more than someone who got good grades because they worked hard.

The hell? People who work hard to get what they have are way more praiseworthy, thought Masachika. However, that wasn't how the real world worked. Plus, he figured it would be more in character for him to seem like that kind of person. In fact, the entire reason he'd wanted to use the student council room was so that no one would see him study.

"Come on, brain. Just a little more."

After encouraging himself one last time, Masachika had just managed to get up when, all of a sudden, his phone on his desk started to vibrate.

"Hmm? Someone's calling me?"

Flustered, he grabbed his buzzing phone and instantly froze when he saw the name on the screen.

"A-Alya?!"

He was really thrown for a loop because he figured it was going to be his father or sister. Alisa rarely ever texted him, let alone called him. Plus, it was the middle of the night. It was far too late for a model student like Alisa to be calling.

"Oops. It stopped ringing."

The phone had stopped buzzing while he was busy panicking. Judging by the fact that it stopped vibrating after only ten seconds, it was safe to conclude that Alisa had hung up…which would lead one to believe that this wasn't anything important, but Masachika decided to call her back anyway. The phone only had to ring twice before someone promptly picked up.

"Oh, hello?"

"…Good evening, Kuze."

"Yeah, hey. What's up? You needed something?"

"That's not why I called…," Alisa replied vaguely, and it made Masachika grin mischievously.

"What? Did you miss me?" he teased, ridiculously lowering his voice to sound as cool as possible.

"…"

And yet his comment was met with silence. He grew antsy, as if he could sense her cold, piercing glare, and he immediately cleared his throat to change the subject…

"<Is that a problem?>"

The abrupt comment in Russian almost knocked him out cold, and he fell forward over his desk.

"…? What was that sound?"

"Oh, uh… Don't worry about it. By the way, what did you just say?"

"I called you an idiot."

"Uh-huh… So… What'd you need?"

"…You said you weren't motivated enough to study alone, so I worried you were having trouble."

"…"

She'd hit the nail on the head, leaving him silent.

"Wait. Don't tell me you were slacking off," added Alisa, voice deepening darkly.

"No way. I was tempted to watch some anime for a while, but I overcame the temptation and am studying now. I'm serious."

"…"

A few seconds of dubious silence went by before being followed by a brief sigh.

"Test week starts tomorrow, you know. I thought this was when you'd be studying your hardest."

"Yeah, I get that, but…sorry. I have absolutely no willpower. I'm too weak."

"I wouldn't go so far as to say that…"

"I just don't have the motivation to study anymore. Like, how do you do it?"

"…I don't know. I've never lost my motivation."

"Seriously? That's insane."

Masachika smiled a bit incredulously, but after a few moments of pondering, Alisa spoke up and calmly explained:

"If anything, I always feel pressed for time. I'm always wondering if there's something I forgot to do or something more I could do with the time I have, so I don't have the opportunity to worry about being motivated."

"…You really are incredible."

She truly was a perfectionist, and Masachika was genuinely impressed by her never-ending pursuit to reach new heights. He was even starting to feel a little embarrassed that he'd considered calling it quits and reviewing in the morning.

"Anyway, I guess I shouldn't bother you any longer and instead work a little harder like you. Thanks for the call, Alya."

"Huh? Ah…"

"Hmm?"

Right when he was about to hang up, Masachika noticed a twinge of panic in her voice and placed the smartphone to his ear.

"What's wrong?"

"…"

"?"

But what his curious ear was met with was a provocative Russian sentence…

"<It's still…too soon…>"

The whisper made Masachika's head jolt back as if he had just been blasted in the forehead, then his lifeless body rolled down his chair. The soft words had numbed everything from his ear to his brain.

H-how dare she whisper something like that into my ear! And what does she mean by, "It's still too soon"?! I mean, I'm sure she was talking about it being too soon to hang up, but it's still too damn ambiguous, and now my imagination is running wild!!

The words tingled in his ear, overloading his nerd brain! He unconsciously visualized Alisa bashfully averting her gaze while whispering those words in all sorts of scenarios.

"<It's still…too soon…>" Ack! That's what the heroine says before they kiss in movies! The guy goes in for the kiss, and the girl covers her mouth and says that! It's like when you say good-bye and go in for a good-night kiss after the third date! …Oh, this is when things get a little awkward between the two main characters, and a new character suddenly appears to stir the waters, as if they were waiting for this moment.

"…Kuze?"

"And the new character knows a past secret of one of the two main characters and drops hints that they know something, but they have ulterior motives. You can't trust the ones who seem perfect and sweet at first."

"…What are you talking about?"

"Huh? You know. Like, why are transfer students usually bad

people in comics targeting women, while they're usually cute girls in comics targeting men?"

"...Well, I've learned one thing tonight. You absolutely cannot focus on studying for the life of you."

"Oh, uh... Yep."

The awkwardness of realizing what he'd said shut Masachika up. Alisa filled the silence with a brief sigh before redirecting the conversation:

"Okay... If you aren't feeling motivated, then how about we make a little bet?"

"A bet?"

"What's your goal?"

"My goal? You mean for the exams?"

"Yes."

"...I want to make it into the top thirty students in our grade."

"...That's quite a big goal. All right. If you can do that, I will grant you one wish. Anything you want."

"Hmm? 'Anything'?"

"...Within the realm of common sense, of course," Alisa added coldly.

"Oh, uh. Sorry. I felt the urge to react to that. You know, being a nerd and all."

Masachika desperately tried to explain himself as his eyes wandered.

"...I have no idea what you're talking about. Anyway, is it a deal?"

"Uh... What if I don't make it into the top thirty?"

"Then you are going to grant one wish of mine."

"...Interesting. Could be fun."

"Kuze?"

"Oh, uh...! I didn't mean it like I wanted to be bossed around by you or anything! I'm just curious what you might ask me to do!"

A few moments of skeptical silence followed his explanation, then Alisa suddenly whispered in Russian:

"<…First name.>"

"Huh?"

"I was giving you a hint."

"…Not much of a hint when you say it in Russian."

"I know." Alisa laughed smugly.

I actually do understand Russian, thought Masachika, but that still didn't help him understand the hint any better.

"Anyway, do we have an agreement?"

"S-sure… If I make it into the top thirty, you will grant one of my wishes, and if I fail, then I will grant one of yours. Right?"

"That's right."

"Then we have a deal. Heh-heh-heh… You're gonna regret ever making this deal with me."

"Hmph. Good luck."

"…You've gotten really good at brushing me off like that. You really should respect your elders, you know."

"What? We're the same age," replied Alisa as if she were rolling her eyes. Masachika was confused.

"No. We might be in the same grade, but I'm still older than you."

"Huh?"

"Huh?"

Her baffled voice made it easy to imagine the dumbfounded look on her face, which Masachika responded to with a puzzled grunt of his own.

"Your birthday's November seventh, right?" asked Masachika just to make sure.

"Yes… How'd you know that?"

"Didn't you tell us when you first transferred to our school? I'm pretty sure I remember hearing you mention it… Eh. Anyway, my birthday's April ninth, which makes me older."

"…"

"I'm already sixteen."

"…"

An indescribable silence followed until Masachika suddenly cleared his throat to play off the awkwardness.

"Ahem! Anyway, it's getting late, so…"

"…Yes."

"Thanks, Alya."

"No need to thank me…"

"See you tomorrow."

"Good night."

After hanging up, he stretched his arms out wide.

"Mmm…! Let's do this!"

And he faced his textbook once more, as though the phone call had breathed new life into him. His complete lack of motivation from a few minutes ago felt like a dream. It wasn't the bet he'd made with Alisa that motivated him, though. Just having her, someone who took the time out of her night to call him instead of studying, made him happy. He felt like he had to pay her back for her kindness by studying, at the very least.

I'm still surprised she knew I was losing motivation, though…

While it was embarrassing that she saw right through him like that, it made him happy as well. Call it telepathy. Call it a deep bond. Call it whatever you wanted, because whatever it was, it touched Masachika.

"Thank you, Alya."

He smiled shyly as he quietly expressed his gratitude to his partner, then started doing his final preparations for the test.

◇

Meanwhile, his partner…

"I'm okay… I'm okay…"

Alisa was mumbling to herself after opening the door to her room. She wasn't doing anything out of the ordinary, though. She was simply heading to the living room to get some water. Why was getting a mere glass of water making her so taut and nervous? …It all started a few hours ago during dinnertime.

"Lurking in the shadows are beings that are beyond human understanding, with powers of unspeakable monstrosity. Tonight, I invite you to a world of horror."

A haunting video was playing with a frightening background track, muffled with static. When they'd turned on the TV during dinner, a show about the paranormal (which was pretty common during the summer) started playing. Maria, who absolutely hated horror, quickly finished her dinner and went back to her room, but Alisa's stubborn personality wouldn't allow that.

"Tsk. Masha's such a scaredy-cat… Me, though? This is nothing," Alisa seemed to be saying as she slowly finished her dinner and calmly returned to her room like the show wasn't a big deal. As one might imagine, it wasn't until the middle of the night when she started to get scared. It was to the point that she was too afraid to walk down the dark hallway to get a glass of water.

A—a ghost isn't going to just pop up out of nowhere, right?

Alisa's head was filled with flashbacks of the spiritual phenomena she saw on TV, keeping her from taking another step outside her room. With that being said, she still wouldn't allow herself to pathetically run to her family for help. Not anymore. After worrying herself sick, she decided to call Masachika, even though she realized how inappropriate it was for her to be calling this late at night. Saying she was calling to check up on his studies was merely an excuse she came up with on the spot. While a certain someone was bashfully crediting the call to telepathy or some special connection the two of them had, the truth was far from it. That was just how the real world worked.

"I'm fine… Okay, let's do this!"

After firing herself up, Alisa clutched her phone, which she had just been talking to Masachika on, to her chest like a good-luck charm, then rushed out into the hallway on her tiptoes. She looked straight ahead the entire time, not even glancing around her as she swiftly ran through the living room; poured herself a glass of water at the sink, which she instantly downed; and sprinted back to her room.

"Phew…"

She let out a deep sigh of relief after returning to her brightly lit room. But when the fear started to fade away, it revealed discontent. What was she upset about? She was upset that Masachika *never told her it was his birthday* back in April.

"What's his problem? I would have at least wished him happy birthday if he'd told me…"

If Masachika were there, he probably would have said, "If I'd told you it was my birthday, it'd feel like I was pressuring you to get me a gift or celebrate it with me," but it couldn't be helped. It was a cultural difference, after all. While it was normal in Japan for friends or families to throw birthday parties for their loved ones, it was more common in Russia, where Alisa was born, for someone to host a birthday party for themselves and invite their friends and family. They'd say something like, "Thank you all for being here today on my birthday! Eat and drink to your heart's content!" In other words, not telling Alisa about his birthday = not inviting Alisa to his birthday party = he didn't even consider her to be a friend.

"And you said we were friends…"

While Alisa didn't invite him to celebrate her birthday last year, either, it was an entirely different situation. It wasn't as if she hadn't wanted to invite him, but if she'd only invited Masachika, she would never have heard the end of it. Her family would have teased her day in and day out, but she didn't have any other friends she could invite, either, so she gave up.

...I wasn't crying. It didn't make me sad when I compared my birthday with Maria's exciting party. Not even a bit. It only made sense that her birthday was so full of life because her birthday is on Christmas Eve. That was why her birthday was more fun. I wasn't making excuses to make myself feel better! I wasn't! Really!

"...Hmph! Whatever," Alisa muttered under her breath before she threw herself onto the bed to relieve some stress. She squeezed her pillow to her chest while burying her face in it. And then she suddenly released her tight grip, pouted, and whispered:

"...You're such a jerk."

CHAPTER 4 | **I-it's a cultural difference...**

"Yes! Nngh…"

Masachika stretched his arms out wide, feeling accomplished after finishing the first week of exams. When he looked around the room, most of the class was already enjoying their freedom and discussing what they were going to do after school, despite still having homeroom after this. Masachika, on the other hand, wasn't planning on hanging out with his friends once school ended. Instead he would watch all the anime he'd recorded—or at least, that was the plan. But there was one thing he couldn't get off his mind…

"Hey, Alya."

"Hey."

It was the fact that Alisa seemed somewhat, truly only a little bit, distant—kind of cold. Ever since Monday, it had felt like something was off, but it was exam week and it could have all been in his head, so Masachika decided to let it go. But he wasn't comfortable going into the weekend without figuring out what this strange, unsettling feeling was.

"Alya, uh… What are you doing after school today?"

"Nothing in particular."

"Oh. Then do you want to walk home together? I want to talk about the closing ceremony if that's okay."

"…Sure."

"Great. Then let's head out together after homeroom."

"Okay."

The conversation itself was extremely normal, and Alisa's behavior didn't seem much different from normal, either, but…something still felt off.

She hasn't been whispering anything sweet in Russian… I don't know why, but…

It had been five days, and he hadn't heard a word of Russian from Alisa. Of course, from Masachika's point of view, that was a good thing. The sudden whispers weren't good for his heart, and the muscles in his face got to relax for a change, since she would usually glance in his direction after whispering in Russian, which made his face tense. So not hearing any of her whispers had its upsides, but…he couldn't help feeling concerned. And the more he thought about it, he realized Alisa had been a bit withdrawn from him this week.

Hmm… I'm sure it's all in my head, but…

Next Saturday was the closing ceremony, which was a huge event in regard to the election because they had to give speeches and greet the student body. That was why they needed to remove whatever was causing the friction between them before then. But, well…

Did I do anything to make her hate me?

He was a sensitive man, frustrated and unbelievably curious as he wondered what he possibly could have done.

After homeroom, Masachika and Alisa left the classroom together as planned, but they felt as though more people were staring at them now than ever as they walked side by side. Alisa's otherworldly beauty had always caught everyone's attention, but eyes were also on Masachika. It seemed as though many students were already recognizing them as candidates and running mates for the student council presidency and vice presidency thanks to the debate last week.

"…So? You wanted to talk to me about our speech at the closing ceremony?"

"Yeah, about that…"

Alisa was as cool as a cucumber despite their onlookers, but Masachika hesitated for a few moments before asking her directly:

"Before we talk about that, I need to ask you something, Alya. Is everything all right?"

"What do you mean?"

"Well… I feel like you've been acting a bit off since Monday."

She suddenly stopped in her tracks, then turned to look at him in amazement.

"Judging from how you're looking at me…I'm guessing something did happen?" commented Masachika with a forced grin.

Alisa, however, stayed silent, turned about-face, and began to walk away.

"…It's just your imagination," she replied with her best poker face.

"Come on. Do you seriously think you can fool me like that?"

"…"

Knowing how stubborn she could be, Masachika made a conscious effort to continue looking forward as he went on:

"Did I do something? Because if I did, I want you to tell me."

"…I don't want to tell you."

"Mmm… All right, then…"

"*Sigh*… I'll make sure to work on my behavior. Besides, I'm sure I'll be back to normal by the time Monday comes around. Isn't that enough?" asked Alisa, glancing up through her eyelashes at him after letting out a brief sigh. Her somewhat uneasy, childish expression would make anyone want to rub her head and dote on her while saying, "That's more than enough." Nevertheless, Masachika managed to get rid of the unholy thought with a shake of his head, and he looked at her seriously.

"Hmm… I don't know… It has already been five days, and you're still in a bad mood. I mean, I guess it would be okay if you really were back to normal next week, but…"

"Was I that obvious?"

"Yeah…"

"Oh… I really was trying my best to hide it."

And, well, it really was difficult to tell anything was wrong just by her facial expressions, but the lack of her occasional Russian whispers betrayed her. She didn't seem to notice, though.

"Actually, you did a good job of hiding it, so I think you are very self-aware. In a good way, of course. I still noticed, though." Masachika shrugged.

"O-oh? You did, huh?"

Alisa arched an eyebrow while fidgeting with her hair.

"In other words, you were really concerned? You couldn't get me out of your mind, even though it was exam week?" she asked a bit provocatively.

"Of course I'm worried. You're my partner, and I care about you," he replied with a dead serious look on his face.

"O-oh… Huh."

"And I care about you. And I care about you. And I care about you…" Those words of his echoed in Alisa's mind, and her fidgeting increased. The ends of her hair were going to get tangled at this rate… but her fingers suddenly froze, and her eyes narrowed in frustration.

"Then why…?"

"Hmm?"

"…"

Alisa looked away from his confused expression and pouted. Masachika changed out of his school slippers and put on his shoes, wondering about her sudden change in mood. Then they began to walk toward the school gate, and Alisa eventually muttered:

"…Your birthday."

"Huh?"

"Why didn't you invite me to your birthday party?" complained Alisa, still avoiding his eyes…but Masachika had no idea what she was talking about.

"Birthday party? What do you mean?"

"You know what I'm talking about. Your…"

Thinking he was playing dumb, she glared at him, but that still didn't help Masachika understand what she was going on about.

"Uh…? A birthday party? Me?"

"…Yes, you."

"…This is the first I'm hearing about it. Who told you I had a birthday party?"

"What do you mean this is the first you're hearing of this? Don't be ridiculous."

"Wh-what the…? I'm telling the truth! I have no idea what you're talking about! And why would I even have a birthday party anyway? What am I, a first grader?!"

"Huh…?"

That was when Alisa realized something wasn't adding up, and she looked at him quizzically, her brow knitted. At the same time, Masachika came to a sudden realization.

"O-oh, wait. Hold on. Do teenagers in Russia usually have birthday parties?"

"Y-yeah. Are things different in Japan?"

"You usually stop having birthday parties in Japan once you hit middle school… Wait. I take that back. There are probably a good number of students at our school who still throw birthday parties. Some kids apparently even throw huge parties at their house. At any rate, I, personally, haven't had a birthday party since middle school."

"Oh…"

"How are you only realizing this n—? …Oh. Sorry."

"What are you apologizing for?"

"Oh, uh. Nothing."

She never had any friends to celebrate birthdays with. That was why. It wasn't like he could say that, though, which was why he decided to hold his tongue, but his lips curled a bit as he looked at her slyly.

"...What?" she asked grumpily.

"Don't worry about it. I just had no idea you wanted to celebrate my birthday with me that much."

"...!"

Alisa scowled and immediately looked away, but she wasn't fast enough to prevent Masachika from seeing her snow-white cheeks flush pink.

"...Not telling someone your birthday in Russia is no different than saying you don't want to be friends with them."

"Ohhh?"

"What?"

"If you say so, Alya. Wink, wink."

"Tsk...!"

He could almost see a vein bulging from her forehead, so he decided he should stop teasing her and make her feel better instead.

"So... Wanna go do something for my birthday? We're three months late, but..."

"Huh?"

"Of course, I still want to be friends and hang out more. How about we go somewhere for lunch next Monday, since it's a half day? We can talk about the closing ceremony and whatnot then, too... Or is it bad luck to wish someone a belated happy birthday in Russia?"

After pondering it for a moment, she shook her head.

"It's not good to wish someone happy birthday early, but late... should be fine."

"All right, then. Let's do it. Ahem. While I know it is late, it would be an honor if you would grace me with your presence at my birthday party, which I will be holding next week," announced Masachika with an unnecessarily grave expression.

"Are you okay in the head?" Alisa scoffed, but Masachika was relieved to see that she appeared to be in a better mood. That look of relief on his face made Alisa stare at him with suspicion once more. Perhaps she realized he was trying to humor her to make up for teasing her, like an adult rattling a toy for a baby. Alisa glared at him out of the corner of her eye with a look of disgust…until they reached a fork in the road, and he faced her.

"Well, I'm going this way. Anyway, see you Monday. Have—…?"

Alisa's eyes suddenly began wandering, darting around in every direction.

Is she looking for something?

It was easy to imagine a question mark hovering over Masachika's head, and he began looking around as well until he suddenly realized Alisa was grinning at him. This set off alarm bells in his head.

Ack! Something bad is going to happen, isn't it?

He instinctively took a step back, but Alisa took a step forward before he could effectively make his escape. They were so close that they could almost feel each other's breath. Alisa placed a hand on his shoulder as he stood frozen, then placed her cheek against his and whispered into his ear:

"<I can't wait. ♡>"

But in the blink of an eye, she stepped back and glared at him.

"There. We're friends again. See you Monday," she spluttered before instantly spinning on her heel and walking off.

"Yeah…"

Masachika watched her leave in mute amazement, then walked awkwardly in the opposite direction on autopilot. But the moment he turned the corner, he grabbed a nearby fence as his legs gave out.

Ha-ha-ha… The first thing she has said in Russian to me in four days… Shouldn't have let my guard down.

"I'm pretty confident I could actually cough up blood right now if I wanted to," said Masachika tensely, clutching at his chest.

I feel like the bar has been raised twice as high now...

He thought he could get away with taking her to some cheap chain restaurant in the neighborhood, but not after she said that. It was going to have to be somewhere more high-end and proper now.

I'm going to have to look for a nice restaurant over the weekend...

This is going to be a pretty difficult mission for someone ignorant about these kinds of things, thought Masachika bitterly with a tight smile, but at least he now knew what had been bothering Alisa, so he decided to call it a win. However, there was something he understood even more than that, for he had discovered...

Having her whisper into my ear like that...could actually kill me.

The following Monday had arrived. The week after exams was essentially for going over the tests in the mornings, and in the afternoons, they discussed summer homework while others attended parent-teacher conferences. The conferences went by student number, which meant Alisa's and Masachika's were the following day.

"So? How'd you do on the tests?"

"I did okay, I guess. My grades were higher than the class average in every subject, at least," replied Masachika, who was working out a crick in his neck on their way out the school gate. That morning, the students were given a brief transcript of what they'd scored on the exams along with the class average. While they went over the tests in class, students would sometimes find mistakes the teachers had made while grading, which was why the official class rank would be posted on Saturday. So they would be using tentative report cards during the parent-teacher meetings. It so happened that they had a half day of school every other Saturday, and this coming Saturday was the closing ceremony, where they would receive their finalized grades for the semester.

"Anyway, I don't know whether I achieved my goal, but I did a lot better than last time."

"Oh? Congratulations."

"Right? Feel free to shower me with praise now."

"Wowww. Good job," replied Alisa robotically.

"…Gee. Thanks."

Masachika shot her a piercing glare, but she completely ignored him and feigned innocence.

"*Sniffle.* You're so mean, Alya."

"If you're trying to act like Masha, please stop. It's grossing me out."

"Yes, ma'am."

The fact that not even her eyes were laughing wiped the goofy look right off his face. His eyes wandered for a few moments until he suddenly changed the subject without even trying to be subtle about it.

"So… Pretty hot to be walking around in the middle of the day. Doesn't help that it is so bright out, either…," commented Masachika, tugging at his collar and fanning himself while frowning down at his clothes. "Why do our school uniforms have to be so hot? It's summer, and we're still wearing long sleeves."

"Oh, this isn't normal in Japan, is it?"

"Not even close. Most schools pass out short-sleeved shirts for the summer. Even businesspeople get to wear short-sleeved button-downs nowadays."

The shirts they were wearing were made of a thinner material than the winter uniforms, but the long sleeves retained too much heat. But why was the school so set on keeping the uniforms this way, even in this day and age? For the same reason their schoolbags hadn't changed in years. Because it was tradition. Seirei Academy's school uniform was rather well-known. People would instantly recognize it around town if they saw it. In a way, the uniform itself was a famous brand of clothing, and the students of Seirei Academy were proud to wear it. However, it also kept the students in-line so they would act proper even outside of school because they were always being watched. Masachika, on the other hand, thought differently.

"They're really downplaying the effects of global warming, aren't they? At least let me take this blazer off."

"Wasn't the student council president trying to do something about the uniforms, though?"

"That was one of his campaign pledges… It sounds like he's having a tough time. Even if he does get the rule changed, I'm guessing we won't be seeing it implemented until the next school year."

Touya, who was on the same page as Masachika when it came to the school uniform, was apparently working toward updating the uniform requirements, but it was a difficult task, especially since a decent portion of the student population didn't care how hot it was, as long as they looked good. The alumni association, which consisted of past student council presidents and vice presidents, was strongly against changing the summer uniform as well, which made the situation even more difficult. Meanwhile, Masachika couldn't help but wonder if they were only being stubborn because they had to wear these uncomfortably hot uniforms back in the day, so they wanted everyone else to suffer as well.

"Anyway, I hope the president gets it done, especially for the sake of middle-class students like us who have to walk home, since we don't have our own personal chauffeurs."

"Are you sure you don't just want to see girls scantily dressed?"

"So you're saying I'm still gonna feel hot and heavy even if we change the summer uniform? Heh! I like the way you think!"

"…"

"Because the thought honestly never crossed my mind. I mean, the first day of summer uniforms is supposedly a pretty important event in a nerd's life, but I've gone to this school basically my entire life, so it really hasn't occurred to me."

Alisa glared coldly as he explained his twisted thinking, but she suddenly smirked provocatively, flipped her hair over her shoulder, and flirtatiously glanced at him out of the corner of her eye.

"So you don't want to see me in a short-sleeved shirt?"

"I mean, if I had to choose, then yes. I do."

"Heh. Oh, you do, huh?"

And if he were being a little more honest, he would tell her what he was *really* interested in seeing: the fabled see-through white shirt with that ever so incredibly faint glimpse of the bra. He was a teenage boy, after all.

But that's something you want to see when the girl's sitting in front of you in class…and Hikaru sits in front of me, which is something I'm definitely not interested in seeing.

"Ahem. Are you thinking about something you shouldn't be?"

"Huh? No way. I was just thinking about how unpleasantly sweaty the president would look in a short-sleeved shirt."

"That's… Yes…" Alisa nodded, her eyes wandering. Within seconds, her smug grin had transformed into a criticizing glare before changing once again at Masachika's innocent response. It was unfortunate that Touya had to be defamed by such an "innocent" comment.

"I bet Chisaki would take everyone by surprise as well. Her biceps and shoulders must be huge. She doesn't really stand out usually, but she apparently has a really athletic build."

"I could see that," agreed Alisa, checking out Masachika from head to toe and grinning almost mockingly.

"You in a short-sleeved shirt would probably leave much to be desired, though, hmm?"

"What the…? Why are you dissing me like that all of a sudden? I have a decent amount of muscle, just to let you know."

"Oh, you do?"

"Don't underestimate a homebody. Don't make me show you this sexy, toned bod."

Masachika immediately imagined himself in a beach lounge chair in a short-sleeved collared shirt (unbuttoned, of course) with his pecs and abs showing…and he instinctively covered his mouth.

"…? What's wrong?"

"Oh… I just imagined something really disgusting. Being ripped only works if you're good-looking, too, huh?" he contemplated with a heavy heart, and erased the narcissistic image from his mind. She looked up slightly, then began to fidget with her hair as if she had an idea of what he'd imagined.

"<I don't think it's disgusting at all.>"

"What was that?"

"I said, 'Great. Now I imagined it, too, thanks to you.'"

"Uh-huh… You didn't have to actually tell me the truth, you know."

"You shouldn't have asked, then," Alisa scoffed, flicking back her hair. After rolling his eyes at her, Masachika stared into the distance.

How does Alya see me?

"<Besides, you are good-looking.>"

Gwah! S-seriously, what do I look like from her point of view?

He desperately tried to keep a straight face while a cyclone of emotions tore through his heart. Fortunately (?), they were approaching their destination, so he was able to focus on that instead, and before long they arrived at a large clothing store by the station that was geared toward teenagers. Why were they stepping inside a clothing store before they went out to lunch? Well, the answer was simple: to change. Masachika was fine with wearing what they had on, but

Alisa didn't seem keen on the idea of wearing a school uniform to a restaurant during this time of day, so they decided to change. That said, they weren't going to do any shopping. This store actually had a changing room Seirei Academy students could use for free. Masachika had been impressed when he'd first heard about it. Of course, Seirei Academy students were still human. They were young. They wanted to hang out after school before going home, but it was against school rules to fool around in the uniform. While you could probably get away with eating at a restaurant, going to the arcade or karaoke was a definite no-no.

One of the worst things about having a well-known uniform was the fact that a local could easily call their school and report them if they were breaking any rules, and they wouldn't be able to avoid punishment if that happened. Therefore, they had no choice but to change out of their uniform when hanging out after school. Nevertheless, Seirei Academy had quite a number of privileged students who would be disgusted by the thought of changing in a public restroom, which was why this clothing store opened their changing room to them. Students from wealthy families made the best customers, so if letting them use the changing room was all it took to get them inside, then it was an easy trade-off.

I still feel like we're kind of taking advantage of them, though.

Masachika sneered at the twenty or so small changing rooms at the back of the store. Just how many customers did they expect to get at once? Did tourist groups stop by the place from time to time? No... They probably just didn't want to let a single Seirei Academy student escape their clutches.

"All right. I'm going to get changed in here, okay?"

"Oh, all right."

Masachika admired how commercially minded the store was as he stepped into a changing booth a short distance from Alisa's and began undressing.

"Phew… I thought I was going to melt outside in this thing."

He quickly wiped the sweat from his body, enjoying the sense of freedom he now had, and pulled his everyday clothes out of his gym bag. After placing his uniform in the bag, he tossed it along with his school shoes into a large tote. Transformation complete.

"The cool air feels *so* good."

While he waited, he realized just how grateful he was for short-sleeved shirts and air conditioners. Alisa eventually came out of the changing room as well.

"Sorry to keep you waiting."

"I-it's fine…"

When Alisa came out, she was wearing the pure-white dress that she had tried on when they went shopping not too long ago. Was there a specific reason for her to be wearing that dress now, though? Regardless, Masachika wouldn't be a self-proclaimed gentleman if he didn't compliment her.

"You really do look good in that dress."

"Heh. Is that so? Thanks."

Alisa proudly brushed back her hair with evident satisfaction. Even her light-blue sandals matched her dress, which seemed very dignified. And was she striking a pose, or was it merely Masachika's imagination?

"Ready to go?"

"Yes, let's."

After bowing and thanking the store employee, they left the clothing shop.

Is it just me, or is this really starting to feel like a date?

This was likely the first time they'd ever hung out alone together in the middle of the day while not wearing their school uniforms.

This is insane… They're all doing double takes.

Each and every person who passed by looked back at Alisa as if their soul had left their body. It was an incredible sight. People stared hard at Yuki when she walked by, too, but nobody ever blatantly turned their head and stared like this.

I guess it's no surprise when you look like Alya, though.

Her silver hair glittered in the summer sunlight, and her snow-white skin radiantly glowed as if every tiny hair on her body was emitting light. That was enough to catch the attention of others, but when you combined that with her extraordinary looks and body, how could you take your eyes off her?

"…What?" she asked.

"Everyone's staring at you."

"Worrying about that will solve nothing. This is just how life is when you're beautiful," Alisa said casually, and what she was saying was true, so Masachika didn't have a response. Looking around and seeing everyone staring was more than enough proof.

"You'll probably be fine, since I'm with you, but what about when you're alone? Surely a lot of guys try to hit on you."

"Yes, I do have people trying to talk to me almost every weekend."

"Figured. But what do you do when that happens?"

"I ramble in Russian until they leave me alone."

"…Interesting."

From Masachika's point of view, Alisa looked slightly different than your average Russian. She had a decent amount of Japanese features. But most people definitely would give up if she started speaking fluent Russian.

Anyway, I'm just glad it's not worse. I was worried she'd be using violence or at least a tongue-lashing.

"You're thinking something very rude right now, aren't you?"

"What? Not at all. I'm just glad you haven't been tricked by a bad person trying to pick you up," responded Masachika with an air of innocence, causing Alisa to raise an eyebrow and smirk provocatively.

"Oh? Is that because you want me all to yourself? You're acting like you're my boyfriend."

"My bad. But I've got to act like your boyfriend when we're in the middle of a date, at the very least."

"…?! Ah, right… A date… Yes…"

Masachika's counterattack immediately wiped the smug look off her face. After blinking for a few seconds, she bashfully fidgeted with her hair before suddenly glancing up at him and whispering:

"<This is the first time…>"

"The first time we've ever gone on a date," right? That's what you were going to say, right?

Alisa suddenly struck with a powerful attack that can be uttered only a few times in every girl's life: "First Time!" But Masachika softened the blow, using his special move "Convenient Interpretation!" Think of it like this: If the special move "Hard of Hearing" was like, "Hmm? What was that?" then "Convenient Interpretation!" would be like, "Oh, she must have meant something else." It was the ultimate special move for defense!

HA-HA-HA. Because there is no way this is the first time a beautiful girl like Alya has ever gone on a date.

Masachika desperately tried to persuade himself of that in order to stay calm, for he did not have the courage to carry the weight of something this big—the pressure of taking this perfect, beautiful woman on her first date. *If you want to call me a chicken, then knock yourself out*, he thought.

Besides, I didn't mean "date" as in a date-date. Alya knows I wasn't being serious, right? …Right?

He timidly glanced in Alisa's direction, and their eyes suddenly met, making Alisa quickly turn her head the other way and whisper in the tiniest of voices:

"<M-maybe we could…hold hands, then?>"

A faint blush stained her cheeks as she glanced back at him.

Okay, then… She definitely took what I said seriously.

Masachika stared into the distance. He felt as if he had an itch he couldn't scratch—an itch that ran down his spine. He shivered. But fortunately, he could see the restaurant up ahead, so he used his special move "Save for Later" and managed to change his mindset. It was like saying, "I'll deal with this later," which he obviously wasn't going to do. More accurately, it was, "Let's ignore my problems until they blow up in my face later."

"Oh, hey. There's the restaurant."

"…The place with the meat on display?"

"Yep."

Masachika had brought Alisa to a restaurant a good distance from the station that specialized in dry aged meats. It was a rather expensive restaurant, with the average price of dinner being five thousand yen and up, which would usually be far too much money for a student (except for a handful of students at Seirei Academy), but you could actually enjoy a nice lunch of aged beef there for a little more than one thousand yen per person. This was the fruit of Masachika's labor after he'd spent hours on the internet and explored the neighborhood over the weekend to find the best restaurant for someone who was new to dating.

Boom! I did a pretty good job if you ask me! Tasteful, right? Alya likes meat from what I can tell, too. I didn't take the easy way out and go with ramen or curry or cheap barbecue meat! I was a real man today!

While visualizing himself with his arms raised high as though he had won a boxing match, Masachika checked to see how Alisa was reacting…which was when he realized he'd made his first mistake: Alisa was new to dating as well. She was inexperienced, which was why she could honestly say:

"Oh, this place is really good, isn't it? I came here once with my family a while back."

Alisa's heart was in the right place, but it felt like a kick to the groin to Masachika, and the champion Masachika in his mind, who'd been raising his hands in the air in victory, turned to stone.

Okay, then… Uh… I guess that's better than her telling me she has been here before, and it sucked…

He had managed to make himself feel better before he came crumpling down…when Alisa innocently swung a bardiche (it's like a Russian halberd) through his body.

"I vaguely remember the venison being really good."

"Petrify" × "Heavy Weapon" = "Break."

Masachika was mentally broken at that point. Despite being so proud of himself a few seconds before, there was not even a fragment of that confidence left. On the contrary, he almost wanted to run away, especially since…

"Sorry… They don't serve venison during lunch hours…"

"Oh… Okay."

Alisa suddenly seemed to notice Masachika's disappointment and, panicking, tried to make him feel better.

"But all the other types of meat were really good, too. I'm really happy you took me here. Come on, let's go inside."

"…All right."

Masachika stepped inside the restaurant, wondering why she was the one taking the lead. After they were escorted to their table and they ordered their lunch and drinks, he decided to bring up the closing ceremony right off the bat in order to clear his mind.

"So, uh… About the closing ceremony…"

"O-oh, right."

"I'm sure Touya will explain things in detail to us the day before the ceremony as the student council prepares for it, but let me give you a brief rundown of what's going to happen. Normally, the president takes the lead during the ceremony and summons each member of the student council to the stage. When your name is called, you walk up to the mic and introduce yourself. The order goes like this…"

He raised his right hand into the air and lowered one finger per person as he explained.

"Student council presidential candidate, their running mate, another candidate, their running mate…et cetera. Everyone is called to the stage in pairs, regardless of their position in the student council. There, they will introduce themselves and talk about how they're running for student council president. Then their running mate will talk about why they're running with said candidate and why they're the best candidate."

"Okay…"

"Now, this next part is important. While there isn't any real voting, the audience is essentially casting a ballot."

"What?"

Alisa's eyes widened in surprise.

"The audience will *only clap for the candidate they want to win*. After you give your speech, they either clap for you in support or they don't. There aren't any rules saying you can only clap and cheer for one pair, but it's kind of an unwritten rule. An invisible vote, if you will."

"So that… That means…"

Alisa gulped before timidly continuing:

"There's a chance nobody will clap, and the room stays completely silent?"

"Of course. Something like that supposedly happened once a long time ago, and the unfortunate pair apparently never showed their faces around the student council again."

"Errr…"

She grimaced at the terrifying story, and Masachika nodded and scratched his head as though he knew how she felt.

"These elimination rounds are one of the downsides of being a student council member. Purposely not becoming a member of the student council and then running for president is actually a decent strategy when you have a lot of talented candidates like this year... A little late for that in our case, though."

He shook his head, realizing information like that wasn't going to help her now, and he continued:

"Anyway, what I'm trying to say is we need to avoid a situation where everyone cheers for Yuki and Ayano while our speeches are followed by silence."

"Yeah... It would probably hurt us in the long run if they got way more applause than us."

"We humans sure are interesting creatures, aren't we? Even if we like someone and want to support them, we won't if those around us aren't. Of course, this goes both ways."

"Yeah, I've heard that many people like what they like mainly because the people around them liked it first."

"Exactly. Peer pressure at its finest." Masachika nodded, then became a bit more serious.

"To be honest, though, I highly doubt we're going to get as much applause as Yuki. But don't get me wrong. We don't want absolute silence, either, because if we mess up this time, then it's going to be really hard to get support later on."

"I figured as much... How hard do you think it'll be?"

"Very. She already has plenty of supporters. I know this isn't the most encouraging thing to say right now, but our goal should be maintaining what we have. We don't need to win. We just need to avoid being the obvious losers."

"You're being rather pessimistic today."

Alisa looked upset, but Masachika shrugged calmly.

"I'm just rationally analyzing our current situation. The first semester closing ceremony is nothing more than a prologue to the presidential race, so we should be able to turn things around as long as we don't get crushed."

"…Yeah, you're right," agreed Alisa, swallowing her dissatisfaction after realizing his judgment was logical and farsighted. She then looked up as if she'd just thought of something.

"By the way, is Yuki going to be doing her speech before or after us?"

"That's what we need to find out. We played rock-paper-scissors in middle school to decide the order, but who knows what we'll do this time."

"Huh. So your position within the student council doesn't matter here, either."

Masachika waved his right hand dismissively before shrugging.

"Not at all. Besides the student council president and vice president, everyone is equally ranked. It's not like being the secretary makes you better than a general member. We used to not even have a publicist, so it would have been a nightmare trying to re-rank everyone if we did."

"Wait. Really?"

"I didn't tell you?"

He pointed at himself, blinking in surprise.

"I was actually the one who created the position of 'publicist.'"

"What?!"

"Honestly, I only made it to make Yuki even more popular back in middle school… You know how she uses the PA system to make announcements about the student council every other week?"

"Y-yeah, I'm aware."

"Well, that's also something I thought up."

"Really?!"

Once every two weeks, Yuki would make an announcement on the school radio during lunch regarding the student council's recent activities and results in addition to discussing student opinions from the suggestion box. It ended up being extremely popular among the students, and while Yuki was an exceptional speaker who usually maintained her perfect ladylike demeanor, the "real" Yuki would occasionally slip out in the middle of her announcements, which was another reason they were so popular. Word on the street was that they were even more popular than what the broadcasting club aired during lunch, which obviously didn't exactly win the students over.

"Yuki was originally a general member of the club like me, which is why I came up with the idea. I wanted to get her name out there and make her more popular. Before long, it ended up becoming its own thing, so Yuki decided she would continue doing it along with making newsletters and whatnot, and that's how we ended up creating the position of publicist for her."

"In other words, what she was doing was officially recognized as a brand-new position by the student council."

"Yeah, that's basically what happened… I know I have no right to say this, but it's kind of unfair, isn't it? The students have the chance to get to know Yuki biweekly. Not even the student council president gets that many chances to talk to the student body. So it's no surprise that more people know and like her, which will give her the advantage during the upcoming election," Masachika informed her with a forced smile before he altered his expression and continued.

"Anyway, there's nothing we can do about that, so back on topic… I know I already told you this, but you can talk about whatever you want when you give your speech at the ceremony. If you're having trouble coming up with something to talk about, I'll chime in and help."

"All right, I'm counting on you."

"You've got it… Oh, right. If you want to go for a draw, you need to make the first strike during your speech. One of the benefits of attacking first means you set an example for the others. So it doesn't matter if they do a better job at striking back because you were the one who set the standard, which gives them an unfair advantage, and everybody realizes that."

"Hmm…"

Masachika smiled awkwardly in response to her obvious aggravation.

"Come on, don't look at me like that. There are plenty of other ways we could go about this if you wanted to play dirty."

"For example?"

"Uh… Like we could try a psychological attack to throw them off their game? But that would go against your beliefs, right? Because I know you like to fight fair."

Merely listening to the suggestion made Alisa grimace.

"Yeah…"

"Right?" Masachika shrugged. "Of course, if they try to do something like that to us first, then it's on, but I doubt they'd try something like that, especially since this isn't even a debate."

"…Would they try something like that if it were a debate?"

"If they needed to," he replied, as extreme as it sounded. He then looked over at Alisa to assess how determined she was.

"Would you think less of them if that happened? Or of me?"

"…I wouldn't. It would be hard for me personally to do something like that, but those kinds of tricks are also necessary skills if you want to be a member of the student council. So no, I wouldn't think less of anybody if they resorted to something like that."

"I'm glad to hear that." Masachika nodded with a little smirk. "Anyway, I'm not going to do anything cheap like that. It's not like I'm Nonoa."

"…? What is that supposed to mean?"

"Huh? Oh, uh… Hey, look. Our food's here."

He cut the conversation short the moment the food arrived. He didn't have it in him to tell her that Nonoa brainwashed a few students in the past, so he grabbed his drink to avoid Alisa's suspicious gaze and proposed a toast, raising his glass slightly.

"So, uh… Thank you for celebrating my birthday with me today. Cheers."

"…Cheers."

Seeming self-conscious, they lightly clinked their glasses together before each taking a sip and moving on to their meals. On their plates were sautéed vegetables and two slices each of various cuts of meat with three types of salts to go with them. Masachika started his meal with a slice of beef (although he forgot to ask the brand and what part of the cow it came from), which he dipped in the red wine salt.

"Wow. This is good."

"It is, isn't it?"

The taste went beyond what he'd imagined, and he enjoyed trying each flavor profile, helping him forget what they'd been talking about.

This salt's really good, too. I wonder where I can get some of this to use at home.

While he was thinking about the new and unique flavors, Alisa suddenly muttered:

"Those rumors about Miyamae… Was that you?"

"Hmm?"

He wondered what she was talking about for a split second before almost immediately realizing what she meant, and he shrugged with a slight grimace.

"Oh, that? No. Nonoa made up and spread that rumor herself. I did go talk to her to see what we could do about you-know-what, but I had no idea she was going to do that."

"Oh…"

The rumor Nonoa had created spread like wildfire across campus during exams. By the end of the week, opinions were mainly split down the middle. Half the students believed Sayaka and Nonoa lost due to being disqualified, and the other half were unsure how the debate would have ended if it had continued.

"Anyway, on one hand, it helped squash all the terrible rumors about Sayaka. On the other hand, it made our victory at the debate less credible."

"..."

Alisa lowered her gaze until she was staring hard at her plate without saying a word. Perhaps something unrelated was bothering her...and Masachika had a good idea what that was. There were a few people around school criticizing Nonoa for using plants at the debate. "Oh, you goofball" and an eye roll were the most common responses among the students, since Nonoa had admitted it herself, and it aligned with their image of what kind of person she was, but there were some students who were definitely not happy about what she did.

"If you are worried about Nonoa, you don't need to be. Seriously. She decided to do this herself, and she's mentally as strong as an ox, so she doesn't care what anyone says about her at all," Masachika explained to his concerned-looking partner. He then paused for a few moments to think before quietly adding:

"I'm sorry. There was probably another way I could have done this."

"...!"

"I left the whole thing to Nonoa, which is why it turned out like this. I should have asked her what she was planning to do. Then we could have actually—"

"No, it's fine," blurted Alisa, shaking her head and cutting him off. "I couldn't do anything to help. No. I *didn't* do anything to help, which means I don't have any right to complain about what happened," she stated with a note of sorrow in her voice, but eventually her expression brightened, and she smiled.

"So...thank you, Kuze. Thank you for doing all that for me."

Masachika felt uncomfortable before her somehow fragile smile.

"Oh... Don't mention it."

Those were the only words he managed to stammer out before he lowered his gaze toward his plate and started eating again.

"Oh my. What's wrong? Are you blushing?" said Alisa with a smug grin.

"...Tsk. Shut up."

He was far too flustered to say anything smart or sensible, but her smile only creased even more at his childish response.

"You're so cute."

Hold up! Now she's saying stuff like that in Japanese?!

Alisa's eyes narrowed like those of a cat who had found a new toy to play with, and she grinned, reaching for her chopsticks. After picking up a slice of meat, she dipped it in the rock salt and brought it toward Masachika's lips.

"Here, I want to pay you back for everything you've done for me. Open your mouth."

She was feeding him again, but unlike when they were at that chain restaurant last time, there wasn't a partition around the table for privacy, so it was really obvious when other customers started staring. Alisa, however, continued to hold the meat out as if it didn't bother her at all.

Getting cocky now, huh? She's going straight for the kill because she thinks she caught me off guard. Did she forget about the spoon incident already?

He recalled that she hadn't been able to use her spoon anymore after doing this the last time they went out to eat together, and he slowly narrowed his eyes. That was when he made up his mind to show her who was boss...and sunk his teeth into the meat like a wild animal, wrapping his jaws around not only the meat but her chopsticks as well. He didn't even hesitate as he looked her straight in the eyes before swallowing and leering a bit.

"Thanks. That was delicious."

"Good."

But Alisa smiled back, calm as could be...and she even started using her chopsticks again.

Wh-what?! She didn't even blink!

She seemed to be faintly blushing, but her smile didn't waver. If anyone was flustered, it was Masachika the moment he saw the chopsticks touch her lips again.

…?! Th-this… This is… No. I don't know what's going on, but I feel like she just turned the tables on me.

He shifted his gaze to his plate to take his mind off it, but he hardly had any food left. After only a few more bites, he was done and already back to facing Alisa, who finished almost immediately after him.

"That was delicious."

"…Yeah, it was."

"I got you a little something."

"…?"

Only when she pulled a gift-wrapped box out of her bag with a smile did Masachika finally remember this was technically his birthday party.

"Here."

"Really? You even got me a birthday present? …Thanks."

After accepting the gift, he unwrapped it at Alisa's insistence, revealing a white ceramic mug with an elegant round design and a blue plant painted on the side.

"Oh, wow. This is a very classy mug…"

"*Giggle.* Right?"

Both the design and the slick surface of the cup were impressively luxurious. He wasn't just trying to be nice. He honestly liked the mug.

"Thank you. I'll put it to good use."

"You're very welcome," Alisa replied with a cheerful nod.

A mug… Something I can use every day… I thought most people would prefer to give consumable goods to someone on their birthday…

Masachika thought that to himself while he put the cup back

inside the box. A mug, of all things… Maybe giving people cups or plates was customary in Russia? When he shot Alisa a look with that thought in mind, her expression filled with curiosity.

"…? What?"

"Oh… I thought only couples bought each other matching cups or plates. That's all," replied Masachika, trying to get back at her, but Alisa simply smiled without showing even a hint of shock.

"Oh my… You're good. I actually did buy matching mugs. In fact, I've already been using mine at home."

"Seriously?!"

"…What if I told you I *was* being serious?" she asked, grinning cheekily from ear to ear. This sent Masachika into full panic mode, unable to say another word or make eye contact. He had lost all hope of beating her today.

"By the way, Kuze…"

"…Yeah?"

He briefly glanced at Alisa and saw that she was still smiling.

"In Russia, the birthday boy or girl is usually the one who foots the bill… Can I expect the same from you?"

"O-of course."

After all, he had originally planned on paying anyway. He only stuttered a bit because he was flustered.

I can handle this. It should be around 2,500 yen per person with drinks included… Yeah, I have more than enough.

After doing the math in his head once more, he nodded at Alisa… and she suddenly grabbed the bill before he even had a chance.

"I'm kidding. This is my treat."

"Oh… Wait. No. I'm serious. I can pay."

"Don't worry about it. In return, you can pay next time, okay?"

She then grabbed her bag, stood up, and went straight to the register. Masachika hastily put his gift in his bag and went after her, but it was too late. She had already paid.

"Thank you for coming. Please come again."

The worker at the register saw them out the door. It was like Alisa was always one step ahead of him.

Man, I just can't win against her today.

He gazed into the sky, dancing in the palm of her hand.

"...Are you that bothered that I paid?" asked Alisa, looking concerned with his behavior.

"Huh? ...Oh, uh. I guess?"

"Oh..."

Alisa turned around and shot him a radiant smile so wonderful that it reflexively made him want to smile back...until a chill ran down his spine.

"By the way, it wouldn't be a birthday without cake, right?"

"Hmm? Oh... I guess?" agreed Masachika, although he was avoiding eye contact. As Alisa's grin deepened, he suddenly recalled what she'd said only a few minutes before.

"In return, you can pay next time, okay?" The bad feeling in Masachika's gut evolved into a conviction...then became a reality.

"Kuze, there's a bakery nearby with the most amazing cakes."

She got me!

He clenched his teeth after realizing he'd been had, but whining and complaining weren't gentlemanly, so he proudly puffed out his chest and put on his most magnificent smile.

"Want to go? My treat."

"Really? I can't wait."

They smiled once more but for a different reason than before, then set out for the bakery... As it happened, Alisa ate five pieces of cake all by herself, and her half of the bill alone totaled a little over three thousand yen with drinks included.

CHAPTER 5

Blinding for more than one reason.

"Wow… I wasn't expecting to see everyone here today…," muttered Chisaki, forcing a smile and surveying the student council room. Touya sat at the head of the long desk in the seat farthest from the door. To his right were Maria, Alisa, and Masachika—in that order— and to his left were Chisaki, Yuki, and Ayano. Every member of the student council was present. Of course, they had all gathered there that day because they had business to attend to… They were waiting to be called in for parent-teacher conferences. The meetings took place in the classrooms after they went over exams in the morning. Each meeting was thirty minutes long, but when you got to go home depended on your seat number. Your meeting could be right after lunch, or you could be there waiting until night. Many students used their clubroom or the library to kill time until it was their turn. Each student council member found themselves drawn to the student council room for some reason or another, as though they had planned to meet here all along.

"Yeah, I never really thought about it, but our last names are really close alphabetically: **Ki**mishima, **Ku**jou, **Ku**ze, **Ke**nzaki, **Sa**rashina, **Su**ou… Every one of us lands between *Ki* and *Su*, huh?"

"That is a really big coincidence," Touya said, and replied to Chisaki's comment with an awkward smile.

"Just to be clear, though, Ayano actually finished her student-parent-teacher meeting yesterday," chimed in Yuki, eyeing Ayano beside her.

"Wait. Really? Then why are you still here? You could have gone home after class this morning," questioned Chisaki. She blinked curiously.

"I told her she could go home, but, well...you know how she is."

"The only place I belong is by Lady Yuki's side," promptly replied Ayano as if the thought of leaving was preposterous. With a slightly forced smile, Yuki shrugged as if to say, "See?" The others smiled stiffly until Maria suddenly clapped her hands and suggested:

"Then how about I put on a pot of tea for us all?"

"Yes, please!" Chisaki cheered, and Maria stood up.

"Ayano, you can stay seated. Allow me," added Maria, smiling down at Chisaki without even glancing in Ayano's direction.

"...?!"

Ayano, who had started to stand and was hovering silently over her chair like a shadow, looked stunned. It was as if her eyes were saying, "What the...?! I could never!" as she stared at Maria with a fixed gaze until Yuki lightly tugged her arm, and she sat back down.

"Ayano, let Maria take care of this."

"Lady Yuki... Very well."

Maria headed over to the shelf with the cups after waiting for Ayano to settle in her seat.

"Kuze? What's wrong?" Alisa asked with a curious tilt of her head.

Masachika had been quietly observing Maria.

"...It's nothing."

But he shook his head and faced forward before turning to Touya, seemingly having suddenly remembered something.

"By the way, I was talking with Alya yesterday about changing our summer uniform, and I was wondering how that was coming along. Does it sound like we're going to be getting new uniforms next year?"

It was a casual thought half-heartedly put into words, which was why Touya's reaction was so surprising. He smirked proudly and replied:

"This is just between us, but we should have a new uniform ready for us at the beginning of summer vacation if we're lucky."

"What?! Seriously?!"

"Yeah, I was planning on surprising everyone at the closing ceremony, but it's basically a done deal already."

"Oh my. What wonderful news. While I do like this uniform, it is far too hot for summer weather."

Yuki cheerfully put her hands together. But after cackling at her reaction, Touya looked apologetic.

"But it hasn't been a completely smooth process...so I might need everyone's help during summer break."

"That's not a problem at all. We'll gladly do everything we can to help, especially after you went through all that trouble for us."

"Thanks... I have to admit, though, this plan would have fallen through without Chisaki's help."

Everyone looked in Chisaki's direction as she stared back at Touya with an awkward smile.

"That's not true. You made this happen because you never gave up and fought for it."

"Only because you were there to support me. Not a day goes by when I'm not grateful to have you as my partner."

"Touya..."

"Chisaki..."

"Look at 'em. They're in their own little world now. I don't know how they do it."

Masachika rolled his eyes at the couple, who were passionately gazing at each other, then turned to Yuki and shrugged as if to say, "Unbelievable." Yuki then shifted her gaze to Ayano and began passionately gazing at her for whatever reason.

"Ayano…"

"Lady…Yuki…"

"Wh-what the…?"

A world of flowers and rainbows celebrating the love between two women materialized before Masachika's puzzled, blinking eyes, but after exchanging a swift glance with Yuki, he figured out what she was trying to say, so he decided to play along as well. He anxiously scratched his head, then let out a deep breath to brace himself before he turned toward Alisa, creating the sweetest mood he possibly could.

"Alya…"

"Not a chance."

"Oof!"

He was shot down the moment he faced her with that troubled expression, causing him to collapse in defeat. Yuki, being herself, then provocatively leered at Alisa.

"Oh my. I thought they'd be closer by now, since they're running together."

"…!"

"Will they really be able to defeat us like that, Ayano? After all, nothing is more important than teamwork when it comes to campaigning."

Yuki smiled softly as she traced her finger across Ayano's cheek, making Ayano shut one eye and tremble as though it was tickling her. A rose seemed to bloom behind them as if to bless their love, and Masachika's heart raced slightly, much to his surprise.

"Kuze…"

There wasn't even a smidgen of sweetness in Alisa's almost defiant stare.

"Just stop. You can't let people provoke you like that."

Masachika wanted to roll his eyes, but he ended up gazing into Alisa's because she wouldn't look away for some reason. And when he saw her up close like this in the light…he once again realized just how beautiful she was.

It's like she's from another world. Hard to believe she's really human, too… Wait! Just how long are her eyelashes?! I seriously feel like I'm being drawn into her eyes… Her almost translucent skin is so beautiful, too. Not even a single wrinkle, either… Where the hell are her pores? Is she seriously not wearing any makeup? …Hmm? Her skin is turning kind of red… Wait. Is it just me, or is she slowly getting closer?

But the instant his numbed mind came to this vague realization, Maria's voice dragged him back to reality.

"Sorry to keep you all waiting. ♪ Hmm? What's going on? Are we having a staring contest?" wondered Maria, who couldn't be further from the truth. Nevertheless, Alisa jumped in her seat the moment she heard her sister's voice and looked in her direction. Masachika slowly blinked a few times before facing Maria as well, but the moment she saw the look in his eyes, she winced, and her smile tensed. She almost immediately began handing out cups of tea as if nothing had happened.

"We ate all the snacks last time, so it's just tea today."

"Oh, we did?"

"Well, summer break is coming up, so we didn't have much of a choice."

"Oh, right… I guess we can't just leave snacks in a hot room during vacation. At any rate, your tea's so good that we don't need any snacks to enjoy ourselves."

"*Giggle.* Thank you."

Maria smiled after hearing Chisaki's compliment, and she placed cups of tea on the table before Alisa and Masachika as well.

"Here you go."

"Thanks."

"Th-thank you."

But Maria seemed to just barely avoid Masachika's gaze once more. He watched her hand Yuki, Ayano, and the others cups of tea and gradually realized he wasn't imagining it.

She really won't make eye contact with me… The whole hypnosis thing from two weeks ago must still be bothering her.

He'd apologized to Alisa once more the day after the hypnosis incident and was forgiven. Although she probably had plenty of things to complain about, she wasn't too harsh, perhaps due to her sister being the main reason she got into that whole mess. Instead, she commanded that he immediately forget what he saw, but there was no way he would ever forget something so exhilarating. Regardless, while Alisa had forgiven him, he had not seen Maria since the incident, and she still seemed bothered by what happened.

Yeah… I should probably apologize again to her, too.

He didn't want to start summer vacation like this, so he decided he had to apologize to her later that day. Just as Maria took a seat at the table, Touya suddenly spoke up as though he were waiting for this moment.

"Oh, right… What's everyone doing during summer break? I was thinking we could get together somewhere and hang out. Maybe stay the night at an inn or something. You know, like what sports teams do when they go to those weekend training camps."

"An inn, huh?"

It wasn't common for the student council to do something like that unless it pertained to student council work. At the very least, Masachika had never experienced anything similar in middle school. Touya suddenly laughed to lighten the mood, seeming to have noticed the first-year's bewilderment, and added:

"It's only to get to know one another better. I'm not going to make you work, and it's not an actual training camp, either. Think of it like a vacation and my way of thanking you in case I do end up needing your help during summer vacation as mentioned earlier. So what do you say?"

"Sounds like a lot of fun to me!" said Chisaki enthusiastically.

"Yes, that does sound like a wonderful idea," Maria agreed.

The first-year students started to consider it once Chisaki and Maria expressed interest.

"Hmm... I believe I could open up my schedule as long as we do not wait too long to decide on a date. *Giggle*. I have never done something like this in the student council before. I cannot wait."

"Lady Yuki's wishes are my own."

"I'm fine with it as well..."

"Yeah, I don't have any plans, so I'm cool with that. Just like a weekend thing, right? Where do you want to have it?"

"First, we need to check everyone's schedule to pick a date. And place? Well, I was thinking about my family's vacation home if that was okay with you all."

"Wait. 'Vacation home'?"

Masachika and the others doubted their ears as Touya grinned confidently.

"My family has a small house by the ocean in a somewhat touristy city... It has its own private beach, and they have festivals almost every year as well."

"Seriously?! Wait. Hold up... I don't mean to be rude, but never in a hundred years would I have guessed you come from a wealthy family."

"I get that. It's not like my father is some top CEO or anything, but my grandfather was apparently a pretty savvy investor, and the vacation house was one of his assets."

"Ha-ha. Ohhh. All right."

"Anyway, it's only an option. We don't have to go if everyone wants to go somewhere else," added Touya, looking at the others. Chisaki thought it over for a few moments and replied:

"It's not really a vacation home, but my relatives own a mountain, so I think I could pull some strings if more people would rather go to the mountains than the beach."

"They own a *mountain*?! That's incredible!"

I swear, this school...! shouted Masachika in his mind at the startling admission, but the next thing Chisaki said turned his face to stone.

"Well, I guess the building on the mountain could be considered a vacation home. It is a villa used for lodging athletes. Like, it has a big dojo in it. Anyway, while there isn't a beach, there's a cemetery nearby, so we could go check it out at night, which might be fun...or scary. Oh, they also have festivals in town every year. They're martial arts festivals, though."

"Sounds like we're comparing heaven to hell. 'There's no beach, but we have a cemetery.' Uh... What? ...Wait. Don't tell me the graves in the cemetery belong to the people who died in past martial arts tournaments..."

"Ha-ha-ha. No way."

"Y-yeah, I figured."

"Maybe some of them do, but it was mostly during training when—"

"President Touya! I vote we go to your vacation home!"

"I would prefer the beach as well."

"If that is what Lady Yuki wishes, then that is what I wish as well."

After Masachika interrupted by energetically raising his hand, Yuki and Ayano soon followed. Alisa and Maria looked over at Touya as well, not uttering a single objection. Their eyes said it all. Touya nodded with a troubled grin, then turned to Chisaki and admitted:

"While I am interested in the mountains, I don't think it would be the best place for us to get to know one another better, so maybe some other time."

"Really? Then...maybe just you and me can go together?"

"...?!"

Touya's expression froze at Chisaki's slightly bashful reply, and as his girlfriend shyly glanced up at him, he robotically forced his stiff lips into a smile.

"Yeah... That...would be nice... I'd love to go...if that's what you want to do..."

"Yesss! Then it's settled! I can introduce you to my master when we get there, too!"

"Your martial arts master...? Okay..."

Touya's mind naturally played out the situation in his head.

Introduced to Chisaki's martial arts master → "So you're the man who fooled my dear pupil into going out with you. Let's see what kind of man you really are!" → Death.

There was a semivacant look in his eyes because of how easy it was to imagine such a future, but Chisaki simply continued the conversation, showing no signs of even noticing.

"Oh, hey. Why not join the martial arts tournament at the festival while you're there?"

"Uh-huh..."

Enter tournament → Die.

The light in Touya's eyes faded into darkness as his girlfriend continued to obliviously open doors that all led to his death.

"Don't worry! There's an amateur division, too! Anyway, I just want to see you fight. You'd be so cool."

"Er..."

But he was no match for Chisaki's adorable charm.

"Then I hope you're ready for this because I'm going to give it everything I've got!"

"Really?! I'm so happy to hear you say that! I honestly cannot wait!"

"Ha-ha..."

He firmly nodded with a dry laugh. *Now that's a real man,*

thought Masachika in admiration…while clasping his hands together and promising himself that he wouldn't be disgusted when he saw Touya next semester in his second form. "This isn't even my final form," Touya might say, but even then, Masachika swore he would accept him for who he was.

They chatted for a while after that. With cups of Maria's tea in hand, they discussed the student council, talked about school, and announced their plans for summer break. After around thirty minutes, Touya suddenly took out his phone and stood up after checking it.

"They're early… My parents seem to be here already, so I have to go."

"Oh, okay. See you later."

"Yeah, good luck… I don't know why I said that."

Touya promptly exited the student council room, smiling at his girlfriend's odd words of encouragement. It wasn't long before Maria stood up and began collecting everyone's empty cups and saucers.

"It's almost my turn, so I should start cleaning up. ♪"

"Oh, let me help you."

Now's my chance! thought Masachika, immediately standing and grabbing Ayano's and Alisa's cups. Telling Yuki and Ayano to stay down with his eyes, Masachika stacked the cups and plates before turning to Maria. As she held a tray in her hands, her eyes wandered for a few moments before she smiled cheerfully.

"Really? That would be a huge help."

"Great. I'm right behind you."

After placing the plates and cups on the tray, he took the tray and left the student council room with Maria. While there was an electric kettle, small fridge, and other similar conveniences in the student council room, there was unfortunately no sink, so they had to borrow another clubroom's sink whenever they wanted to wash dishes—which was a small pain in the butt at times. They usually borrowed a sink in the home economics room, but they used the science room from time to time as well. Of course, they only did that if they had no other choice, since it didn't really feel all that hygienic. Fortunately, the home economics room wasn't being used that day, so they decided to borrow the sink there. Standing side by side and washing the dishes, Masachika subtly glanced over at Maria, who appeared to be acting completely normal but still seemed uncomfortable in a way.

Yeah… It looks like I was right.

But right as he breathed a soft sigh of resignation in his mind and looked away, he accidentally bumped his hand into hers.

"…!"

Flustered, she immediately pulled back, and the plate that was in her hand clanked.

"Oh, my bad."

"N-no, it's fine. Sorry about that. Must have been…static electricity or something."

I highly doubt there's much static electricity when it's this humid and we're washing dishes, thought Masachika jokingly, but he kept his opinions to himself and replied:

"Oh, all right."

He stealthily glanced at Maria once more after that…and noticed her ears were slightly red, and she was forcing a smile as though she was trying to hide something.

"…Masha."

"Hmm? What is it?"

"…You already washed that cup a few seconds ago."

"Oh my. Did I?"

Does she think she's going to find a clue if she keeps staring at it like that? thought Masachika as she stared hard at the cup in her hands. He wasn't sure if she was panicking or merely being a ditz. Regardless, it was clear she was still upset about what had happened the other day, so he decided it was time to talk after they finished washing the dishes and drying their hands.

"Hey, uh… Masha?"

"Yes?"

"I just… I wanted to apologize again for what happened the other day…with the hypnosis and all…"

"Oh, it's perfectly fine. Besides, I was the one who wanted to do it…"

Slightly panicking, she told him to lift his bowed head, but the instant he did and their eyes met, she blushed and looked away.

"Ah. Um… I forgot to ask the other day, but…did I do anything to you while I was hypnotized?" she asked, bashfully glancing at him. Masachika swallowed his breath, caught off guard by how unusually nervous she was, since she always gave off a mature air of confidence. Absolutely embarrassed, he instantly attempted to take his mind off it and think back to what happened that day…and he was hit with an unbearable sense of shame, almost causing him to writhe in agony, which he desperately fought to contain.

"Well, uh… You held Alya and me in your arms…then rubbed our heads."

He gritted his teeth after putting the uncomfortable memory into words, but Maria simply blinked slowly before a faint glow of relief brightened her expression.

"…That's it?"

"Yeah, basically."

He actually had his face buried halfway in her cleavage, but that fell into the realm of being "held in Maria's arms." He technically felt her thigh from over her skirt as well…and after thinking about it further, Masachika realized his fingers may have traveled to even more risqué locations, but she didn't ask what he did to her. She asked what *she* did to *him*. Therefore, there was no reason to bring it up. He was a gentleman, after all…with the broadest definition of the word possible, of course.

"Oh… Thank goodness."

She sighed in pure relief, seemingly oblivious to Masachika's somewhat twisted logic, but her innocent expression elicited an uncomfortable sense of guilt.

"Uh… Are you sure you're okay?"

"Yes, if that's all it was. But…"

Maria swiftly wrapped her arms around her body as though she had remembered something.

"Hey, uh… Did you see my…?"

"U-uh…"

Masachika's eyes naturally wandered as she looked up at him with an ever so slightly angry, accusing gaze.

If my only options are if I looked or not, then yes, I looked. I mean, I looked away when she started undressing, but what Chisaki did was so shocking that I instinctively glanced over…and that was when I just happened to see her…in an extremely sexy pose without her skirt on and her shirt already unbuttoned two buttons down from the top. Her sister's shirt was already almost completely unbuttoned, though, so that definitely left a deeper impression, but, well…I definitely remember Masha's also snow-white skin.

He racked his brain, trying to think of how he was going to explain that, but it was already too late when he didn't immediately deny it. Maria pouted a bit resentfully as she looked at him.

"Pervert."

"Oh, uh… Sorry. I didn't mean to."

While somewhat surprised things like this made her angry, he still lowered his head apologetically. In fact, *surprised* was an understatement. He actually thought she would say, "Don't worry about it. I don't care at all," and shoot him a bubbly smile. That was why he wasn't really expecting her to react like any other girl would…and yet, at the very same time, he enjoyed a small taste of the immoral delight he got from angering *the* school Madonna.

"Kuuuze?"

"Huh?! Yes?"

"Are you really sorry about what you did?"

She still pouted, but there was nothing scary about her sweet baby face glaring at him.

"Yes, very much."

If anything…

Thank you for this extremely rare experience, Masha. She looks so cute. There's something about seeing this childish side of her, when she's usually so much more mature than the rest of us, that almost brings a tear to my eye. I'm pretty confident that if she started pointing at me and scolding me, I would immediately drop on all fours and scream, "Yes, ma'am! Thank you, ma'am!" at the top of my lungs.

"Kuze! You're not sorry at all, are you?!"

Puffing out her cheeks, she reached for his face in the midst of his ridiculous daydream, pinching each cheek and pulling them to the side as if she were playing tug-of-war with herself.

"Wha' aww you 'ooin'?"

"I'm punishing you!"

Maria glared menacingly at Masachika and frowned as she tugged his cheeks in opposite directions, but even that didn't really hurt. In fact, compared to Alisa's relentless slap, it was cute in more ways than one. If anything, Masachika felt like he was being rewarded right now. She eventually let go, as though she was content with her work, before gently wrapping her hands around his face, guiding his eyes until he was looking into her serious gaze only inches away.

"Kuze, you shouldn't embarrass girls like that, okay? And when someone is angry, your apologies need to be sincere."

And yet she still didn't really seem angry. In fact, one wrong

move, and any spectator would think they were going to kiss. There wasn't a teenage boy on the planet who would be able to remain calm this close to a beautiful older woman. Whether Masachika realized this was another story.

If I argue with her, maybe we can stay like this a little longer while she lectures me.

The thought swiftly came to mind, but he felt it might make his sweet older schoolmate actually angry, so he decided to obediently nod back in agreement instead.

"...All right."

"Good."

Maria let go of his face after he nodded and lightly rubbed his head as if to praise him for being a good boy, then she faced the sink once more. But when she reached out to grab the rag to dry one of the washed plates, her pocket vibrated and made a faint buzzing sound.

"Oh... It looks like my mother has arrived."

"Oh, great. Don't worry about the dishes. I'll take care of it."

"Mmm... I'm really sorry. Are you sure?"

"Positive. Now, go see your mother."

After Maria somewhat regretfully left the room, Masachika quickly finished drying the dishes, restacked them on the tray, and returned to the student council room. The remaining five members chatted for another thirty minutes until Chisaki had to meet her mother at the school gate as well. Alisa's parent-teacher meeting would begin when Maria's finished, so she got out of her chair soon after Chisaki left.

"See you all later."

"Have fun."

"See you."

"Enjoy."

The door closed. Only three students remained, and a few

seconds of silence filled the air. Yuki's usual archaic smile vanished, and she swiftly looked in Masachika's direction.

"It's finally just the two of us," she stated in an absurdly low, cool voice.

"Well, I guess I should go wait for Grandpa by the gate."

"Hey, wait! Don't ignore me!"

"Says the girl who's pretending Ayano isn't even here!"

Yuki threw herself over the table and roughly grabbed his arm—behavior unbefitting someone believed to be a proper young lady at school. Masachika looked down at his sister as if he were staring at garbage.

"What are you looking at me like that for?! It's been so long since we could just be siblings together like this because things have been so hectic lately!"

"Oh... Now that you mention it, you're right."

His eyes wandered before he came to the realization that they hadn't been spending time together as brother and sister lately. He also realized it had been over ten days since they last hung out, which was rare for them.

"I'm sure you were fine, though, since you were having sooo much fun with Alya."

"What? No..."

After Masachika awkwardly averted his gaze to avoid the disdain in her eyes, Yuki rolled onto her side over the table, then placed her hands under her eyes and began pretending to cry in the most obvious way.

"*Sniffle. Sniffle.* I'm so lonely."

"Uh-huh. All right, all right. Let's get you off this table first, okay?"

Yuki smoothly slid off the table, her long black hair slowly crawling after her before vanishing off the corner. She then flicked it back like wings, throwing her disheveled hair neatly behind her and taking a seat in her chair, smugly reclining with her chin up.

"You may spoil me now."

"What happened to the whole 'I'm so lonely'–crying bit?"

He rolled his eyes at his sister's rapid mood swings, and Yuki overdramatically raised her eyebrows as if she wasn't bothered in the least.

"What's wrong? Hurry up."

She was acting like a mean boss who asked far too much of her subordinates, but Masachika still decided to play along, albeit reluctantly. He felt like a crooked banker being forced to apologize in public, placing his hands on the table and pressing his lips together.

"Here…?" he asked, his voice trembling in bewilderment and humiliation.

"Yes, here. I told you to spoil me right now, Masachika."

"But look where we are! It's…!"

"It's what? Can you do it or not?"

"…!"

He deeply lowered his head, hands trembling, and painfully grunted:

"I—I can do it!"

After slowly sitting back down, he swiftly lifted his head and placed a hand on the back of the chair next to his.

"Come here."

That was all he said in the coolest voice he could manage while doing everything possible to look like a badass.

"Pfft!"

"That's it—I'm done."

Masachika promptly got up out of his chair.

"Awww. ♪ I was kidding. You're the coolest brother in the whole world. ♪" gushed Yuki in a conveniently sweet voice as she ran over to his side. She was finally able to sit next to him and be his sister for the first time in what felt like forever. Though he smirked wryly, he indulged his sibling. Ayano, meanwhile, turned into air. Masachika continued on his quest to make his sister feel better for the next fifteen minutes until his phone vibrated, telling him that his grandfather had arrived.

"Oh! Looks like Grandpa's here."

"Oh, great. Have fun."

"Yeah, see you later… Where did Ayano go, by the way?"

He took a sweeping look around the room in search of his childhood friend, but she was nowhere to be found.

"Huh? Maybe she read the room and decided to stand guard outside?"

"Seriously? You— No, I don't have the right to complain. I didn't notice, either, after all."

Shaking his head, he gently opened the door to the student council room, revealing Ayano, who actually kind of looked like she was standing guard just like Yuki had said. In fact, it probably was safe to assume she *was* standing guard to protect her master's honor.

"Oh, hey… Uh… Sorry."

"…? For what?"

The guilt Masachika felt for completely forgetting Ayano's existence after scolding Yuki for the same thing was unbearable, but Ayano genuinely didn't seem to realize how he felt, let alone why he felt that way, so she curiously tilted her head with a blank expression. Nevertheless, he patted her on the head a few times in appreciation and for forgiveness, causing her to close an eye as if ticklish.

"All right, I'll see you two later."

"Later."

"We await your return."

After saying good-bye to them with an indescribable feeling in his heart, Masachika grabbed his bag and headed toward the front gate to meet up with his grandfather. Cutting through the school building, he made his way to the shoe lockers at the entrance, where he changed shoes before taking a step outside...and...immediately felt the uncontrollable urge to make a U-turn. But it was already too late.

"Oh, Masachika! There you are!"

"Grandpa..."

Standing at the gate was a jolly old man with a perfectly bald head. It was his paternal grandfather, the man who'd introduced Masachika to Russian culture and Russian movies when he was a child. Unlike with his grandfather on his mother's side—Gensei Suou—Masachika got along with this man, Tomohisa Kuze, extremely well. This was obvious, considering Tomohisa had come all the way there to act as his grandson's guardian on behalf of Masachika's father, who was extremely busy with work. Straightening his posture, Tomohisa lifted his white fedora slightly, smiling mirthfully at the sight of his grandson. He was what people usually imagined when they thought of a nice old man... The only problem was his clothing.

"Why are you wearing a white suit?"

"Hmm? I look dapper, don't I?"

"The only people who wear white suits are massive narcissists or foreign mafiosi!" shouted Masachika, laden with prejudices.

"Hmm... Oh, right... I know what I'm missing."

Sensing something was off, he readjusted his hat, then reached into his inner pocket before pulling out a pair of sunglasses and putting them on.

"Now I look good."

"You look even more like you're in organized crime now! Like a retired don! All you need is a massive trench coat or whatever those scarf things are they have around their necks, and people would honestly be scared of you!"

"An ascot? I have one of those right here."

"Why do you have a scarf with you?!"

Tomohisa pulled a folded white piece of cloth out of his other inner pocket, but Masachika immediately stopped him and brought him inside before he did anything else that would make him stand out.

"*Sigh*... Couldn't you have worn something less embarrassing?"

"I thought I looked cool..."

"Let me guess. You saw a movie, and there was a guy in a white suit in it. I'm surprised you even had a white suit."

"I was saving the little pension I had left for a day like today and bought it not long ago."

"I hope Grandma beats you," joked Masachika in a muffled voice of anger and embarrassment as he briskly trotted toward the school building. In all honesty, he didn't want anyone seeing him with this old man. After changing back into his school slippers at the shoe lockers, he helped his grandfather into some guest slippers, then began walking straight toward their destination.

"Hey, Masachika. We still have time before the meeting. Let's take a walk around campus while I'm here."

"Absolutely not."

"Why? Are you really that embarrassed to be seen with your grandfather?"

"Yes."

"Hmph... Fine. Then I'll just go for a walk without you."

"I'd rather not have to talk to the police today after they get a suspicious-person call and show up on campus."

Masachika somehow managed to calm his grandfather, who had way too much energy for a seventy-one-year-old man, and got him into one of the chairs set up in the hallway outside the classroom for waiting. A few minutes went by before his father eventually became the topic of conversation.

"Hmm... So Kyoutarou's been busy, huh?"

"Well, he's apparently working at the embassy in the UK this year…so I guess he'd be really busy."

Masachika's father, Kyoutarou, being a diplomat, had been working at the Ministry of Foreign Affairs up until last year, but he began working at a diplomatic establishment abroad starting this fiscal year. His father, who was usually never home to begin with, was now coming home even less since he started working abroad. The man was so swamped with work he even had to start asking his own father to show up to his son's student-parent-teacher meetings like this.

"I see… But he could have at least been here for the parent-teacher conference." Tomohisa frowned slightly.

"Eh, I can't blame him for not being here. I mean, it'd take him at least half a day to even get here."

"You've always been a good kid."

"Quit it."

Masachika brushed his grandfather's hand off his head bashfully, a heartwarming scene between a loving grandfather and his grandchild that you'd see in any neighborhood…but the entire mood changed the instant the door to the classroom rattled open.

"Thank you for your time today."

"Thank you very much."

Alisa and a woman who appeared to be her mother stepped out of the classroom, and the second Tomohisa saw them—saw Alisa—his eyes widened.

Oh, hell no! Things have been so hectic since he got here that I forgot to warn him!

Masachika regretted not mentioning it to his grandfather beforehand, but regret wasn't going to fix anything now.

"Oh, Kuze. H—"

"An eastern European miracle!"

Tomohisa jumped out of his chair with his arms spread wide as if he was praising God.

"Grandpa, stop!"

Masachika desperately latched on to his grandfather and tried to pull him back down as he attempted to explain things to his startled, retreating classmate.

"Alya, I'm so sorry. This is my grandfather, and he's kind of obsessed with Russia…"

"…?! Oh…"

"May I ask your name, young lady?"

The look on his face and the words he used made it almost clear he was trying to pick her up.

"I said stop! Please!"

He grabbed his grandfather and dropped to his knees, begging the old man to stop before he got any closer to Alisa.

"I'm sorry. I'm really sorry. You can just ignore him, okay?"

"Oh, your grandfather seems very…cheerful."

Her thoughtful words unfortunately felt like being stabbed in the heart to Masachika. He grabbed his grandfather's collar with his left hand while waving Alisa along with his right in an attempt to get them to leave before his grandfather embarrassed them any further, but the woman who appeared to be Alisa's mother took a step forward and asked:

"I don't mean to bother you, but…are you Masachika Kuze?"

"Huh? Oh, yes. That's me. You're Alisa's mother, correct?"

He instantly let go of Tomohisa and politely greeted her. Good manners had been beaten into his head ever since he was a child, after all. The woman placed a hand over her lips as if she was impressed by his entirely composed demeanor, despite the fact that he had been freaking out up until a few seconds ago. Alisa's eyes were wide in shock as well.

"Oh my. What a polite young man you are. It is a pleasure to meet you. I am Akemi Kujou, Alisa's mother. I've heard so much about you from her."

"I really hope only good things."

"*Giggle.* Her eyes light up with joy whenever she talks about you."

"...Really?"

While he didn't know exactly what they'd talked about, he at least knew that Alisa enjoyed talking about him. That alone was enough for him to get a good idea of what was going on. He carefully examined the woman in front of him once more. She had gentle, refined features with wavy shoulder-length black hair and a body brimming with both a maternal vibe and sex appeal. It was easy to imagine how popular she must have been back in the day. Her face... resembled Maria's.

I guess this is what Masha would look like if you took away her Western features. Maybe? But I guess it's her overall energy that resembles Masha more than her face.

She had a very motherly aura overflowing with kindness and acceptance, as if she were the Holy Mother—a Madonna—herself. If she were an actress, she'd surely be a huge hit with the middle-aged and older demographic. But she wasn't just beautiful and kind; her eyes also sparkled with wit.

Wait. Is she trying to see what kind of person I am? I should probably be careful with what I say, then...

Masachika came to that conclusion after observing her with a smile for only two seconds before sharpening his gaze. Akemi's lips curled even more, albeit slightly, as though she could tell he was tightening his guard...which made him tighten his guard even more. A tense air reigned over the space. Akemi slowly opened her mouth to speak as Masachika braced himself behind his smile.

"By the way, are you a good ballroom dancer?"

He froze for a few seconds at the completely unexpected question, slowly blinking before naturally repeating:

"'Ballroom...dancer'?"

"Yes," promptly replied Akemi, causing him to be even more confused.

Ballroom dancer… What? Is that code for something? What's she trying to ask me, dammit?! It doesn't make any sense!

Perhaps he should be honest and admit he wasn't that bad of a dancer? No, a mediocre reply like that wouldn't be enough. He debated his options in his mind, but Alisa spoke up, clearly aggravated, before he could give an answer.

"Mom, why are you asking him that? You're making him uncomfortable."

"Hmm?"

"Why'd you ask him if he could ballroom dance?"

"'Why'? Because he has slightly sloping shoulders," replied Akemi unexpectedly with an innocent look on her face. There was no hidden meaning behind what she was saying, let alone critical thinking. She really was Maria's mother.

Masachika's body almost went limp, especially since he'd had his guard so tight, but his relief was short-lived. Tomohisa smoothly slid over to Alisa's side and wrapped his hands around hers in an alarmingly natural manner.

"Will you be my granddaughter, my fair lady?"

"H-huh?"

"Hey?!" Completely forgetting his good manners, Masachika shouted at his grandfather, who looked like he was about to propose.

"What do you say? Are you interested in being the wife of my grandson, Masa—"

"Shut up already!"

Masachika covered his grandfather's mouth from behind and forced him to shut up while peeling him off Alisa.

"So, uh… We've got a meeting to get to, so I'll see you later!"

"Oh. Yes."

"See you again soon, I hope."

Cutting the conversation short, Masachika said good-bye to Alisa and her mother. Only once they finished bowing and started to walk away did he let go of his grandfather.

"So, Masachika, are you gonna marry her or what?"

"Shut up."

"So, Alya, are you going to marry this Masachika Kuze boy?"

"Be quiet."

Around the same time he resentfully glared at his obstinate grandfather, he heard Alisa and her mother having a similar conversation in the distance. *Looks like we both have it rough,* he thought, deeply empathetic. But it was now time to collect himself and face the classroom before them…where his homeroom teacher was sitting with a tense, awkward smile.

"He heard everything, didn't he…?" Masachika whimpered, gazing up into the heavens.

◇

"Thank you for your time…"

"Much appreciated."

After finishing the student-parent-teacher meeting, Masachika and Tomohisa exited the classroom, and perhaps since they wrapped up somewhat earlier than planned, there was no one waiting outside yet.

"So about that—Alisa, was it? About her…," he asked as they made their way to the staircase.

"Can you stop already?"

Masachika was relieved that the meeting was over, even if it meant he had to deal with his grandfather still pressing him for answers… And that ended up being a mistake. There was still one thing he should have been careful about, but it had completely slipped his mind, perhaps due to his grandfather wearing him down the whole time. It happened right when they stepped into the hallway that led to the entrance: a fateful encounter.

"…!"

The instant Masachika saw her, he could feel the blood leave his head, and when she saw him, her eyes widened before she swiftly averted her gaze.

"Oh! If it isn't Yumi. Long time no see."

"It has been a while…Grandpa."

Maybe she hesitated because she didn't know if she should still call him "Grandpa," since she and his son were divorced. Or maybe she was concerned about their relationship, since they weren't family anymore. Maybe it was both. Whatever the case, Tomohisa cracked a smile, showing no concern and demonstrating only kindness toward her.

"I'm glad to see you're in good health. What about you, Yuki? How have you been?"

"I have been doing very well, Grandpa. By the way, you're dressed…very interestingly today."

"Oh? I look dapper, don't I?"

"*Giggle.* Very much so."

"Right?! Masachika here has been criticizing my attire since he saw me for some reason," he added, cheerfully grinning at his granddaughter's compliment before glancing at each of them once more and asking:

"Are you and your mother getting along?"

"Yes, of course. Isn't that right, Mother?"

Yumi nodded modestly at her daughter's elegant yet innocent smile…as Masachika watched with cold, dead eyes.

Yeah, that's a load of bull. Fake smiling and all. If they were really getting along, then Yuki would be showing her real self right now.

And she calls herself Yuki's mother. She can't even get Yuki to be herself. And because of her, Yuki...

"...!"

Tightly clenching his teeth, Masachika frantically pushed down the hatred that burned in his chest, but the sight of his mother revived old memories he had sealed away long ago, and a muddy stream of nauseating emotions began to well up from the pit of his stomach. A chill ran through his body and down to his fingers and toes with every breath he took to calm himself, and sweat beaded on his skin. Nevertheless, Masachika didn't take his eyes off Yumi—as though that would mean defeat. Yumi, on the other hand, wouldn't even look directly at him. Despite it being the first time she'd seen her son in who knew how long, she had no words for him, nor would she look at him. She had nothing.

...Hmph. That's what I thought.

It was then that the fire burning his lungs and the flames brushing against his skin passed, and he was swallowed in perhaps despair or maybe even resignation. It didn't matter to him either way. Nothing did anymore.

"We should get going, Grandpa. I don't want anyone seeing us here," suggested Masachika in a voice void of all emotion. Tomohisa seemed to show a little concern about being seen as well and lightly nodded.

"Oh, right... See you two around."

"I will see you again during summer break, Grandpa."

"...! ...See you around."

Yumi opened her mouth for a brief moment as if she was going to say something, but whatever she wanted to say perished before it could escape her lips. After slightly bowing their heads, Yumi and Yuki left and headed toward the staircase, but Masachika promptly changed into his shoes without watching them leave. Even Tomohisa changed out of his slippers without saying a word.

"Oh, wow. I almost forgot how hot it was outside." Tomohisa frowned, squinting at the blinding sunlight outside the entrance.

"You wouldn't be so hot if you weren't wearing that ridiculous suit."

Masachika rolled his eyes.

"I couldn't just wear a polo shirt, though."

"Honestly, that would have been way better than this…"

"Well, Yuki said I looked good."

"She was obviously just trying to be nice," replied Masachika with a half smirk. After frowning at the comment, Tomohisa looked up at the sky and commented:

"Yuki looks more like her mother every time I see her… She's still a little short, though."

"…Yeah," he perfunctorily replied to his grandfather, who then felt compelled to answer, albeit with a slightly cruel smile on his face:

"What? Do you still hate your mother?"

"…"

After Masachika replied to the straightforward question with silence, Tomohisa stroked his chin as though in deep thought.

"It really is strange. If you ask me, you and your mother are so much alike."

"Excuse me? Ha-ha!"

He scoffed at what seemed like a bad joke, but Tomohisa calmly nodded back.

"You do. While you look just like your father did on the outside when he was your age, you are just like your mother on the inside. I feel like Yuki's the opposite. She has Yumi's looks but Kyoutarou's personality."

"…"

"But, well, neither you nor Yuki have your parents' eyes. I wonder whose DNA you got those from."

"Beats me."

Masachika touched his eyes, the only identical feature he and Yuki shared—a sign that they were siblings—and shrugged. Tomohisa shrugged back at his grandson, who was still sticking to his stubborn, brief replies, before changing the subject.

"Anyway, I stand by what I said, and it's hot out today. Want to go grab some shaved ice?"

"Shaved ice? That's not really something you can find just anywhere."

"Really? Let me check…"

Tomohisa whipped out his smartphone and actually began searching for a place. *I can't believe how with the times he still is,* thought Masachika in both admiration and shock before lethargically replying:

"No, wait. I think I'll pass. I just wanna go home."

"What? Are you tired already? Oh, you don't look so good. Hold on…"

Masachika stepped away from his grandfather's approach and worried gaze, facing forward.

"It's just the strong sunlight making me look pale. Anyway, I just want to go home and take a shower. That's all."

"That's it? That's cold, boy."

"Maybe if you were wearing something at least seminormal, I would have gone with you."

He glared at his grandfather, who was fanning his face with a folding fan that seemed to have had magically appeared in his hand. Masachika looked like his everyday, ordinary self…but there was also something about him reminiscent of a small child who had cried and cried until he wore himself out and couldn't cry anymore.

CHAPTER 6 | **Hot for more than one reason.**

It wasn't anything super dramatic like my mother abused me or she cheated on my father. In fact, looking back, my mother had always been a soft-spoken, kind person. Things weren't perfect between her and my father, but she was kind to Yuki and me. She would shower me with praise whenever I did well in whatever I was learning outside of school, and she would even bake us sweets from time to time. Any regular person would probably think she was a good mother. My sister and I loved her as well.

...It all began because of something so small—something that would make any ordinary person say, "Wait. That's it?" Honestly, thinking back, it really was not a big deal at all. But one day...my mother suddenly stopped looking me in the eye. She used to always look into my eyes, pat me on the head, and praise me as a kid. "Good job. You must have worked really hard on that" and "Wow, that's amazing," she would say...until one day, she started to avoid eye contact. Her once sweet smile became awkward, and that was when I realized she was forcing herself to act this way. I thought maybe I wasn't doing enough. I had to work harder. If I did better, then surely she would be genuinely happy for me from the bottom of her heart.

Hey, Mom. Look. My flower arrangement teacher said I did a really good job. I got my black belt in karate, too. I've already studied ahead with these books that middle schoolers use, and I know you like piano, so I—

"Stop! Just stop!"

...That look in her eyes. That wasn't what I wanted to see. All I wanted was to—

"Mmm..." Masachika groaned, feeling abnormally hot all over.

"Oh..."

He stirred in his bed, and just that slight movement made his entire body and head ache. He was miserable. He'd had a bad feeling last night, and it turned out his gut was right. He had a cold. A sore throat was the least of his problems because he felt like a sack of potatoes. He definitely had a fever. That was when the alarm by his bedside started to ring, so he turned it off by dropping his heavy arm onto it. He grabbed his phone, which was lying there as well, then rolled onto his right side. A sharp pain shot through his arm and shoulder, but it was still far better than having to lift his arm.

"This isn't going to work..."

After turning on his phone, he decided to call school to tell them he was going to be absent today, but he didn't know the school's phone number. He felt like he wrote it down somewhere, but he couldn't remember where. *I guess I'll just search for it online*, he thought, but even that became far too aggravating to handle right then.

"Takeshi... No, Hikaru."

He thought about which of his friends he could ask to relay the message to their homeroom teacher and decided he could trust Hikaru more for some reason. He imagined Takeshi screaming, "What the hell, man?!" But he didn't care. He didn't have enough energy to care.

"...Hello? Masachika?"

"Hey... Sorry about the random call. I caught a cold."

"What? Are you okay?"

"I'll be fine, but I can't make it to school today. Do you think you could tell our homeroom teacher for me?"

"Sure, no problem. How about I stop by your place after school? You're the only one home these days, right?"

"Don't worry about it. I already have someone else who can stop by to check up on me."

"If you say so. Take care and rest well."

"Thanks."

After hanging up, he used what little energy he had left to text Yuki.

> Sorry. I caught a cold.

> Do you think you could ask Ayano to get me some medicine?

Right after he sent the second message, he feebly dropped his phone before rolling onto his back.

"Sigh..."

He would kill for a glass of water at the very least, but even getting out of bed was too much work. Fortunately, however, he still felt tired, so he decided to go back to sleep.

...I feel like I was having a terrible dream before waking up a second ago.

Perhaps it had something to do with running into his mother the previous day for the first time in forever. He felt as if he'd had an old recurring dream that he'd chosen to repress.

Now that I think about it, I've been remembering a lot of old things lately.

The memories of when he was Masachika Suou were something he wanted to seal away and forget forever. Remembering all the bad things and sadness he endured tore at his heart.

Maybe it's actually because I'm trying not to remember any of it.

He tried to never think about the details of what happened in the past. He stopped himself whenever he almost did, in fact. But the truth was, they weren't all bad memories. At least, that's what he believed. But if he tried to remember the good things, his mind would remind him of when he said good-bye to his mother…and what happened with that little girl that day. That was why he had to seal away all his memories in the darkest recesses of his heart. Eventually, the past = bad in his mind, and that belief only grew stronger every time he tried to look away from it.

They say anger and hate slowly fade with time, but they don't completely go away.

If anything, he still felt deep sadness and pain from his past, despite his memories slowly dissipating. Nevertheless, he no longer knew where the pain and sadness came from. Even now, whenever he tried to remember the past, his brain wouldn't let him. The fear of facing whatever happened to him prevented him from so much as putting a hand on the lid sealing away his memories.

Sigh… Whatever.

Even using his brain became tiring, so he forced himself to stop thinking. There was no reason to do something that was going to make you more depressed, especially when you were already sick. He simply happened to run into his mother the previous day. He wasn't planning on facing her now or ever. The past wasn't worth remembering, for the memories of Masachika Suou were of no use to Masachika Kuze. That was what he told himself as he fell back asleep.

Ding-dong.

"Mmm…?"

Masachika woke to the sound of the doorbell ringing. Although his mind was hazy, he figured it was either Yuki or Ayano at the door, but then he realized that Yuki had a key to the house. She and Ayano wouldn't need to ring the doorbell. Plus, if he wasn't hearing things, then maybe that wasn't the doorbell to his house. It sounded more like the buzzer at the entrance to the apartment building. Even if Yuki rang the doorbell to tell him she was here, why would she be trying to get him to buzz her in at the entrance?

"Did I order something…?"

He tried to roll his sluggish body out of bed, but he depleted every bit of energy he had the moment he rolled onto his side. The thought of pretending not to be home crossed his mind, but the bell immediately rang once more.

"Yeah, yeah… I'm coming…"

Masachika fired himself up and managed to slide out of bed, figuring he should probably get up and walk around at least once that day. However, every step was like taking a hit to the head, making him grimace as he made his way to the intercom…but when he saw who was on the screen, he honestly believed he was seeing things.

"Huh?!"

But there was no way to mistake that silver hair, those blue eyes, and that otherworldly beauty. Alisa, dressed casually, was standing at the entrance to the apartment complex.

"…Huh? Why is she…?"

Masachika couldn't recall ever telling her his address. Of course, he had never invited her to his house, either. Questions flitted through his mind, but he had only a few seconds to buzz her in before running out of time, so he pushed the answer button.

"…Alya?"

"Oh, Kuze? Are you okay?"

"Huh? Wait… Did Yuki tell you what happened?"

"She told me you had a fever and couldn't get out of bed, so she asked me if I could bring you some medicine…"

"Oh, all right… Let me buzz you in."

"Okay. Thanks."

He pressed the unlock button and watched until Alisa safely stepped inside the apartment complex. After returning to his room, he grabbed his smartphone off the bed, turned it on, and saw a message from Yuki pop up on the screen… He instantly tossed the phone back on the bed.

> Hey, what's the problem? A silver-haired maiden's about to nurse you back to health. You're welcome.

The message was accompanied by a grinning emoji.

"You could have at least told me before she got here… Gaaah…!" shouted Masachika weakly, taking his frustrations out on Yuki as he threw himself facedown onto the bed. While he honestly just wanted to stay like that for the rest of the day, he felt he had to at least wash his hands before Alisa came inside, so he mustered up every last bit of strength he had and headed to the bathroom. After relieving himself, he'd just begun to wash his hands when the doorbell rang, so he clung to the wall and dragged his feet to the front door. He was wearing pajamas and had bedhead so messy it was a surprise no birds had made a nest in it yet, but he was far past caring anymore. *It is what it is*, he thought.

"Coming…"

He had slid his feet into his slippers and was reaching for the doorknob when he realized he probably should wear a mask.

Wait… Where'd I put my mask?

Nevertheless, his hesitation quickly passed because he couldn't make Alisa wait any longer, so he unlocked the door before modestly cracking it open.

"Alya…? Thanks…for taking time out of your day…to do this for me…"

He peeked through the crack in the door, using it as a shield, but even holding the door slightly open like this honestly felt like heavy labor to him. He had to bear with it for her sake, though. Alisa's eyes, however, fluttered in what seemed to be surprise, which might have been Masachika's fault for showing his face at all.

"Yeah, it's…it's fine. You look worse than I was expecting, though."

"…I bet you were thinking, 'Even an idiot can catch a cold, huh?'"

"Not at all."

Alisa softly sighed because he was still cracking jokes, even at a time like this. She then gestured to the bag in her hands.

"Can I come in for a little bit?"

"Huh? Oh, you shouldn't. I'll just take the medicine and…"

"…Yuki asked me to stay with you for a while and take care of you," admitted Alisa almost reluctantly as she slightly pouted.

My dear, dear sister… I do not mind that you have the brain of an otaku, but I wish you would keep other people out of your schemes…

Masachika instinctively began complaining to Yuki in his mind.

"<Sorry. That was a lie.>"

Oh. Apologies, Yuki. Looks like you were framed.

Alisa glanced at him, fidgeting with her hands as he inwardly apologized to his sister. Yuki was used as a scapegoat so Alisa could hide her embarrassment.

"But really, I should be fine. All I need is to take some medicine and get some sleep."

"You still need to eat something, right? Are you telling me you're feeling good enough to cook for yourself?"

"Oh, right… I don't want you to catch my cold, though."

"Don't worry. I brought a mask."

She took a mask out of the bag and put it on, but Masachika had mixed feelings about how thoroughly prepared she was. She was perfect, even at a time like this.

I mean, she's right. She's doing the right thing, but…

What was this feeling of disappointment? It felt as if his body had become a filthy pathogen, and his thrilling fantasy of being pampered by a sexy nurse had transformed into something more innocent and medical.

I was a fool for ever believing the most beautiful girl in class would pamper me!

Masachika stared off into space, once again realizing that fantasies born from 2D worlds were nothing like reality.

"Besides, I brought a lot with me, and I'd rather not have to lug it all back," argued Alisa, lifting the bag filled to bursting with various items. It looked like she had brought food in addition to medicine. Telling her to go home after carrying all this here on a hot day would be a sin, regardless of whether Masachika had asked her to or not.

"All right… I guess I could use a little help if that's okay with you…"

He gave up and welcomed her inside, since he was both physically and mentally at his breaking point.

"Thanks."

But right as Alisa stepped inside and the door shut, Masachika suddenly couldn't relax anymore. The chirping of the cicadas outside receded until the inside of his house was drowning in palpable silence. The fact that he was home alone with a girl was really sinking in, and even something as innocent as locking the door started to feel wrong.

"Kuze."

"Y-yeah?"

"Here, put on a mask."

"Oh… Right…"

Despite feeling somewhat nervous, his expression turned dead serious the moment she handed him a mask. It felt like she was saying, "Put on a mask, you filthy scum." Of course, Alisa would never really think something like that. At any rate, he still felt that masks were the enemy of romantic comedy scenes.

You can't kiss if you're wearing a mask... Now that I think about it, having half your face covered basically kills any chance of a game or movie even being a romantic comedy... Wait. There have been some heroines as of late who have had their entire faces hidden behind masks. But even then, these heroines are cute because anime and comics can use effects and whatnot to make them expressive, even when you can't see their faces, but it'd be terrifying to actually see an expressive mask in real life. Anyway, if you're going to cover your face, then I definitely prefer a blindfold over the eyes more than a mask over the mouth. If Alisa were actually blindfolded, I'd look and feel like a criminal, and I don't even want to talk about the fanfics that would be written about her, and what am I even thinking about anymore?

Masachika's nerdy imagination ran wild as he put his mask on, standing in a bit of a daze and swaying slightly.

"Kuze? Are you okay?" she asked with a worried expression.

"Now I get it... You get a sense of guilty pleasure *because* it seems bad. It's the thrill of doing wrong. I guess that's just another thing that makes blindfolded heroines better."

"...You're definitely not okay."

"...I agree."

Feeling embarrassed by her pitying gaze, Masachika decided it was best to take Alisa to the living room before he said anything worse.

"This is the sink, and this is the toilet. And that...don't go in there. That room over there is my room... And this is the living room. Just put your stuff down wherever you want. Oh, and there's some water and barley tea in the fridge if you're thirsty. Grab a cup and help yourself. Any questions?"

"I'll let you know if I have any. Anyway, you really should lie down and get some rest."

"Yeah, I think I'll take you up on that offer…"

He was quick to agree, since simply standing was hard enough for him, and he headed back to his room. After collapsing onto his bed, he reached to move his smartphone out of the way…and it suddenly started vibrating. Another text message from Yuki popped up on the screen.

> Stop imagining Alya in a blindfold.

"What the hell? Is she psychic?" muttered Masachika, wondering how her timing could have been so perfect, unless she really could read minds. His phone suddenly vibrated once more.

> This isn't mind reading. It's just love.

"How do you say something like that without dying of embarrassment?"

> How do you complain to a phone like that without dying of embarrassment?

"You little…! There's no way you're *not* reading my mind! Damn esper!" barked Masachika, straining his throat and immediately coughing.

> Your throat must be hurting. Don't scream too much, okay?

"…"

> By the way, only a nerd would use the word esper. Most people probably don't even know what that is.

Masachika tossed his phone somewhat roughly toward the bedside, not even in the mood to argue with an inanimate object anymore, and pretended to not see a message that suddenly popped up saying, Ouch! She was far too good at knowing what her older brother was thinking, and they weren't even twins.

I need to check my room for hidden cameras and bugs later...

He rolled onto his back with that decision in mind.

"Kuze? Can I come in?"

"Hmm? ...Sure," he replied after taking a sweeping glance of his room and checking if there was anything embarrassing lying around.

I should be fine. I don't keep dirty magazines under my bed like they do in comics for boys, and I don't have any picture frames suggestively placed facedown like they do in comics for girls.

If someone searched his closet, they might find something that suggested he used to be a part of the Suou family, but there was nothing like that in plain sight, since Masachika himself obviously didn't want to be reminded.

"Okay. I'm coming in."

Alisa was holding an unfamiliar water bottle when she hesitantly stepped into the room, and she held it out to him after she had a hard time finding a place to put it.

"Here. I brought you some tea with honey if you want it."

"Oh, thanks. Sorry, but do you think you could pull out that thing with a knob on my desk? Looks like a shelf. It turns into a side table..."

She pulled the shelf on wheels out of the study desk, then rolled the side table next to the bed before placing the water bottle on it.

"So, uh... Do you want anything to eat? If you are feeling well enough to eat, of course."

"Yeah, sure. You don't have to be so nervous, by the way."

"I'm not nervous... I'm just feeling a little restless," she claimed, her eyes wandering.

"<And it smells like teenage boy in here, too…,>" she added in a whisper.

That's not something you should whisper! And don't act bashful after saying that, either!

Alisa began to anxiously play with her hair while glancing at Masachika, making him feel uncomfortable as their interaction morphed into a rom-com.

"So, uh… Which do you prefer? Porridge or borscht?" she asked shyly.

"Nobody has ever asked me that before," joked Masachika with a straight face, taken aback by the bizarre, seemingly mismatched options. Alisa pouted somewhat and rambled:

"Borscht is really good for you, you know? You boil the vegetables until they're really soft, so it's really easy to eat, even if you're sick. Plus, it has garlic and onions, which can boost your immune system. And beets are great for your digestive system, so—"

"All right, all right. I get it. You're starting to sound like some little old lady from the countryside."

"…"

Although that was a pretty rude thing to say to a young lady her age, Alisa fell silent as if she was at a loss for words. Perhaps she really did learn all that from her grandmother in Russia.

"So? Which is it going to be?"

"Well, it's not often I get offered borscht, so let's go with that…"

"…Okay. It should be ready in four hours, so—"

"You're asking me to wait four hours? *Four whole hours?*" he exclaimed after hearing what he thought must have been a joke, but she frowned as though she was dead serious.

"I mean, a lot of ingredients go into making borscht… I could make it quicker if I used a pressure cooker, but that's sacrilege."

"Yeah, I wouldn't even know the difference. Anyway, if that's the case, I'm fine with regular ol' porridge. Oh, sorry. I mean, as long as you don't mind making it, because I feel really guilty about asking you to cook for me…"

Even speaking started to hurt, his voice gradually weakening before he collapsed lethargically back down onto the bed.

"All right. I'm going to use your kitchen to make you some porridge, okay?"

"Thanks…," he muttered somewhat lifelessly, watching Alisa open the door to his room, take out her phone, and type something. He followed the movement of her fingers…and narrowed his eyes, pulling his lips back.

"She is legit looking up how to make porridge…," said Masachika unenthusiastically after Alisa left.

All you do is cook rice in water or soup stock, then add some salt, right? Surely there's no way you could mess that up.

At least, that's what Masachika thought.

"Ohhh… You flavor it with salt, not sugar? I guess that makes sense. This isn't kasha, after all," Alisa mused to herself.

Okay, she could definitely mess it up. Big-time. Kasha is one of Russia's versions of porridge, where oatmeal or buckwheat groats are used instead of rice, milk instead of soup stock, and sugar instead of salt. Therefore, Alisa made the right choice looking up how to make Japanese porridge. One mistake could have led to a truly bizarre conversation.

"Blech! You used sugar instead of salt!"

"Yes. Of course I did. So what?"

"Huh?"

"Huh?"

"Hmm… So if I use one of these microwavable rice packets…can I just dump it into the pot? …Wait. I should probably microwave it first."

With a smartphone in one hand, Alisa placed one of the rice packets she bought into the microwave.

"'With plenty of water'? How many liters is 'plenty'?" she muttered in annoyance at the vague instructions, referencing a few different recipes and filling the pot with water.

"Oh, the rice is done… Ouch, ouch, ouch! That's hot! Ow, ow, ow!"

Not only was she startled by how hot the rice packet was, but the instant she peeled off the top, she was hit with a gust of hot steam, startling her once more. She managed to bring the rice packet over to the pot by holding the edges, but she was in such a fluster to rid herself of the hot food that she tilted it too far sideways, causing the entire pack of rice to fall into the pot as if it were a giant rice ball, splashing water into the air. And because she held the pack right in front of herself, some water splashed onto her stomach as well.

"…"

Drops of water splattered about the kitchen, and her clothes were wet enough that she would have trouble brushing off any suspicion if Masachika asked her what happened. She looked hard at herself, frozen in place…until she eventually lifted her head slowly and wiped her clothes and the kitchen dry with a handkerchief.

"I'm fine. I just need to put on an apron, and problem solved."

Alisa pulled an apron out of her bag, swiftly slipped into it, and began cooking once more as though nothing had happened. "How did that solve anything?" one might wonder, but perhaps she was referring to saving her dignity, because Masachika wouldn't be able to tell that she had spilled water on herself now.

"…How much water did I lose from that?"

Once again, she found herself worried about the amount of water in the pot. Only after adding what appeared to be an adequate amount back did she turn on the stove.

"…"

She put the lid on the pot, waiting for it to cook. Waiting. Waiting.

"...Is this really all I had to do? I feel like I'm forgetting something..."

Alisa started to grow somewhat anxious with nothing to do but wait, so she decided to remove the lid and stir the pot again for no particular reason, then began to go over the recipe once more to make sure she didn't miss anything.

"'Until it thickens'? Thickens how much? They could have at least been more specific, like, 'Until there's no liquid left.'"

She continued to mumble to herself until she eventually finished cooking the porridge.

"This looks about right...I guess?"

After pouring the porridge into a bowl, she topped it off with long onions (which took her an entire five minutes to dice), then grabbed a spoon and the saltshaker so Masachika could make it as salty as he wanted.

Why is there a dent here?

But when she arrived in front of his room, she wondered why there was a small dent underneath the doorknob before stepping inside.

"Kuze, I brought you some porridge."

"Oh... Thanks."

Masachika was lying limply over the bed, his voice slightly hoarse and eyes somewhat hazy. He was uncharacteristically show-ing Alisa his weaker side. And because of that...

I want to rub his head until he falls asleep...

Her maternal instincts kicked in, but she immediately trashed that idea, crushing it into a million pieces before they drifted off into the dark depths of her mind. And during that time, Masachika slowly raised his right hand and gave her a thumbs-up.

"An apron, huh? ...Nice."

"...Sounds like you're feeling better already," barked Alisa with disgust, thankful that her mask was covering her lips and cheeks as she walked over to his bedside... Little did she know, her ears, which weren't hidden behind a mask, were completely red as well. Masachika obviously noticed.

"Are you well enough to eat?"

"Yeah... I think."

He shuffled his body until he could sit up and dangle his legs off the side of the bed. After tiresomely ripping the mask off his face, he grabbed the spoon next to the porridge.

"...You're not going to blow on my porridge to cool it down for me?"

"Do you want me to?"

"...I was joking," said Masachika awkwardly before thanking her one more time and taking a bite of his meal.

"...It's good," he softly muttered to Alisa, who was sitting in his chair watching him.

"Good."

She didn't really know what made rice porridge good or bad or if there even was such a thing as good porridge. Nevertheless, she was glad he didn't say it tasted awful. She continued to watch him eat for the next few minutes until she realized how uncomfortable it must be to be stared at while eating. She shifted her gaze and focus to his room.

"..."

The first thing she noticed was how (surprisingly) clean his room was. He didn't have much stuff, to be more precise. Despite always claiming to be a nerd, he didn't have a huge bookshelf stuffed with comics and light novels, nor did he have anime figures on his desk. In fact, there was almost nothing like that in sight, save for a few comics stacked on his study desk.

"...All my nerdy stuff is in another room," interjected Masachika as if he knew exactly what she was thinking.

"O-oh."

Alisa awkwardly looked forward and promptly tried to change the subject.

"So… Where are your parents?"

It was a question that had been on her mind for a while now.

"My dad's at work, and I don't have a mother."

"Huh…?"

"Oh, it's not like it's a secret or anything, but it's just me and my dad here," he casually added.

"Oh… I had no idea…"

She seemed to be shaken up a little, but Masachika sluggishly continued to talk as if it wasn't a big deal.

"It's not like she's dead. My parents are divorced, just like plenty of people nowadays."

"Yeah…"

Despite probably feeling awful due to his fever, he still spoke of his mother as though she was a pain in his ass, and it made Alisa feel somewhat sad. Only now had she realized why his grandfather came to the parent-teacher conference the day before, and she was disappointed in herself because she believed she was sharper than that. And at the very same time, she was shocked because she suddenly realized she didn't know Masachika that well, after all.

I didn't know when his birthday was until the other day, now that I think about it…

She hadn't known his birthday, even after sitting next to him for over a year, and she'd never thought about his family situation until he brought it up. Coming to this harsh reality only made Alisa more disappointed in herself. And seeing that it wasn't a secret, it would be safe to assume his childhood friends Yuki and Ayano already knew. Just the thought of them celebrating his birthday in this lonely house while she was left in the dark filled her with frustration, but perhaps she would have never known about Masachika's family situation if Yuki hadn't asked her to check up on him. So perhaps she should be grateful and thank Yuki instead…as much as she didn't want to.

Once Kuze gets better, I'm going to start talking to him more to get to know him better.

Right when she secretly came to that decision, Masachika finished his porridge.

"Masha made that tea, by the way, so I'll pass along your appreciation."

"Thanks."

"Now for your medicine. Oh, wait. Maybe you should change first?" she suggested after noticing how sweaty and messy his pajamas were.

"Come on, Alya. What kind of fan service would this be if you weren't the one undressing me and wiping the sweat off my body?" jested Masachika.

"Stop joking around and get changed already. I'll go get you a glass of water and your medicine."

"…Yes, ma'am."

"Do you need a towel and some hot water?"

"Nah, I'll just use these pajamas to wipe off the sweat."

"Okay… Oh, where do you keep your thermometer, by the way?"

"It's…"

After learning where they kept the thermometer, Alisa took his empty bowl and spoon to the kitchen sink, where she washed them, but right when she was going to put them on the rack to dry…

"Oh…"

She found the mug she gave him for his birthday.

He's actually using it…

It warmed her heart. Her hand naturally grabbed the cup as she grinned bashfully from ear to ear. An entire ten seconds went by before she suddenly came back to her senses and put the cup back down quickly. Her eyes darted to her left, then right, confirming that no one had seen her. After clearing her throat for no good reason and calming herself down, she filled a glass with water and grabbed the medicine along with a few other items before heading back to his room.

"Can I come in?"

"…Come in."

When she stepped inside the room, Masachika had already changed into a different pair of pajamas and was waiting for her, sitting on the edge of the bed. The freshly stripped pajamas he had been wearing were nowhere in sight, but perhaps he hid them in fear that she'd see such an embarrassing monstrosity.

"Here, this is your medicine, and this is one of those cooling patches you put on your forehead… And here's your thermometer."

"Thanks."

Masachika placed the thermometer under his armpit, then washed down the medicine with a glass of water. After a few seconds went by, the thermometer beeped, so he reached to pull it out…and a mischievous smirk suddenly curled his lips.

"Want to take a guess at my temperature?"

"Just show me the thermometer."

"Mmm… Fine. *I'll* guess! Let's go with…38.4 degrees Celsius!"

"…"

"Ugh! I was so close! Looks like I've got a 38.6-degree fever. *Cough! Hack!*"

"Stop playing around and get some sleep."

"*Cough!* Ngh… Fine."

After Alisa combed back his bangs, she stuck a cooling gel sheet on his forehead, and he collapsed onto the bed with a thud. He squirmed around for a bit to get comfortable, pulled the mask back over his nose, then relaxed every muscle in his body.

"…I really appreciate everything you're doing for me today.

Seriously. I'll pay you back once I get better. Just leave the receipts on my desk."

"Don't worry about it."

"No, I need to pay you back. Please."

"Okay, okay. Whatever you want."

"Thanks. Now...I should get some sleep. You can go home now. The key should be..."

"You don't need to worry about me. I'll be in the living room studying."

"What? You don't need to stay here anymore. You—"

"You're sick. Stop worrying about me and get some sleep."

"Okay..."

She turned off the lights, and Masachika closed his eyes in resignation, but after a few moments went by, he heard what sounded to be Alisa's footsteps walking back to his room.

She probably came back for the cup and thermometer...

Or so he thought, up until the moment he heard a chair squeak nearby, contrary to his expectations, and it was followed by a hand gently patting his chest in a rhythmic manner, like a mother trying to soothe her child to sleep.

"...Alya?"

"What?"

"This is kind of embarrassing," was what he wanted to say after instinctively opening his eyes, but he held his tongue the moment he saw her piercing gaze.

"Thank you...for so much. That's all."

"It's the least I can do... You're always helping me, after all..."

"Not as much as you help me."

He closed his eyes once more after adding, "Like when I forget my textbooks," and instantly felt the land of dreams rapidly pulling him into another world, perhaps thanks to Alisa's hand gently tapping his chest.

"That's nothing compared to how much you have helped me with the election… And that's far from the only time you've been there for me. You—"

"You don't need to thank me… I only do these things…because I want to," he whispered, almost completely out of it. That was the end of the conversation. It was time to sleep, believed Masachika, but Alisa was still saying something, much to his surprise.

"Because you want to? What does that mean?"

"Hmm? What…?"

"Why do you always help me?"

"That's because…I…"

"…Kuze?"

"…"

Alisa was asking him a question he knew he had to answer, but he couldn't overcome the sandman dragging him down, so he let go of his consciousness. But right as he was about to pass out, he heard these words:

"Good night…Kuze."

"Nngh…"

When Masachika finally awoke, it was pitch-black outside.

"Ah…"

He felt a lot better already, perhaps thanks to the medicine. While his senses were still slightly dulled and his mind foggy, it might have been because he slept too much. When he looked up at the clock, it was already past eight, which meant he had been in dreamland for over five hours. It became clear to him that he had snoozed way too long after he added in the hours he had already slept that morning.

Alya must have already gone home…right?

But before he left his room to check, he grabbed his phone out of habit and curiously raised an eyebrow. There were two messages from Yuki displayed on his lock screen: Did you order a maid? and Sent you a ticking time bomb. BOOM! ☆

Masachika instantly started to worry. His gut twisted as he opened the door to his room…and he immediately imagined himself in a different world in an attempt to escape reality…because two beautiful young women were quietly…oh so quietly glaring at each other in the living room.

I see… So this is what a cold war is like. I had no idea Russia and Japan were about to go at it again.

Only his absurd imagination was keeping him from breaking down, but he was too loud when he opened the door. The two girls in the living room looked over in his direction and greeted him, dragging him back to reality whether he liked it or not.

"Kuze, are you sure you had enough rest?"

"How do you feel, Sir Masachika?"

One was Alisa, and the other was a young lady who usually always had her hair down sloppily covering her face at school but now had it neatly tied up, exposing her face, and was fully equipped (?) in a maid uniform: Ayano. Incidentally, her maid uniform was frilly, like one of those so-called maid uniforms you would see in Akihabara, but this wasn't the Suou family staff's official uniform. This was something she wore because Yuki wanted her to. The Suou family staff's official uniform was far simpler. They didn't even wear those frilly headbands. Ayano only ended up with this outfit because Yuki went straight to her grandfather and demanded, "Young women should wear cuter clothes!" Her grandfather reluctantly agreed but only if Yuki promised Ayano would not dress like that when they had guests over. Therefore, Ayano's maid uniform was something Yuki fought for. That was how much it meant to her.

It is a cute uniform, but there's a time and a place for it…and that place isn't here or now.

Masachika's eyes unfocused, staring into the distance after seeing Ayano dressed as a maid for the first time in a long time. Meanwhile, Ayano, who was sitting across from Alisa, stood swiftly and silently from her chair and slipped under his arm like some sort of teleporting wizard.

"Allow me to lend my shoulder."

She was under his right armpit before he realized it, with her left arm wrapped around his waist and her right hand on his chest.

"Come on, now. I can walk on my own."

"I do not want you overdoing it."

He tried to walk away, but Ayano immediately tightened her arm around him, stiffly pressing herself against his right side.

"You need to relax, Ayano. You're making me feel like some underground syndicate's boss who sexually harasses his slaves."

"You're the one who needs to relax, Kuze... Ahem. Let go of him already."

"I will not. It is my duty as a maid to take care of him."

"You're Yuki's maid, not his."

Ayano immediately froze...allowing Masachika to softly slip away. However...

"Lady Yuki gave me orders to take care of Sir Masachika, so it has become my duty to take care of him."

Ayano squeezed him in her arms once more as if to say, "I won't let you escape!" Alisa's eyebrow suddenly twitched.

"Therefore, I will be taking over from here. You may go now. It is late, so I will have the Suou family driver take you home."

Ack! I know she probably means well, but the way she said that sounds like she's trying to start a fight!

"It's getting late, so you should probably go home and get some sleep. I can handle the rest," was what Ayano probably meant, but thanks to her detached tone and the fact that she was holding Masachika tightly in her arms, you could also interpret her words as, "You're

of no use now that I'm here. The driver's already waiting for you outside, so hurry up and get out of here."

Alisa raised her eyebrows sharply before fixing Ayano with a
fierce glare, but Ayano stared right back at her without blinking.

Wait... Ayano did mean well when she said that...right?

*Wouldn't she look more confused if she meant well? You wouldn't
glare back at someone like this, right? Hold on... Is there going to be a
bloodbath? Did I walk into a battle zone?*

Right as the suspicions started popping into Masachika's
mind, he suddenly remembered the second message Yuki had sent
him: Sent you a ticking time bomb. BOOM! ☆ Were the chills
running down his spine caused by his cold...or was it something
else?

"Besides, shouldn't you be preparing for tomorrow?" added Ayano.

"..."

Alisa's eyebrow twitched again...but Masachika had no idea
what Ayano was talking about.

"Tomorrow? What's happening tomorrow?"

"Nothing. It's a school day. That's all," replied Alisa quickly, talking over him, but her answer didn't really make him less concerned.
However...

"Kuze, who do you want to stay here to take care of you?"

A small question instantly came to mind.

What kind of question is that?!

It was a question that led nowhere good, and it made Masachika
inwardly scream.

*I'm more used to Ayano taking care of me, and I feel guilty for
keeping Alya this long already, so my answer is Ayano...but that's not
what kind of question this is, is it?*

This wasn't about logic or reasoning. Women want to hear how
you really feel about them when they ask you questions like this, and
Masachika knew that.

How do I really feel? What do I want?

He spaced out somewhat, as if his fever was slowly returning, and he asked his heart what it wanted—what it desired. Whom did he want to stay with him? That answer was simple and naturally rolled off his tongue.

"I want a harem."

Dammit! I forgot I was human garbage! recalled Masachika suddenly as the light in Alisa's eyes vanished.

"Oh, uh. No. What I meant was, uh…"

"…"

"Very well. Shall I call for Lady Yuki?"

"No!"

"Lady Alisa, could you support Masachika's left side for me?"

"I don't need anyone supporting anything."

"You do not need to be embarrassed. We understand that all men desire to impregnate as many women as possible."

Ayano's eyes were crystal clear, a complete reverse of Alisa's.

"I know your heart's in the right place, but do you think you could stop making me sound even worse than I already do?!"

His painful shout was met with Alisa's deep sigh, which tickled his ear and made him jump.

"I suppose there's nothing to worry about if you're feeling good enough to scream that much."

"Huh? Alya?"

"I'm going home. I made you some borscht, so feel free to help yourself whenever you get hungry."

"B-borscht? Oh, is that what that smell is?"

Masachika looked around the living room as an aroma filled the air. Alisa quietly nodded, then picked up her belongings and started to walk out.

"A-Ayano? I'm having a hard time walking with you holding me like that, so do you think you could let go?"

"…Very well."

After finally managing to break free from Ayano, he followed Alisa before stopping at the front door and apologizing.

"I'm really sorry, especially since you came all the way here to help me… Anyway, I really appreciate what you did for me today. Thanks."

Her expression softened.

"It's fine… I helped you…because I wanted to, too."

"Hmm? 'Too'?"

"…Don't worry about it."

She shifted her gaze away from his curious expression and locked eyes with Ayano, who was standing diagonally behind him.

"Take good care of Kuze for me."

"I will."

She bowed slightly to Ayano before looking at Masachika again.

"…?"

Alisa's eyes. Her eyes harbored a strong will, as if she was determined to do something—something unknown to him.

"Alya?"

"Good night, Kuze."

"Y-yeah… Good night."

But she smoothly turned on her heel, pushed the front door open, and left without responding to his call. He watched, feeling like something was off, but his worries were pushed aside the moment Ayano locked the front door after quietly slipping past him.

"Are you okay? Do you need me to lend you my shoulder?"

"No, I'm fine. Really."

Ayano took a step closer to him, but he retreated.

"Hold on. Something has been stabbing me in the leg. Do you have something in your pocket?" he whined, painfully rubbing the outside of his thigh. She froze for a moment and tilted her head before blinking hard as if she had just realized something.

"Oh, that's…"

Out of nowhere, she grabbed her skirt and confidently lifted it in one quick swoop.

"What the…?!"

Ayano's white knee-high socks were revealed in all their glory before Masachika's wondering gaze, including her…bare thighs…?

"…Ayano. What're those?"

Something inside him died when he saw what was wrapped around her thighs: two black bands on each leg holding what appeared to be silver pens.

"Weapons."

"They're what?!" shouted Masachika in an almost shrill voice. Ayano suddenly swung her right arm, slapping her skirt and causing it to flutter, just *barely* covering the secrets to the universe. No man could resist staring in anticipation, Masachika included. She then thrust a palm forward but stopped before his eyes.

"They're weapons."

"…What are you doing?"

Wedged between her fingers were three extremely pointy metal pens. With enough force, a hit to the throat with one of these could easily kill someone, but…why was she hiding something like this under her skirt?

"Lady Yuki told me it 'wouldn't be right' without these."

"Yep. Figured."

"She told me that a maid dress was a type of combat uniform, so I had to be prepared for battle at all times."

"Huh, I wonder who she plans on fighting."

Masachika returned to the living room, not even in the mood to comment on it anymore.

"Are you hungry? There is borscht in the kitchen, as you know."

"Oh, right. Do you think you could get me a bowl?"

"Very well. I will be back shortly."

Long after sitting down in a chair and checking his temperature, a wonderful aroma wafted by.

"Sorry to keep you waiting. What was your temperature?"

"According to this thermometer, it's 37.4 degrees Celsius, so way better already."

"I am glad to hear that. Here, I reheated it for you."

"Thanks."

When he grabbed the spoon and peeked into the bowl, he found exactly what one would expect to see with borscht: a dark-crimson soup. Alisa apparently didn't put any meat in it and only went with thoroughly boiled vegetables, probably due to him being sick.

"So... Let's see how it tastes."

He scooped a spoonful into his mouth, nearly wincing at the soup's acidity, but the sweetness from the vegetables almost immediately followed. Masachika could feel his dulled senses rapidly awaken.

"This is delicious..."

His appetite returned in the blink of an eye, and he scooped up a large helping of vegetables next, each one perfectly boiled, melting in his mouth without him even having to chew. The cabbage and onions were sweet, and the beets didn't have much of an earthiness to them, either.

I really wasn't a fan of the earthy beets in Grandpa's borscht back in the day... He always laughed and said they wouldn't be beets without the flavor, but I prefer these beets way more.

He continued fervently eating in a daze until he realized his bowl was completely empty.

"There is still some borscht in the pot if you would like seconds."

"...Yeah, I could go for a little more."

He ended up finishing off the pot after that. Even Masachika was kind of surprised he could eat that much.

"That was delicious... I really owe Alya one."

She'd said something like it takes four or so hours to make borscht, and Masachika felt nothing but gratitude for someone who spent that long doing something for him.

"Phew…"

His head started to feel a little fuzzy again after eating. It could have been because he was stuffed, but maybe his fever was returning, too.

"I brought you your medicine."

"Oh, thanks."

He took his medicine once more, then stood up so he could go lie down. After stopping Ayano from helping, he sluggishly dragged his legs back to his room and crashed onto his bed.

"Hff…"

"Would you like me to draw a bath for you?"

"Hmm… I think I'm good for today."

"Then at least allow me to wipe your body for you."

"I think I'm gonna go hop in the shower."

He immediately reversed his first decision when he saw the glowing determination in Ayano's eyes and her clenched fists. His gut told him that something really bad would happen if he allowed her to help when he was in such a weakened state.

"Then allow me to wash your back—"

"No. I'm fine."

"There is no need to worry. I will put a blindfold on."

"Huh, I was wondering when the blindfold setup was going to show. Anyway, blindfolded body washing? Sounds dangerous."

"Then I will not put on a blindfold."

"Sounds dirty."

"You can feel comfortable around me. As your maid, I promise not to look at your nude body sexually."

"What kind of declaration is that? Like, who declares something like that?"

"And if I break that promise, you can do whatever you want to my—"

"Okay, okay, okay. I've heard enough."

After his shower, Masachika continued to do whatever he could to keep Ayano from trying to help him do every little thing, and by the time he was ready to go to bed, he was utterly exhausted both physically and mentally.

"Sleep well."

"Yeah… Good night." He waved, pretending not to notice how restless she was acting.

"Perhaps I should sleep by your side and—"

"No. I don't want you catching my cold."

"Then how about a lullaby?"

"No thanks."

It was as if she were saying, "Really? Are you sure?" as she refused to completely close the door to his room, peeking inside through the crack.

"Ayano." Masachika sighed softly and narrowed his eyes.

"…! Yes? What can I do for you? You do need me, don't you? You want me to sing you a lullaby, don't you?" said her glittering eyes as she opened the door.

"This is an order. Go to Yuki's room and go to bed," he sternly demanded.

"…! Very well. Good night."

The instant he uttered the word *order*, she sprang into the air, and she promptly bowed before withdrawing from the room.

"I should have said that an hour ago…," said Masachika with an exasperated smile, and he grabbed his phone to check it before going to sleep, discovering yet another message from Yuki displayed on the screen: Ayano VS Alya—Match 1: Ayano wins.

"You make it sound like there's gonna be a second match," he joked in a whisper, placing his phone down before rolling over.

Although he figured it'd be hours before he could fall asleep after
sleeping so long that day, the urge to get some shut-eye came quickly,
so he surrendered himself to the force, and he slowly fell asleep.

...Yes, he fell asleep without even revisiting what was bothering
him about Alisa's attitude when she left...and without thinking
deeply about what Yuki said in her texts. But by the time he realized
that, it was already over. It was all too late.

CHAPTER 7 — Apparently, it's sort of like Ishikawa's 5M method.

It was already a little past eleven when Masachika woke the next day.

"Wow... I slept *way* too much. I'm kind of impressed I could even sleep this long."

While he may have been on the verge of going bankrupt after all the sleep debt he had accumulated through countless days of being chronically sleep-deprived, sleeping almost half the day away was still too much. He slept an entire day if you included the previous afternoon as well. His body felt like a bag of garbage after resting that long. His head felt heavy as well, but that might have been because of his cold for all he knew.

"Wait... Did I just inadvertently play hooky from school?"

He was suddenly hit with anxiety as a cold sweat broke out because he had overslept and didn't even call the school. A few moments of panic went by when a sudden knock at the door interrupted his thought process.

"Are you awake?"

"Y-yeah...," he replied, baffled by the familiar voice. The door opened and in walked Ayano wearing her maid uniform. She looked captivating as she clasped her hands in front of her chest and gracefully lowered her head—revealing the frilly headband on top.

"Good morning."

"Yeah, good morning. Did you skip school today because of me?"

"Yes, taking care of you is far more important than getting my exams back. Your grandfather Tomohisa already contacted the school and told them you wouldn't be coming in today, so you have nothing to worry about."

"Grandpa called them for me, huh?"

Ayano checked him out from head to toe as he sighed in relief, then handed him the thermometer.

"Your thermometer, sir."

"Oh, thanks."

"How do you feel?"

"I feel a lot better…but I think I slept too much. My body feels really heavy…and my throat still hurts, too. I might just be a little dehydrated from sleeping so long and not drinking enough water, though."

"…I see."

In the midst of his explaining, the thermometer suddenly beeped, so he took it out and checked his temperature.

"Oh, 36.7 degrees Celsius. My fever's basically gone."

"I am so glad to hear that. What would you like for breakfast? Rice porridge or udon?"

"Let's go with udon."

"As you wish."

After thanking Ayano for her kindness, Masachika headed to the bathroom to rinse his mouth and take a quick shower, then changed into a new pair of pajamas and returned to the living room. The udon's broth was rich and delicious enough for him to easily finish half an extra helping. His body was finally starting to feel better by the time he had finished eating.

"Phew… Thanks a lot, Ayano."

"I am glad you liked it, and I am glad you seem to have your appetite back."

"Yeah, I'm basically back to normal. Even my sore throat feels a lot better already."

"I am relieved to hear that. However, you should still rest today, just in case."

"Yeah, school's already over anyway."

When he looked at the clock, it was already 12:35 PM. While it'd usually be lunch around this time, today was a half day, and while the student council members had to meet the following day to discuss the closing ceremony and prepare for it, they didn't have a meeting today.

"Here is your medicine."

"Oh, thanks...?"

All of a sudden, Masachika felt like something was off when he saw the medicine and the glass of water being handed to him.

Hmm? Hold up. Something doesn't feel right.

It felt as if there was something extremely important right under his nose, but he couldn't figure out what that something was, and his instincts weren't allowing him to ignore it, either.

This pill...?

He stared hard at the pill in Ayano's hand before suddenly realizing what was most likely the problem. The previous day, Masachika was out of it due to his fever, so he hadn't really thought much about it, but he recognized these pills.

"Is everything okay?"

Ayano tilted her head, her expression blank. And yet she looked almost nervous.

"Ayano, show me the box you got this medicine from," he quietly demanded, staring right into her eyes.

"..."

Panic...could not be seen in her eyes, but she wasn't able to immediately answer him, either. Her quiet hesitancy only solidified his suspicions.

"Ayano."

"...As you wish."

She closed her eyes in resignation before returning with the box the medicine came in. And after checking the front and back of the box, he was sure of it.

"Ayano, this medicine makes you sleepy, doesn't it?"

"...Yes."

It all made sense now. No wonder he slept so much. He wasn't sleep-deprived. It was simply one of the cold medicine's side effects. Mystery solved. But what he didn't know was why Ayano was making him take this medicine, which Alisa had bought, when she knew it made him sleepy. Furthermore, *who* chose this medicine?

"Ayano, you know this medicine makes me really sleepy, right? Why didn't you warn me?"

"..."

She didn't answer his question but instead dropped to her knees smoothly and bowed.

"You have my sincerest apologies."

"..."

"What I did was unforgivable. I should have never made you, my master, take medicine that has such strong side effects. Please punish me however you will."

She kept her head perfectly lowered over the carpet as she apologized.

"Ayano, was Yuki the one who told Alya to buy this medicine?" he quietly asked.

"..."

His question was met with her silent admission, for she could not sell out her master (Yuki) or lie to her master (Masachika), either.

"What is Yuki scheming? Let's assume she didn't want me to go to school today. Why would that be?"

"..."

But Ayano maintained her silence, ready to take the fall for her master. Masachika sighed, then softened his tone.

"Ayano?"

"Yes?"

"Tell me everything you know, and I will let you take care of me for the rest of the day however you'd like. I won't complain. You can do whatever you'd like to me."

"…?! N-no, I refuse to be seduced."

"Nobody's seducing you."

She jumped a bit, still bowing her head on the floor, then she turned down his offer. Masachika scratched his head at her somewhat bizarre reaction and thoughtlessly improvised another proposal.

"Then how about this? If you tell me everything you know, I will ridicule you. Like 'How dare you sell out your master, worthless scum,' or something like that."

"Oh?!"

Ayano swiftly lifted her head, eyes brimming with surprise and expectation, before promptly looking away and returning to a bowing position.

"Okay, I just saw you waver."

"I—I did no such thing."

"Don't lie to me. That was the most expressive I've seen you all year. I can't remember the last time I heard you squeak like that." He sighed, rolling his eyes.

"H-hey… Master?" she timidly stammered, slightly lifting her chin.

"…What?"

"Out of curiosity…were you also planning on stepping on my head when you ridiculed me?"

"…Would you like me to?"

"I only thought it would make sense if you did, seeing as you are standing over me like this. In addition, I noticed you were barefoot, and I thought that might be why, so I wanted to make sure just in case. That's all."

"Stop avoiding the question and answer me. Do you want me to step on you?"

"..."

"The silent treatment again, eh?"

Fast-talking, excuses, and silence: Everything she did was an admission of guilt. *Wow, what wonderful weather today. It's so bright outside*, thought Masachika, staring out the window and into the distance. Something he'd done partly as a joke and partly because he'd wanted to see if she really was a masochist had far exceeded what he could have ever imagined. His childhood friend was not just a masochist, no. She was a freak. Oh, and a *hard-core* masochist. You could describe Ayano in a few words: **B**lank expression, **D**evoted, **S**ilent, **M**aid. Oh god! It had been right there in plain sight the entire time!

"Sigh..."

Masachika exhaled, holding his head as if his brain was hurting. Then he stood up and began heading to his room.

"I'm going to school. And I'm not going to reprimand you for something like this, so you can stand up already."

"I mustn't. I must pay for my sins."

"Then clean the house for me while I'm at school. That's your punishment."

"...As you wish."

She finally stood, but she turned to him with worry in her eyes.

"Are you really going to school? Shouldn't you get some more rest?"

"The fever's gone. I'll be fine."

"Shall I call the chauffeur and have him take you?"

"Nah, walking's faster."

"But you just recovered from your fever, and it is an extremely hot day today. Besides…"

"Hmm?"

Ayano's gaze wandered in hesitation, as if she was having trouble telling him something.

"I believe it is already…too late."

"…What is?"

Distressed by Ayano's ominous words, Masachika got dressed as quickly as he could; ignored Ayano's efforts to stop him; and headed straight to school. The burning-hot sunshine was like a whip beating his recovering body as he ran, eventually arriving at school at a little past one o'clock. Students were shuffling out the front gate, perhaps having finished lunch in the cafeteria. They shot him curious glances here and there for coming to school late on a half day that was already over, but he continued to press forward against the current until he reached the school building.

"Where are Alya and Yuki…?"

He panted heavily as he changed into his school slippers and decided to check out their classroom first before heading to the student council room. He swallowed some of the phlegm in his throat, and as he walked briskly toward the classroom, he heard three guys passing by talking excitedly about something.

"Man, the noble princess is such a good talker—very fun to listen to and unlike anyone else."

"Princess Alya did a really good job, but they're just on different levels, ya know?"

"I thought Kujou did a good job at the debate the other day, but she's not really good at improvising, it seems. Like, at all. Did she memorize some sort of script before the debate last time?"

"Yeah, I bet she did."

"Totally."

They continued chatting as they passed by, seeming not to notice him at all, and anxiety began to swell in his heart once more.

*What? "Improvising"? "Script"? Don't tell me there was a debate...
No. There's no way they'd decide to do a debate on the one day I'm gone, especially not the following day.*

But he didn't have enough information yet to produce an answer. What he did know was that while the details were unclear, it was obvious that Yuki did something to put herself above Alisa in popularity.

*Dammit! I can't believe I let my guard down! I was an idiot to think nobody would make a move before the closing ceremony...
Dammit!*

He beat himself up over his own carelessness and peeked into the classroom...where he found Alisa sitting alone at her desk.

"Alya..."

When he opened the door, Alisa, who was staring in a daze at her desk, lifted her head, and when she saw that it was Masachika, her eyes opened wide in shock.

"Kuze?! What are you doing here?!"

"I heard from Ayano that Yuki was up to something, so I came."

"Oh... How do you feel?"

"My fever's gone, so don't worry about me. More importantly, what happened?"

He sat at his desk so that he was facing her, and she bit her lip, lowering her gaze.

"...I'm sorry."

"Alya?"

"I messed up. You went through so much to help me, and I failed! I...!"

Her voice cracked, tainted with regret, and her clenched fists trembled in her lap.

"Okay, okay. Take a deep breath. Can you tell me exactly what happened?"

He spoke in a soft, soothing voice to calm her down until she eventually began her explanation.

◇

It had all started the day prior, before morning homeroom. Alisa and Yuki were facing each other in the student council room after Yuki stopped by Class B and asked her if they could talk.

"Alya, I know this is sudden, but do you think you could stop by Masachika's house after school and give him some medicine for me?"

Although Alisa was puzzled by the sudden request, Yuki continued with a hand on her cheek in a troubled manner:

"Masachika has a fever right now and can't get out of bed."

"Wait. Really?"

"Yes. Normally, I would be more than happy to stop by and take care of him, but I unfortunately have business I must take care of today, so I was wondering if you, his partner in the election, could go in my place?"

"Oh… Sure, I can do that."

Despite feeling kind of annoyed at being asked by Yuki to help him, Alisa accepted the job, since it would have bothered her more if Yuki decided she had no choice but to go herself. Yuki then pulled a sheet of notepad paper from her pocket as though she already knew Alisa would accept.

"Thank goodness. This is the name of the cold medicine he usually takes, along with his address. Are you sure it's okay?"

"Of course."

Alisa took the sheet of paper, feeling frustrated that there was yet again something she didn't know about Masachika.

"All right, I'll stop by his place after school," she promised. She was standing up to go back to her classroom when Yuki suddenly stopped her.

"Oh, Alya? There is actually one more thing I would like to ask you before you go."

"…? Go on."

"If it is okay with you, I would like for you to join me as a guest for the afternoon school announcements."

"Huh?"

Yuki intertwined her fingers, clasping both hands together.

"As I am sure you know, during lunch once every two weeks, I, as the student council publicist, give reports on what the student council is doing, has done, or is going to do. Therefore, I thought I should discuss the debate from two weeks ago tomorrow, and who better to have as a guest than you, Alya?"

"T-tomorrow?"

"Yes. I believe it would be a great opportunity for you to leave a good impression on more students, since you won the debate. Think of this as a postgame interview in sports. They almost always interview the winner, right?"

"I guess…"

Alisa hesitated. She wasn't sure it was her place to discuss what happened at the debate. The negative comments going around school about Sayaka had been contained thanks to Masachika's and Nonoa's efforts. Even though there were still some students who had a problem with Nonoa putting plants in the audience, Nonoa didn't care in the slightest, and there was nothing Alisa could do anymore to help, either.

Would it really be okay to stir things up again after they worked so hard to get everything under control?

She never planned on announcing her victory to begin with, but would it really be right claiming it was a no contest? Would making it a no contest actually end up making things worse, as Masachika suggested when he talked about the victor pitying the loser?

Yes... I should be careful about what I say.

Masachika and Nonoa were far more social and good when it came to relationships, and she didn't want any shallow thoughts of hers to destroy the outcome they created. Only after coming to that decision did Alisa decide to convey how she really felt to Yuki.

"...I apologize, but I don't feel like I actually won that debate. That's why I don't plan on doing any winner's interview, let alone bringing up something that is already long over."

"Oh my. Is that so?"

"That's so," Alisa said with a nod. Yuki leaned back as though she was shocked before eventually smiling confidently.

"Then how about you join me during the show as a guest, and we can simply not talk about the debate?"

"Huh?"

"This will be the last student council report of the semester, so I thought maybe we could make it a little special. So? Will you do it?"

"S-sure, if that's the case..."

"Wow! Really? Thank you so much!"

Yuki clasped her hands in front of her face again, and Alisa nodded back. But after smiling innocently, she suddenly lowered her tone a few notches and added:

"However, it appears that you and Masachika really do plan on letting your victory at the debate go to waste. It's almost as if you are *trying* to make it seem like your victory didn't count."

"...! I'm impressed you noticed..."

"Of course I did. There have been rumors going around as of late that Nonoa broke the debate rules, and you two are not doing anything about it. That alone tells me everything I need to know. If you really were serious about proving you won at the debate, Masachika would have spun the information in your favor and put a stop to it."

"..."

Alisa was considerably disturbed by the fact that their opponent had completely seen through them, and Yuki capitalized on that shock by suddenly changing her smile.

"Ha-ha! Oh my, *Alisa*. You must be very confident, throwing away your victory at the debate like that. Do you seriously believe you can defeat me with a single win under your belt?"

"What...?"

Yuki's entire vibe instantly changed. Peeking out from the shadows of her perfect ladylike expression was a different her—one with a menacing sneer like nothing Alisa had ever seen before, making her eyes widen in disbelief.

"You casually stepped foot into my territory as if it wasn't even a big deal. Don't you think you are being a little naive? In fact, you are being so careless that I just had to warn you myself." She snickered, blissfully narrowing her eyes in a cold glare. Although the ominous smile sent a chill down Alisa's spine, she began to deeply ponder Yuki's proposal. And then it hit her. What Yuki said about her being a guest was a lie. What she was really inviting Alisa to do was to come on her show to argue it out.

"Did you finally figure it out? *Giggle.* This is not an invitation as a friend. This is an invitation as a rival. You should have been wary when I asked you to do this when Masachika was absent."

"Don't tell me that was your plan all along?"

"Of course it was. I figured this was a wonderful opportunity to destroy you while your strategist was gone."

Her smile didn't break when any of those foul words slipped off her tongue. However, the utter shock of seeing her friend act like this roused Alisa's rebellious spirit.

"In other words, you think you can do whatever you want to me if we play ball in your court."

"Yes, of course. Obviously, I didn't need to warn you of my plan, but I figured I wouldn't need to resort to surprise attacks if you were alone. Furthermore…"

Yuki paused for a second, looking at Alisa with a contemptuous smile.

"You can't make excuses if someone challenges you to a fight, and you lose fair and square, right?"

"…! It sounds more like you're underestimating me."

"Oh my. Do you not realize that you are already dancing in the palm of my hand? I believe I am estimating you just right."

"…!"

Yuki's taunting completely altered Alisa's way of thinking. The woman in front of her wasn't a friend who she worked together with on the student council. She was an enemy who needed to be defeated.

"Oh. Of course, you can rely on Masachika if you want to. You could even ask him for guidance when you deliver the medicine to him today." Yuki smirked smugly, perhaps having sensed Alisa's change of heart and realizing she didn't have to hide it any longer. Alisa knew she was being taunted, but her pride still wouldn't allow her to depend on Masachika after being insulted like that.

"That won't be necessary. He's sick and needs to rest, so I'm not going to bother him. No matter what."

"Oh my. Are you positive? Surely having his assistance would only benefit you."

It was as if her eyes were saying to Alisa, "Go cry to Masachika for help because you're not going to get anywhere without it," and that made her snap.

"Ha…ha-ha… Are you sure *you'll* be okay without Kuze's help?"

Alisa implied that they both relied on his help, but Yuki didn't even blink.

"Of course I'm sure. At any rate, I hope you work as good alone as your title suggests, Solitary Princess."

"…! I'm not going to lose to you!"

Although Alisa was essentially baring her fangs, Yuki confidently cackled back.

"I am looking forward to tomorrow."

And just like that, out of nowhere, the two beautiful princesses were going to battle it out face-to-face the following day. Soon after that, Alisa began to prepare for their fight. She checked the questions from other students in the suggestion box and imagined which contribution would be brought up during the radio show. Even while taking care of Masachika, she tried to remember as many of Yuki's radio show announcements as she could and simulated likely topics and responses in her mind as well. And then…after school the next day, she headed to the broadcasting room, having done everything she could to prepare in such a short time.

"Are you here?"

She knocked on the door before stepping into the room, where Yuki was already waiting for her.

"Good afternoon, *Alya*. You're here early."

"…Yeah. I'm looking forward to it."

"Me too."

Alisa raised an eyebrow at the fact that Yuki was back to calling her by her nickname again, but she sat next to her friend and rival, still ready for battle. That is, until something completely unexpected took her by surprise.

"We still have time before the announcement starts, so… Alya?"

"What?"

"I'm sorry."

Yuki suddenly turned to Alisa and bowed deeply, shocking her.

"Wh-what are you apologizing for?"

"For the way I acted yesterday."

Her voice was heavy with regret, her head still deeply bowed.

"It pains me to challenge you like this out of nowhere, especially since you are such a wonderful friend. I had to act overly aggressive so I wouldn't hesitate and change my mind, but after going home last night and reflecting, I realized what I did was wrong."

"…"

"I know it is selfish of me to say this, but I do not want to lose you as a friend, so…do you think you could forgive me?"

"I-it doesn't matter anymore. Please lift your head," replied Alisa, uncomfortable. Yuki then looked up and glanced at Alisa's expression.

"Does that mean…you forgive me?"

"Y-yeah… It's fine. You're really serious about this. That's all, right?"

"Thank you so much! Oh, thank goodness."

Alisa was honestly not completely satisfied with Yuki's selfish apology, but when she saw the smile on Yuki's face…she didn't have it in her to complain anymore. Yuki's look of relief, as if a weight had been removed from her shoulders, made Alisa smile softly as well.

"I am truly sorry. I know I am making excuses, but there is a reason I have to become the student council president, no matter what," confessed Yuki with a grave expression, tightly clenching her fists in front of her chest. Alisa, who had an idea what that reason was, slightly sympathized with her and almost reflexively asked:

"Did your family tell you to become the student council president?"

The reason she asked went back to when she first joined the student council and Yuki opened up to her. She didn't think much of it at the time. She thought, *Well, everyone's family is different* and *It must be rough being constantly pressured by your family like that*, but…

"Well, that is part of the reason."

Yuki's eyes wandered as if she didn't know how to say what she wanted to say, but after some hesitation, she gazed right at Alisa and revealed:

"I had an older brother."

"What?"

Alisa was caught off guard by the unexpected confession, since she had always heard that Yuki was an only child. Yuki looked away from Alisa's wide eyes, stared off into the distance, and eloquently continued:

"My brother was always much more talented than me, so my parents and grandfather expected so much from him. They believed he would make a wonderful heir to take over the Suou family one day… and I looked up to him very much as well."

Her gentle expression almost appeared to be reflecting the memories of a past dear to her when all emotion suddenly faded from her face.

"But now he's gone."

"…!"

Yuki's tone suddenly changed. What she was saying… Alisa was at a loss for words. He was *gone*? Did that mean…?

"Therefore, losing isn't an option for me," she uttered, gazing right into Alisa's eyes, inevitably piercing her heart.

"I have to live up to my family's expectations in his place. That is the responsibility he left with me."

"…"

A strong sense of duty and a firm will could be sensed from her bold declaration…but she suddenly smiled.

"…But everyone has their own problems and their own reasons

for doing something, so I don't know why I am saying all this. I apologize." Yuki smiled, looking apologetic, as she bowed again.

"H-huh? No, it's fine," replied Alisa, trembling. Yuki lifted her head and revealed a vacant, forced smile as she announced with a mood-lightening sparkle in her voice:

"Oh! Look at the time. The show is about to begin. Are you ready, Alya?"

"...I'm ready."

"Ready"? Alisa wasn't mentally prepared to do anything. She even forgot what she was doing there in the first place, and she turned to face the microphone almost unconsciously.

"What about you, Alya?" asked Yuki, getting Alisa's attention.

"Huh?"

"Why do you want to become the student council president?"

The words pierced Alisa's already anxious heart, and her mind went blank. When Masachika asked her the same question long ago, she was able to answer immediately. She told him it was because she wanted to be the student council president. That was it. But after hearing about Yuki's situation, Alisa suddenly began to feel her reason was far too insignificant.

"Oh, we really are out of time. Shall we begin, Alya?"

"Huh? O-oh, yes. Let's."

Even after reflexively replying, there was a part of Alisa still vaguely trying to remember what she was about to do, but by the time she did, it was far too late. The microphones were already turned on, and the program had already started.

"Hello, everyone. This is your biweekly student council announcement with me, Yuki Suou, student council publicist, here to update everyone on what the student council has been doing these past two weeks. And guess what? I have a very special guest with me today, since this is the last announcement for the semester. Say hello."

Alisa found herself lost in Yuki's well-flowing, eloquent voice until it was her turn to speak. Yuki shifted her gaze to Alisa, who nervously faced her microphone...but she had completely forgotten what she'd planned on saying.

"Oh, Alisa Kujou here. Ah! I'm the student council accountant... Uh... I'm happy to be here with you today."

Her stiff and awkward introduction embarrassed her to the point that she could feel her back get warmer.

"Oh my. Alya seems to be a little nervous today. But there is nothing to worry about! I doubt there are that many people listening to this announcement today! I know that isn't something I should admit, though," Yuki promptly chimed in, but Alisa could feel that even her cheeks were getting hotter now.

Pull yourself together! You have to beat Yuki! And how are you going to do that if you need her to hold your hand and help you like this?!

She tried scolding herself, but it wasn't only that. Up until a few minutes ago, she was driven to defeat Yuki, but that drive had almost completely faded.

Why do I want to win, though? If anything, I...

There had to be a reason she wanted to win. A reason that was hers and hers alone. A reason to become the student council president.

No...! I can think about that later. I need to focus on this announcement right now. Uh...

Alisa understood just how important this announcement was, and yet Yuki's question was all she could think about. Why *did* she want to become the student council president? She would surely not be able to defeat Yuki if she couldn't answer with her chest puffed out proudly, but it was like an obsession slowly pushing Alisa into a corner.

"...I suppose that would be the gist of it. What do you think, Alya?"

"Huh? O-oh, uh..."

But the broadcast didn't stop, and the more Alisa panicked, the more difficulty she had trying to think, which consequentially caused her to trip over her words as well.

"What happened after that was…more of the same. I couldn't gather my thoughts, and I didn't get a chance to recover mentally, either, as she toyed with me. Yuki essentially had to dig me out of each hole I made for myself after everything I said…which wasn't much, since I was having trouble conveying anything," she admitted, her voice tainted with bitterness and self-scorn. She ground her pearl-white teeth.

That's cruel…

That was the first thought that popped into Masachika's mind as he quietly watched over Alisa, frowning uncomfortably at how diabolical Yuki's psychological warfare was. First, she took on the role of a sinister villain, challenging and taunting Alisa to fire her up. Then, on the day of the challenge, she did a one-eighty and tried to elicit sympathy right before the announcement, shattering Alisa's will to fight. And as if that wasn't enough, she also told Alisa that she was fighting to become the president to live up to her family's expectations, since her beloved older brother was now gone, then almost immediately switched to asking Alisa what she was fighting for. And because Alisa was a serious and sincere person, she fell right into Yuki's trap. Perhaps the silver lining here was that Alisa was so sincere that she had no idea Yuki was trying to make her doubt herself. If Alisa, who didn't have many friends to begin with, ever knew these were calculated moves Yuki used to defeat her, she probably would stop trusting people, at least somewhat. Perhaps that, too, was part of Yuki's plan.

Wait… Maybe Yuki knew that Alya wouldn't notice. Maybe that was part of her plan.

She maintained her friendship with Alisa, helping her every time she tripped over her words while simultaneously trying to throw Alisa off her game. *My sister meticulously planned this terrifying attack*, thought Masachika.

"It's so frustrating."

When he returned his focus to the strained, weak voice in front of him, Alisa was still frowning and clenching her teeth, her fists trembling.

"I can't believe how easily I let myself get worked up like that… I was so confident when I took her up on her challenge, but in the end, I couldn't do anything—"

"Okay, that's enough. You're moving in the wrong direction with your thinking," observed Masachika, and he clapped his hands to snap her out of it. Alisa lifted her head to look at him.

"…The 'wrong direction'?"

"You're doing exactly what Yuki wants. So you weren't able to say the things you wanted during the announcement that Yuki hosted. That's it? Since when did that become a 'challenge'?"

"What do you mean?"

"Yuki said she was challenging you, or at the very least, she made it seem like it was a match. That's why you thought it was a competition. Am I wrong?"

Alisa blinked for a few moments with her head bent forward before slowly leaning her upper body back. After making sure she pulled herself together, Masachika continued in a matter-of-fact tone:

"Wanting to win is important, but you can't let that obsession take you prisoner. It'll give you tunnel vision, and you'll miss important details, so be careful."

"'Important details'?"

"Yep. Like…what's the headliner?"

After she shot him a puzzled look, he shrugged and continued:

"Fighting head-to-head in these sudden death matches is not what you do. You're the kind of person who puts everything she has into fighting with everything she has, regardless of who her opponent is. You analyze your rival until you are satisfied and ready, and the results simply follow. Right?"

"I suppose…"

"Thinking about your opponents and their problems is a distraction for people like you. Of course, the existence of an adversary could give you motivation, but you don't need motivation. You can keep motivated all by yourself. In other words, worrying too much about your competition for whatever reason only gets in your way and keeps you from giving one hundred percent to whatever you're doing."

"…"

"I get it, though. This is the first time you've gotten so worked up that you completely lost your sense of composure, right?"

"Yes… I suppose I did get worked up now that you mention it…"

Alisa appeared to be deep in thought, as if she had an idea of what he was getting at.

"Listen. Change your mindset. Yuki wasn't trying to use today's broadcast to achieve dominance over you. She was trying to distract you so you wouldn't be able to give it your all at the closing ceremony when you give your speech," suggested Masachika, purposely taking an assertive tone.

"…!"

"Am I wrong? Today was a half day, so there were hardly any students who stuck around to listen to the announcement during lunch. If she wanted to get the upper hand during one of these announcements, she would've done so when the whole school was around to hear."

"But…didn't she decide to do this because you were sick, and you weren't coming to school today?"

"That's part of it, but you would have accepted a challenge from her to fight one-on-one even if I hadn't been absent, right?"

"…"

"So I know I'm repeating myself, but change your mindset. There's no need for you to do things her way. Something this insignificant wouldn't even count as a preliminary skirmish compared to the closing ceremony speech. You were a guest during today's announcement, and you weren't the best talker in the world. That's all. No big deal. None of our schoolmates even knew you two were duking it out, and there weren't that many students who heard the announcement. Plus, nobody's going to care about, let alone remember, what happened today if you put on a good show at the closing ceremony in two days."

He spoke earnestly, his eyes boring into hers. However, even Masachika himself knew that everything he said wasn't completely factual. It was most likely that there had been a shift in the balance of power between Yuki and Alisa after today's announcement. This was their first time publicly clashing, after all, and Masachika had naturally assumed their first altercation, which would draw a lot of attention, would be the closing ceremony. However, Yuki's surprise attack proved him wrong. Right as people were starting to find themselves impressed with Princess Alya after the debate, this happened. *She got us*, thought Masachika, who'd wanted to go into the closing ceremony with Alisa's popularity still on the rise from the debate. Nevertheless, having Alisa change her mindset was what was most important right now. Because he believed taking care of this was imperative after unintentionally learning that her mental state greatly affected how much of her true potential she could tap into.

"So the headliner would be the closing ceremony? And the

announcement was more like an opening performance? Is that what you mean?"

"Basically. It looks like she wanted to throw you off your game... but things probably didn't go exactly how she planned."

"...?"

Alisa blinked.

"She was probably expecting you to be depressed because you couldn't perform how you wanted to during the announcement, and she wanted you to stay depressed during the closing ceremony. But you're frustrated, not depressed. Which means everything's going to be okay. We can simply use that frustration as motivation. So stop letting it bother you," he commanded with a confident grin. He quietly looked her in the eye, and as if his will were conveyed to her, she suddenly closed her eyes and exhaled deeply before collecting herself and facing him once more.

"...You're right. Thank you."

"...Oh, one more thing. While it's fine to be frustrated, don't let the rivalry get the best of you. She wants you to become overcompetitive and obsessed."

"In other words, I need to forget about what happened for now and focus on giving the closing ceremony everything I've got, right?"

"Yep, sounds about right."

"Okay. I'll make sure to change my mindset... And I'm sorry. I'm sorry for running into battle all by myself like that."

Alisa lowered her head, and Masachika grew unbelievably restless because it was extremely rare for Alisa to ever bow.

"No, uh... I mean... It's my fault, too, for getting sick during such an important time. I'm sorry."

"It isn't your fault you got sick."

"But this never would have happened if I didn't let my guard down. I failed to predict that Yuki would ambush us like this. I was being naive thinking she wouldn't go all out before the closing ceremony. I thought it wasn't going to be *that* big of a deal, since it's just the closing ceremony. I got too comfortable, and I hate myself for that."

"I didn't see it coming, either. Besides, I should have gone to you first, instead of letting my pride take over like that."

"You were only looking out for me because I was sick and—… Let's just do better next time, okay?" suggested Masachika, aggressively scratching his head. Although clearly not 100 percent happy with his conclusion, Alisa nodded in agreement. A slightly awkward air filled the space between them for a few seconds until he cleared his throat and added:

"Anyway, depending on how you look at it, I guess you could say this is a good chance to show everyone what a hard worker you are, just like we discussed at the restaurant that day. The protagonist shines the brightest during adverse circumstances, after all. Besides, at the very least, we learned firsthand that Yuki is better at this type of warfare, and it's important to have a good idea of your opponent's skill set."

"…Yeah, I never expected Yuki to attack from the rear like this, so I suppose I could consider this a good learning experience, since I won't be making the same mistake twice," she said as though she was trying to persuade herself of that as well.

"…Are you disappointed?" asked Masachika in a somewhat worried manner.

"Huh?"

"Are you disillusioned with Yuki after learning these are the kinds of things she does?"

Alisa slowly blinked for a few moments before shaking her head.

"No, I'm not disillusioned. While it was a surprise attack, Yuki challenged me head-on. I don't have the right to blame her when I only have myself to blame for losing."

"…All right. I'm glad to hear that."

He let out a sigh of relief after learning that Alisa and Yuki were still friends, but at the very same time…

Yeah… It looks like she still hasn't realized that Yuki basically used psychological warfare against her.

Alisa seemed to truly believe Yuki only acted overly aggressive so Alisa wouldn't change her mind, and she seemed to not realize that even *that* was all part of Yuki's plan to throw her off her game. In actuality, it was all a well-calculated act, but in Alisa's mind, Yuki's behavior and question messing her up was purely coincidental.

It wasn't a coincidence, though. She knew that would happen, which is why she did it. But I'm not sure if I should tell Alya that…

On one hand, if he decided to be completely honest with her, it would most likely destroy their friendship. But on the other hand, he would need to explain to her what happened to make sure she wouldn't make the same mistake again. Masachika began to inwardly debate with himself when…

"Kuze? What's wrong?"

"Oh… It's nothing."

He saw the innocent look on her face and decided to keep quiet. Besides, strategizing was his specialty. All he had to do was handle the things Alisa wasn't good at for her.

"If it's nothing, then why are you smiling?"

"Huh?"

Masachika blinked in wonder, and only after touching his face did he realize that he actually was smiling.

"Wow, you're right. Good question."

"'Good question'?"

He thought about it before her perplexed gaze…until it finally hit him.

Am I excited? Am I having fun…because Yuki and Ayano got one up on me?

Yuki once expressed her love for sibling rivalries and how excited she was to fight him, but it seemed that Masachika was no different.

"Interesting... Ha-ha! She really got us this time. That's all."

The instant he realized the reason he was smiling, his smirk twisted into something sinister.

"It's strange. I'm even a little surprised myself how excited all this has made me."

Neither Yuki nor Ayano had acted that differently the previous day, but they actually had been hiding daggers behind their backs, eagerly waiting for an opening to strike, and they managed to beautifully unsheathe said daggers without Masachika noticing. The fact that they pulled it off so well was surprisingly amusing to him. While undoubtedly an arrogant feeling, what he felt was similar to the joy a parent would feel when they saw just how much their child had grown up. His usually unmotivated demeanor was nowhere to be found, and his lips were curled in exhilaration as if he was about to lick them any moment now. Alisa gazed in wonder...then softly placed a hand over her mouth and looked away.

"<Wow... I could get used to seeing him like this...>"

Masachika curiously blinked at her because he genuinely couldn't hear what she whispered into her hand.

"Did you say something?"

"I just said that look on your face was creeping me out. You looked like some bad guy scheming something."

"...Did I really look that bad?"

"...Yes."

Although she nodded, her hand couldn't cover her faintly blushing cheeks, and the contrast between what she said and her expression sent him into a tunnel of confusion.

Huh? Why? Wait... Does she like bad boys? Is this one of those "good girls like bad boys" kinds of things?

He suddenly imagined Alisa being tricked by some scumbag, which made him frustrated, since he knew how bad boys were portrayed as a virtue in comics written for women.

"Alya…"

"What?"

"Young, handsome yakuza bosses only exist in comics. Don't even think about trying to get involved with people like that in real life."

"…You sometimes say the most wild, random things, you know that? What are you talking about?"

"What? You're blushing, so…I thought you liked bad boys or something."

"What the…? No way. And I'm not blushing, either… I was just thinking about how that bad-boy grin on your face didn't suit you. That's all."

"Rude."

Now that she mentioned it, it did look like she was covering her mouth in an attempt to keep herself from laughing.

Hold on. The fact that she whispered something in Russian is proof that she said something incredibly embarrassing.

Regardless of whether she meant what she said, she was clearly blushing because of it.

Eh, whatever. I highly doubt Alya would ever let some thug trick her anyway.

That was when Masachika was hit with what seemed like a divine revelation. He seemingly randomly recalled an event that took place at his house earlier today when Ayano's eyes were sparkling because he said he'd ridicule her.

Wait… Don't tell me that Alya's also…?!

Did she blush when she saw that sinister look on his face… because of something like that?! The thought naturally crossed his mind, but he almost immediately ruled out the possibility.

No, no, no… Alya's a sadist, if anything. She always looks at me like I'm trash.

Although satisfied with his terribly rude conclusion, another nerdy cliché trope popped into his mind.

Hold on! Girls who are obviously aggressive sadists most of the time usually turn into submissive masochists in front of the people they like! Hhhnnng?!

But right after he reached that conclusion, he immediately imagined himself punching himself in his stupid face.

Dammit… What is wrong with me? Cocky much? I'm disgusted at myself for letting my imagination run wild like that. All right, I'm just going to stop thinking about it.

With that decision in mind, he fixed his expression and faced Alisa to—

"<I thought it was attractive because it's you.>"

"Hnnng?!"

"Kuze?!"

Masachika suddenly smacked himself on the head (he dropped a fist on it, to be precise), and Alisa's face filled with disbelief.

"Wh-what's wrong? Are you okay?"

"…Hmm? Why wouldn't I be?"

"What? Because—… *Sigh.* Now your forehead is turning red."

She leaned forward with a worried gaze and smoothly ran a finger across his forehead. Perhaps she was fine with touching him now after taking care of him the day before, but the nerve-racking sensation in addition to her being so close made Masachika lean away.

"A-are you okay? You still look a little gloomy," he promptly exclaimed. Although he was mainly trying to change the subject, Alisa instantly froze.

"…"

Alisa slowly sat back down in her chair.

"What's up? Is there still something bothering you?"

After a few moments of silence, she quietly muttered:

"...I didn't have an answer."

"For what?"

"Yuki asked me why I wanted to become the student council president...and I didn't have an answer for her."

She hung her head low, clenched her fists tightly over her skirt, and bitterly explained:

"Yuki is running in the election for her family's sake... She is determined to do it for them... But... But I... I am doing all this for myself, and I started to think that maybe that wasn't a good enough reason... I didn't know what to say to her! I didn't have any answer for her!"

Alisa raised her fists before her chest, enduring the pain in her heart.

"I embarrassed myself in front of Yuki, and I'm frustrated that I wasn't confident enough to give her an answer..."

Masachika fell silent when he saw her bite her lip with a lowered gaze...because he, too, once felt the very same way about his reason for joining student council. He decided to help her run for student council president because he'd felt guilty about tossing his responsibilities to Yuki, and he became the vice president by kicking each and every one of his opponents down. And that was why he had suffered for so long...and that was why he was painfully aware of how Alisa felt.

But...

But he had someone who laughed away all his pain. He had someone who believed in him and was kind to him.

"Alya..."

And now it was his turn to give back. Just like those kind people who were there for him, it was now his turn to be there for Alisa. He was going to keep the promise he made her that time when he said he would be there for her and support her dream.

"Keep your chin up, face forward, and look at me!"

Alisa jumped when he shouted and looked up, pressing her lips together tightly as Masachika stared right into her eyes.

"So your reason for becoming student council president isn't as good as Yuki's? Who cares? Did you forget? I know why Yuki wants to become the president, and I know why you want to as well. And guess what? I chose you."

Alisa looked as though she'd been completely caught off guard.

"I told you already. You're already someone people want to cheer for and support. I know your beauty—how passionately devoted you are and how you always put a hundred percent of yourself into everything you do. I know how you live true to your heart. You deserve to be rewarded more. You deserve to be cheered on by your peers and loved."

He could feel his body flush as he spoke, but he ignored it because he knew he had to speak from his heart if he ever wished to reach Alisa's. Moreover, his gut was telling him that he *had* to tell her how he really felt right now or bear the consequences.

"That's why…you need to keep your chin up. You need to face forward, puff out your chest proudly, and be yourself. You don't have to worry about a thing. You are every bit as charming and attractive as Yuki. Trust me."

It was at this moment he realized his back was sweating profusely. The urge to writhe in agony and slam his head into his desk was strong, but he fought through the impulse and continued to look her in the eyes. After appearing stunned for a few moments…she placed a hand over her mouth and started to laugh.

"Pfft… Ha-ha…! That sounded like you were confessing your love to me, you know."

"Oh, shut up! And just so you know, I'm never going to say anything like that ever again! Got it?!" he instinctively shouted, mainly because she pointed out something he had already somewhat realized himself.

"Ugh! My entire body's burning up now! My fever must be back. This is what I get for doing something I'm not used to doing while I have a cold!"

Masachika looked the other way, tugging at his uniform's collar and fanning himself.

"*Giggle*. Oh, really? Well, I suppose you can't be blamed for how it sounded. You do have a fever, after all."

She smiled, sliding closer to him before placing a hand on his cheek, guiding his face forward toward hers. His eyes opened wide in astonishment as she touched her forehead to his.

"...You really do feel a little warm."

"...?!"

Her eyes were closed, and their noses were only a hair's breadth apart. The situation was like a romantic kissing scene, which rendered him speechless and dumbstruck. Each second felt like an eternity in which he hesitated to breathe, but before long, Alisa leaned back in her chair and gently smiled at him.

"Thank you. I've found my answer thanks to you. I can move forward now."

"...Oh, awesome," replied Masachika briefly, unable to maintain eye contact. Alisa cracked a smile once more after seeing him like that and said in a voice filled with relief:

"You're right. I shouldn't compare myself with others. Whatever I do, that's my decision, and that's all that matters."

"Exactly... Yuki is Yuki, and you are you."

"When you're right, you're right."

Masachika let out a sigh of relief to see his partner back to her old self.

"Yuki may be fulfilling her late brother's wish, but I'm still not going to let that get in my way."

...Hmm? Masachika froze after hearing something he simply could not ignore. Late...to what? Hold on?! Like late-late?! Like... dead?!

Yukiiiiiiiii!! Why is your brother dead?!?! Who killed me?!?!

He screamed in his mind at his sister, who was winking at him with her tongue out, and his entire body began to sweat for an entirely different reason from a moment ago.

Wh-wh-what should I do?! Alisa thinks Yuki has this really dark and depressing past... Should I correct her, since I am supposed to be Yuki's childhood friend? But that might damage their friendship... But still...this is far too...

The unexpected dilemma distressed him, but after worrying about it for a few seconds, he hesitantly opened his mouth and stammered:

"H-hey, Alya—"

But the door to the room suddenly opened, drawing their eyes toward it.

"Knock, knock."

The apathetic voice was followed by the door rattling open, revealing Nonoa, who barged into the room with Sayaka, who politely bowed once, behind her. Both Alisa and Masachika were surprised by the unexpected visit.

"Oh, I knew you'd still be here... Wait. Kuze? I thought you didn't come to school today."

"I actually just got here..."

"Oh? Anyway, good timing," replied Nonoa, unfazed by their reactions, and she plopped herself down in Hikaru's seat...straddling it in front of Masachika.

"Nonoa, that's bad manners."

"Eh, who cares? It's just us in here."

Nonoa ignored Sayaka's scolding and rested her elbow on the back of the chair before cradling her chin in her palm. Her eyes were half-open with her usual unmotivated expression, and her legs were spread wide open...right in front of Masachika.

...And this is probably why she never became one of the school's so-called princesses, for better or for worse.

From Masachika's point of view, Nonoa was popular enough and obviously good-looking enough to be counted as one of the princesses of his grade, and the only reason she probably wasn't included with the likes of Alisa and Yuki was because she felt far more obtainable than them. If Alisa and Yuki were like stars in the sky, then Nonoa would be more like a flower beautifully blooming from the earth.

...She'd definitely be one of those carnivorous plants, though.

He added that one last zinger before slightly raising his guard and asking:

"So... Need something?"

"Hmm? I don't need anything. Saya's the one who wanted to talk to you."

"Oh..."

Masachika shifted his gaze to Sayaka, who was standing behind Nonoa. After her eyebrow briefly twitched, she let out a deep breath, then gathered her resolve and straightened.

"I know this is late, but...I wanted to apologize to you two...for not only the debate but for being rude as well. You have my sincerest apologies."

Nonoa watched Sayaka bow deeply to them before slightly lowering her own head, albeit while still sitting.

"I'm sorry, too. Like, it was totally my responsibility to stop Saya. I knew she stepped out of line, and I did nothing. I know it's a little late for begging, but do you think you have it in your hearts to forgive us? We'll make it up to you, of course."

Nonoa put her hands together in front of her face and winked, and Sayaka continued to bow. Masachika looked over at Alisa.

"I don't have anything against them, so it's up to you, Alya."

"Well…she already apologized for what she said to me, so I don't care anymore, either. And Miyamae didn't do anything she needs to apologize for."

"I'm, like, pretty sure bringing plants to a debate is something to apologize for."

Nonoa tilted her head inquisitively, but Masachika waved dismissively.

"That's just strategy. Since when do the losers apologize to the winners anyway? Come on."

"Ha-ha… Yeah…"

"…You were the ones who forfeited your victory."

Sayaka lifted her head and stared hard at Masachika. It was clear by the look in her eyes that she figured out he was the one who asked Nonoa to squash the rumors about her.

"It was bothering Alya, so I did what I had to do. That's all. Besides, it was Nonoa who actually did everything, so don't blame us for what happened." He shrugged. He wasn't going to accept thanks for helping her, and he wasn't going to take criticism for the hit to Nonoa's reputation, either. Put simply: "If you have a problem, bring it up with Nonoa, not me." Sayaka easily picked up on what he was trying to say, but she turned her gaze to Alisa next.

"That still doesn't change the fact that you two were looking out for me. The fact that you didn't bring up the debate during the announcements proves that. Am I wrong?"

Alisa stared Sayaka right back in the eye.

"…Who knows who would have won if we had waited for everyone to vote. I didn't want to declare victory when it wasn't a hundred percent certain that I earned it. That's all."

Sayaka stared hard, observing Alisa as if she were trying to peer into her soul, but she eventually lowered her gaze with a begrudging smile and nodded.

"…I see you are a woman of great pride," muttered Sayaka before turning on her heel. She walked to the classroom door and went to open it…but stopped.

"…But I am a woman of great pride as well."

Masachika immediately realized what she was up to.

"Hey, wait. What are you planning?"

Sayaka looked in his direction and replied:

"I will not bend the truth just for the sake of my reputation."

"So you plan on announcing you lost? During one of the school announcements? Wait… At the closing ceremony?"

She looked away as though she was unable to answer him, so he stood out of his chair.

"I'm sorry, but as a member of the student council, I can't allow you to waste valuable time at the closing ceremony with something like that. If you want to pay Alya back for her good faith, then there's another way you could do that, you know."

"…'Another way'?"

And after Masachika explained what that way was, not only Sayaka but also Alisa stared in astonishment. Even Nonoa raised an eyebrow.

"…Are you being serious?"

"Completely serious. Are you okay with that, Alya?"

"S-sure…"

"Nonoa, you said you'd make it up to us, right?"

"Uh… Yeah, I guess I did say that."

After seeing Alisa's puzzled nod and Nonoa's half smirk, Sayaka turned to face him.

"It's not like I'm going to cheer you on or support you," she argued as if she was suppressing various complex emotions while staring at Masachika and Alisa.

"Yeah, I know."

"...And I still think you should have run alongside Yuki Suou."

"Really? But you can at least recognize why I chose Alya, right?"

Alisa and Sayaka stared each other down for a few moments before Sayaka finally closed her eyes.

"...Fine."

After seeing Sayaka's slight nod, Nonoa grabbed the back of her chair and leaned way back.

"Whoa. Really? All right, I'm in, I guess."

She slid back in the chair and casually bobbed her head up and down.

"Thanks. I'm counting on you two." Masachika firmly nodded in return before facing Alisa, whose eyes were wide in disbelief, and exclaimed:

"See, Alya? This is the effect you have on people. We're going to beat them now."

"Huh...? We are? W-wait. I thought we were going for a draw."

Masachika curled his lips fiercely at his partner, who was still utterly confused by the sudden turn of events.

"We're not going for a draw anymore. We're going to finish what they started...and crush them."

Alisa gasped at his declaration, Sayaka silently resettled her glasses on her nose, and Nonoa smiled gaily.

CHAPTER 8

A Greeting

It was after school on the following day. Each member of the student council was preparing for the closing ceremony in between meetings relative to their position. They ran throughout school in groups of two to three with copies of the closing ceremony agenda in hand. After Alisa and Masachika finished those responsibilities, they began to practice for their upcoming speech on the stage in the gymnasium.

"Thank you all for your time."

Although they didn't have a microphone to practice with, Alisa finished giving her speech and was showered with Masachika's applause from below.

"Perfect. Just do what you did here tomorrow, and we're set," he advised, walking up the steps to the stage, but Alisa's expression suddenly clouded with anxiety.

"Yes… All I need to do is remember what I practiced…"

"Are you worried? You had no problem speaking at the debate."

"That's because I was focused on my own inner world… But there are going to be a lot more people at the closing ceremony, right?"

"Yeah, I mean…everyone at school has to be there, so this gym's going to be packed," he replied honestly with a shrug, since he felt there was no use sugarcoating it for her. He then brightened and replied:

"But that doesn't change what you have to do. It doesn't matter how many more people there are. You just need to focus on how you're going to speak and—"

"I don't think that's going to be enough. I figured that much when I saw you speaking at the debate the other day. There's a distinct difference between self-righteously regurgitating memorized talking points and speaking directly to the people. This speech is my chance to greet everyone, which is why I need to look them in the eye when I speak. I want to speak *with* them, not at them," she said with a serious gaze at the floor below the stage before turning her eyes firmly toward Masachika. "Hey, how do I converse with the audience like you do?"

She really is always trying to improve herself, he thought in admiration as he scratched his head.

"I mean…it's kind of something you just have to get used to doing for the most part. But first, you need to make sure you can perfectly say your speech without glancing at your script. After that, all you need to do is watch and see how the audience is reacting, then change your tone and how long you pause. Maybe even stick a few jokes in between your lines, but make sure you stay focused."

"…"

Alisa frowned after hearing his advice, and Masachika realized he was demanding far too much, so he smiled and added:

"But this is your first time, so don't expect to be able to do everything perfectly. Like I said, it's something you have to get used to doing. So all you need to do this time is keep your chin up and confidently say your piece."

"…Is that really going to be enough?"

"Trust me. Consider this practice for the upcoming election. I told you yesterday. Remember? We don't want to provoke Yuki or excite her because she'll try to trip us up."

"…!"

Those words suddenly made Alisa realize she was unconsciously feeling pressed that she had to beat Yuki, and she was dumbfounded.

"Alya, do you want to know a little secret to relieve tension and get the audience's attention?" he asked, lowering his voice and gently patting her on the shoulder to calm her down.

"A secret?"

"Yep."

He whispered into her ear as she raised a brow, and ultimately her jaw dropped. She then appeared to be in deep thought.

"That's…"

"Easy, right? And it's very effective as well."

"…All right, I'll give it a try." Alisa nodded with an expression of utmost seriousness. Masachika looked at her confidently…and all of a sudden, a voice called out to them from the wing.

"Are you practicing for tomorrow's ceremony?"

Their eyes simultaneously darted in the direction of the voice, only to find Yuki with her usual curated smile and Ayano standing behind her, bowing with her usual blank expression.

"Oh, you two are done with your work for the day, too?"

"Yes, everything went smoothly."

Their exchange may have sounded friendly, but there was an unusual tension filling the space between them. Yuki slowly walked toward Masachika with a hand over her mouth, her head tilted.

"*Giggle.* Is everything okay, Masachika? That look on your face is scaring me."

"You've got a lot of nerve saying that. Getting rid of that proper-young-lady facade and going full mask off, huh?"

"Oh my. Me? *Giggle.*"

She widened her eyes and smiled a perfect ladylike smile, but the light behind those eyes was cold and distant. While most people would shudder at the terrifying sight, Masachika simply shrugged and looked back at Alisa.

"See? This is the real her. I know I've said this before, but don't be fooled by her act."

"O-okay…"

"Oh dear. Alya? *Giggle.* Did I disappoint you?"

But Alisa slowly shook her head.

"No. I was a little surprised, but I haven't become disillusioned."

"Oh my…"

"We still haven't known each other that long, after all. It's only natural for there to be sides of you I don't know about yet."

"…"

"Besides…you were serious when you said you still wanted to be friends with me, right?"

"…Yes, of course."

"Then everything's okay." Alisa nodded with ease, catching Yuki by surprise.

"Plus…I was able to reexamine myself thanks to you."

"…What do you mean?"

Yuki's fake smile faded, although she was still tilting her head. Alisa then stared her straight in the eye and declared:

"You asked me why I wanted to become the student council president the other day, and you will get that answer. Tomorrow. I'll also receive far more support from our fellow students."

Staring at Alisa, Yuki blinked in genuine confusion for a few moments before dissolving into laughter.

"*Ha-ha-ha!* You really are a sincere, wonderful person."

"Wh-what's that supposed to mean?"

Alisa appeared embarrassed by the unexpected praise, but Yuki continued without even a hint of shame:

"I was only speaking the truth. I am really happy to be your friend, Alya."

"…!"

Alisa swiftly looked away as though she couldn't take anymore bonding, which only made Yuki smile more.

"And because you are so wonderful, I have something I would like to tell you," revealed Yuki.

"…What is it?"

"I told you my brother was gone… I never said he was dead."

"Huh…?"

Alisa looked back at her with a blank expression and saw Yuki's mischievous grin.

"He ran away from home, and while he cut ties with the Suou family, he is still very much alive and well."

"Wh-what?!"

Alisa's face turned bright red as fury rippled through her for being led on like that. She shot Yuki a piercing glare, which Yuki parried with a cool, refreshing smile of her own…until Masachika swiftly jumped in front of Yuki, cheerfully smiling as well.

"Oh, thank goodness. I was worried this was going to destroy your friendship."

His smile was unnaturally joyful, which made Yuki immediately cautious, reverting back to her usual archaic smile.

"Oh my. You make it sound as if our friendship has been damaged in some way, Masachika."

"No? I mean, I think you're a punk for what you did, but what's new?"

He spoke with a bright tone and mirthful smile as he approached Yuki and Ayano. Alisa watched anxiously from behind, but Yuki's smile didn't waver, even when her brother was standing right in front of her.

"Wait… Could it be? Are you angry that I waited until you were sick to attack?"

"Not at all. Striking when your opponent's down is only natural in war. Plus, giving me the medicine without me noticing took a lot of talent. Beautifully done."

"Why thank you. What an honor," she replied, and yet she got chills from her brother's smile. And Ayano, who was glancing in his direction, was no different. Cold sweat trailed down their backs, for there was something eerie about the bizarre energy Masachika emanated. As he continued to exude intimidation, he cheerfully went on:

"It's a weird feeling. Hard to describe it, to be honest. It's like… wanting to pet your cute little dog that is biting you but also wanting to discipline them so they never bite you again. Know what I mean?"

Yuki, however, didn't joke about the frightening things her brother was saying. She even set aside her usual noblewoman facade after seeing just how serious his eyes were—something she hadn't seen in ages. All she felt now was a tinge of fear and exhilaration, which manifested in the form of a fierce smirk and sparkling eyes, and as a result, Masachika's sneer grew even more sinister as well.

"If I were to give some advice, though…," he began, looking down at Yuki without any humor. "You took a bite, so now you better clench your jaw and not let go."

The ambition glowing in his stare was proof enough that he hadn't been driven into a corner, and it was at that moment that both Yuki and Ayano realized they had stepped on the tail of a sleeping lion.

Ha-ha… I think I got them a little worried, but maybe I didn't go hard enough.

There was no simpler declaration of war, but that worked out in Yuki's favor as well, since she had wanted to fight him head-on. Her fighting spirit rose with her elation as she quivered with excitement. Ayano began to quiver as well…but where she was quivering will forever remain a secret.

The terrifyingly tense atmosphere swallowed the stage like a storm. It was almost hard to believe this was the day *before* the closing ceremony speeches, but a hesitant voice soon called out from one of the wings, clearing the air.

"Hey, uh… I wanted to do some final checks before tomorrow, but…"

Everyone looked in the direction of the voice and found three second-year students from the student council in the wing. Touya wore a slightly stiff smile, so Masachika and Yuki rid themselves of their fighting spirit and walked over. Alisa and Ayano calmed themselves before following. Although the air was still tense among the first-year students, Touya began the final checks for the closing ceremony. It wasn't long before the conversation shifted toward the next day's speeches.

"Now, for our student council member greetings tomorrow, I, the president, will speak first, followed by the vice president, Chisaki, then Big Kujou, and then the first-year students will speak after that. There aren't many student council members this year, so I'm not going to give you a time limit, but let's try to keep the speeches to no more than three minutes long if possible. Any questions?"

He had given only a brief rundown of the ceremony earlier, so hands were raised. After making sure everyone was okay, Touya somewhat hesitantly shifted his gaze to the four first-year students.

"Okay, now for the speaking order of the first-year students… What do you want to do? Last year, the candidates for student council president played rock-paper-scissors to decide order."

As Yuki and Alisa exchanged glances, Yuki smiled slyly.

"I wouldn't mind playing rock-paper-scissors," she suggested, but right as Alisa was about to agree, Masachika cut her off and interjected:

"No way. Rock-paper-scissors rewards whoever can read their opponent best."

"Yes, I suppose." Yuki shrugged.

"Hmm?" wondered both Touya and Alisa, raising their eyebrows.

"I get it." Chisaki nodded.

"Whaaat?" said Maria with a confused smile. Ayano, true to form, was one with the air. But these siblings were not joking. Because if you're as big an otaku as either of them, the first game you master is rock-paper-scissors, just in case you are ever drugged and wake up to find yourself in the middle of a death game where you have to bet your life to survive. Once again, these siblings were not joking.

"How about we flip a coin?"

"Yeah, that sounds fair."

"Perfect. Ayano can flip the coin, and Alya can call it, then. How does that sound?"

"Nah, let's have someone else flip the coin."

"*Giggle.* Very distrusting today, aren't we?"

The obvious reason neither Masachika nor Yuki would be allowed to flip the coin was because they could possibly cheat. Ayano, on the other hand, didn't have the skill set to cheat like them. Nevertheless, Masachika still couldn't risk it—not after she casually slipped him the medicine that made him sleepy. Of course, Masachika and Yuki weren't allowed to call heads or tails, either, because they could easily predict the correct answer.

"Um… How about I do it?"

Masachika looked at the second-year students and noticed Maria pulling out a hundred-yen coin, so he glanced over at Yuki to make sure she was okay with that. She shrugged, which was enough for him, so he looked at Maria once more and nodded.

"We would really appreciate that. Okay, Masha will flip a coin, and Alya will guess if it's heads or tails. If she guesses right, she gets to choose whether she wants to go before or after Yuki, and if she guesses wrong, then Yuki gets to do that."

"Sounds good to me. The side with the picture on it is heads, and the side that says 'one hundred' on it is tails. Everyone ready?" asked Maria as she placed the hundred-yen coin in her palm. Alisa, however, shot her a skeptical look and asked:

"Masha, are you sure you can do it?"

"Alyaaa. ♪ Stop making fun of your big sister. Of course I can do it. Just you watch." Maria pouted.

"Ready? Three, two…one!"

She then jumped into the air for some reason and flipped the coin. A part of everyone's soul died as they watched Maria hop up and down once more, for who knows why, while she pursued the flying coin with her eyes until she eventually slapped both hands together and caught it like someone trying to smash a fly.

"I got it! See? I told you I could do it, Alya!"

Maria smiled smugly and bragged with both hands clasped together, but Alisa's eyes were cold.

"So? Which side is up?"

"Huh…?"

Maria looked down at her clasped hands and realized it was impossible to decide which way was up and which way was down.

"Um… How about we say this way is up, then?"

She turned her hands so the left was on the top and the right was on the bottom.

"Heads," stated Alisa with a detached tone.

"What? Don't you think you should think about it a little longer?"

"Just show us the coin."

"Mmm… Fine."

Maria removed her left hand, revealing the number 100. Yuki, who had been watching Alisa's expression the entire time, noticed her briefly frown.

"Tails. All right, Yuki, do you want to go before or after me?"

"Hmm…"

Yuki placed a hand on her chin as Maria and Masachika quietly watched her.

It would have been great if we won the coin toss, but whatever... Let's just see how much of our plan she can see through.

Yuki focused on her own thoughts while her brother stared.

Normally, going last makes you stick out more and gives you the advantage...but if I go first and impress everyone so much that they won't even bother clapping for Alya, then I could destroy her. On the other hand, going first usually means you become the standard for the rest, which will get you at least the bare minimum amount of clapping, so it would be difficult to absolutely crush Alya if I make her go first. She and everyone else could even use that as an excuse. "Oh, she went first, so give her a break." Stuff like that... Maybe I really should choose to go first? That was what I was planning on doing anyway. But...

Yuki tried to analyze the situation from a different angle.

That's only if I wanted to absolutely crush her to the point of no return, but now that my brother's serious about this, maybe it'd be better if I tried to win in the safest way possible... Which means going after her would give me the edge. I should probably see how he is planning to fight first before striking...

That was when Yuki was suddenly overcome with a feeling that something was off. The way her brother was acting a moment ago... and the way he was clearly trying to taunt them...

Now that I think about it...he was really trying to scare us...which is unusual for someone who normally pulls the strings from the shadows to get things done... Was that all an act?

Her gut told her she was right the instant the thought popped into her head. She swiftly looked at Masachika and put on her thinking cap.

If that was all an act...then what is he after? He acted like he was angry that we tricked him and made it seem like we were going to fight

head-on. But he really doesn't plan on fighting fair and square. And…!
He's trying to distract me from Alya! That's it!

It hit her like a divine revelation from the heavens as she stared hard into her brother's eyes. While she couldn't read his poker face, she could tell she was approaching the truth.

Yes… I got so caught up with my brother that I almost lost sight of things. It's Alya I'm after…and she isn't that mentally strong from what I can see. Plus, she is probably still traumatized from yesterday's announcements that we did together, since she was having a really hard time talking. That was why I was planning on forcing her to go after me at the ceremony. The pressure would crush her.

Once she remembered her original plan, she realized that Masachika was trying to distract her with something else, but that was over. She'd seen through his little trick.

He is going for a draw! He wants Alya to go first so she doesn't have to feel pressure while still getting at least the bare minimum amount of applause! Which means I am sticking to my plan and going first so I can dominate!

Around five seconds had gone by while Yuki reached her conclusion with her extraordinarily quick thinking.

"I would like to go first, please," she announced to Touya, seeming smug.

"All right, then. Suou and Kimishima will go first, followed by Little Kujou and Kuze."

Alisa silently nodded in agreement with the terms and slowly grinned.

The next day arrived. Thanks to the student council's preparation the day before, the closing ceremony was going smoothly as the teachers spoke and the disciplinary council made their announcements. Touya, Maria, Alisa, and Masachika were watching the ceremony from stage right while Chisaki, Yuki, and Ayano were watching from the wing on the opposite end.

"Now let's hear from our student council members."

The time had finally come. The emcee from the broadcasting club called out the names of the second-year students to come one at a time to greet their peers. Touya, oozing charisma, proudly greeted the student body and ended his speech with a surprise announcement: They were finally getting new summer uniforms. Chisaki spoke cheerfully, adding jokes here and there, and gave a relatively brief speech. Maria wore her usual bubbly smile and gave a very detailed, well-thought-out speech, despite her friendly tone and demeanor. While each second-year student was unique in their own way, every one of their speeches won the crowd's attention. Their eyes were locked onto the stage with gazes usually reserved for movie stars...until it finally came time for the first-years to speak.

"Now let's hear from the student council publicist, Yuki Suou."

The air in the room instantly changed when the first presidential candidate took the stage: Some waited in anticipation of the silent battle between candidates, some bounced with excitement, and some calmly readied themselves to assess the situation. A myriad of gazes settled on Yuki where she stood onstage and where she was projected onto the large screen behind her, evoking some excitement among the crowd.

"Hello, my fellow students. I am the student council publicist and former middle school student council president, Yuki Suou, and I plan on running for student council president in the election for next school year."

She gave a small bow with her archaic smile and was immediately greeted with cheers from the audience in the gymnasium. She nodded at the crowd and then continued her speech in a lighter tone.

"Therefore, I would like to tell you all a little about my vision for next year. When I become the student council president…I promise to create an environment where your opinions matter. Oh dear? Was that too generic?"

Yuki suddenly smiled mischievously, creating some laughter in the audience and clearing the tension. She then lifted a large box from behind the podium and presented it to the crowd.

"Specifically, I want to talk about this: the suggestion box, which has been around for years at our school. There are probably more of you who haven't used it even once compared to those who have. As you all know, I address many of these during the afternoon announcements I make on behalf of the student council, but it seems to me there are not that many people with problems or requests. Why, though? Perhaps you believe leaving a suggestion in the suggestion box is pointless because nothing is going to get done about it?"

Her specific question prompted the student body to reflect on how they felt. After they nodded back at her individually as though they agreed, she continued to explain why.

"But it is understandable that you would all feel that way. After all, most members of the student council have no experience with the kind of work we do. Even working adults spend their first year learning the ropes at their job, and yet most members of the student council serve out their entire term after only one year, then move on. Trying to listen to student requests and actually realize their demands is an extremely difficult task, especially this year. Because this year… for some reason…! For some *reason*, we hardly have any first-year students in the student council. In other words, we are short-staffed."

The students laughed at Yuki playing dumb. "Whose fault do you think that is?" they joked. Yuki defended the second-year student council members, claiming the problem they had was due to a lack of members in the student council, while peppering her conversation with quips before smoothly transitioning to the main issue.

"However, the moment I become president of the student council, I will meet the demands inserted into the suggestion box," she firmly declared before continuing.

"To be specific, I will be solving at least one suggestion per month. The experience I gain from this will then be used to further implement even more difficult demands. For example, altering or adding new events on field day, expanding upon the school festival's events and length, and increasing free time during field trips. Furthermore, I believe creating new events for Christmas, Halloween, and other holidays would be very fun as well."

Excitement followed the exhilarating proposals for many students, but it came with skepticism as well. "Can she really do that?" wondered more than a few. Nevertheless, Yuki wouldn't be Yuki if she didn't have an answer for that as well. She smiled boldly, her eyes sweeping the crowd before she suddenly declared:

"Furthermore, I believe this is something only I can achieve, utilizing the skills I acquired during my two years in the middle school student council in addition to my achievements and experiences as a member of the student council in high school. And I plan on proving that to all of you soon through my work. Thank you all for listening."

Yuki then bowed once more before being showered with raucous applause and cheers echoing throughout the gymnasium. She raised a hand in response and calmly exited stage left to return to her seat.

"Now, that's cheap. She talked a big game while not giving a single detail about what she's specifically going to do this year. She even made excuses for why we didn't do much about the suggestions in the suggestion box all while making it sound like she was sticking up for our second-year peers...and her argument was convincing, too, which makes it even less fair," Masachika acknowledged with a bitter smirk as he watched her walk away. Touya nodded, his own expression a combination of bitterness and admiration.

"She really knows how to talk a big game and stretch the truth. She's probably better at it than me."

"Ha-ha… Yeah, she has a lot of experience. Plus…I guess she is a bit of a liar as well."

"Wow. Harsh."

They continued to joke back and forth, and Maria checked in with Alisa.

"Alya, are you okay? Are you nervous?"

"I'm fine… Just leave me alone right now."

"Oh my. Alya, come on." Maria pouted at her sister's typical coldhearted response. Masachika smiled a bit at their exchange, and Ayano was called to the podium, but there was a brief stir in the crowd when they saw her projected onto the screen. It was only natural, though. After all, while she may have been wearing the school uniform, her hair was neatly tied back like a maid's. Even her messy bangs, which usually obscured her face, were properly brushed out of the way, exposing her beautiful forehead, and though her expression was as blank as it always was, she seemed highly motivated in a way… Maybe? …Probably not. Regardless, countless guys in the crowd went wild when they saw this girl, who usually never stood out. "Who is that cutie?!" wondered the male students. "Wow! Ayano looks so cute today!" expressed a portion of the female students as well. Ayano was actually extremely popular among a select group of girls at school and was like a school mascot to them.

"I am Ayano Kimishima, a general member of the student council, and outside of school, I am a maid for the Suou household and an attendant of Lady Yuki."

Perhaps the best way to describe the mood in the gymnasium at that moment would be "?!". First, a beautiful girl suddenly appeared, and now she was claiming to be Yuki Suou's attendant? The information overload would be way too much for most people, but the commotion in the crowd didn't stop Ayano.

"I plan on running with Lady Yuki in the election for next school year. I have been by her side ever since we were children, and I plan on using my years' worth of experience as her attendant to support her one hundred percent. She is a wonderful woman of high morals who was gifted with both talent and beauty, and I believe she has what it takes to make the school a better place as the student council president," she stated in a monotone voice as if she were reading from a script. Nevertheless, there wasn't even a hint of exaggeration or deception in her voice as she stared into the crowd with her unclouded eyes, which gave a strange ring of honesty to what she was saying. Before long, the crowd seemed to realize that she was simply stating facts. Besides, Ayano was just speaking her truth, after all.

"Lady Yuki has maintained an excellent academic record every year at this school, and she speaks English at a native level. In addition, she has recently started to study Chinese and is already at the conversational level. Piano, flower arrangement, karate—she is talented in school, the arts, and even sports. And yet never once has she let it go to her head. She always expresses gratitude to those around her and is considerate of others. She even gets me, a maid, something special for my birthday every year."

Ayano then closed her eyes, slightly lifted her chin, and pressed her lips together... It appeared she was trying to look proud, but she wasn't moving any of the muscles in her face. Regardless, a certain group of girls in the crowd squealed with delight at the sight of her incredibly smug (?) expression. Laughter soon followed like a wave throughout the audience. "She's pretty funny." They guffawed. Although Ayano blinked in bewilderment at their unexpected reactions, she proudly and passionately rambled on about Yuki some more. Her unique vibe and way of speaking appeared to be addictive, and before long, everyone was listening on the edge of their seat.

"Yeah, I figured this would happen," muttered Masachika as he listened to Ayano's speech from the wing.

"Yuki gave a very convincing address, and her achievements in middle school really help her case. Then she had Ayano, who has known her since she was a child, essentially vouch for her, strengthening her case." Masachika spoke in a detached tone, praising their rivals after objectively analyzing their speeches. He then looked back at Alisa and said:

"Those speeches were airtight. I can see why Yuki wanted to go first and shoot for a shutout victory."

Masachika calmly acknowledged the severity of the situation.

"...But you think we can win, right?" asked Alisa, showing no signs of concern in her eyes.

"Yep. Thanks to you, of course." Masachika nodded calmly at her unshakable trust, and he smiled with evident satisfaction, relieved that she wasn't letting her rival's speech get to her. He gently placed a hand on her shoulder.

"So you don't need to get competitive or go out there looking for a fight."

They knew their chances of winning against Yuki would be slim if Alisa played by her rival's rules, and Yuki knew that, too, which was probably why she was trying to bait Alisa.

"I know... I'm completely calm now thanks to you."

But Alisa was no longer feeling any sort of rivalry with Yuki.

"Then we're good. Do you remember the official name for these speeches, by the way?"

Alisa smiled a bit at his question.

"Of course. 'Greetings from the Student Council,' right?"

"Exactly. 'Greetings.' While it has become a custom to give policy speeches, that wasn't what this was originally for. First..."

He shifted his gaze toward the students sitting in front of the stage.

"...let's give them a chance to get to know you."

Following those words, Ayano's speech ended at exactly the

238 Alya Sometimes Hides Her Feelings in Russian, Vol. 3

three-minute mark. She bowed and left the podium before meeting up with Yuki, where they both took another bow. Immediately, the gymnasium began to shake...or at least that was what it felt like—a testament to how much applause and cheering followed their bow. The storm continued to overtake the building for a full ten seconds, loud enough and long enough for the emcee to hesitate whether to proceed or wait, until it eventually died down as Yuki and Ayano disappeared into the wing.

"Well, uh... Now let us hear from our student council accountant, Alisa Kujou."

Alisa took to the podium in front of the still extremely excited student body. Only after the silver-haired young lady was projected onto the screen did the audience begin to focus on her. It seemed about 50 percent of the audience was interested, 30 percent was indifferent, and 20 percent felt bad for her. Most of the students were already captivated by Yuki's speech, and there were hardly any students left who were expecting anything from Alisa, let alone wished to support her. It was as if she were standing alone in a foreign land with no one to help her. While the audience's eyes slowly began to focus on her, she opened her mouth and said:

"Спасибо за представление. Я казначей ученического совета Кудзё Алиса. На будущий год я планирую выдвинуться кандидатом на выборах председателя совета. Прошу вас поддержать меня."

Her Russian greeting came out of nowhere and with great force, leaving almost every student dumbfounded in their seat. They all stared at her now as she suddenly fell silent and slowly blinked.

"...My apologies. It seems I was so nervous that I started speaking in Russian."

The crowd erupted in laughter. The princess Alya seemed to be joking around, but she said it with a completely straight face. "Yeah, right!" "Wait. Is she joking?" The crowd went wild, trying to figure out if she was joking. Alisa inwardly sighed in relief, since they'd reacted just as she and her partner hoped they would. This was the secret Masachika had taught Alisa the day before to hook the audience within the first ten seconds.

"First, speak in Russian. This should help relieve some of the tension when your turn comes around, since Yuki and Ayano are going to go before you. You're probably going to be pretty nervous during the ceremony, and you still might be somewhat traumatized after what happened during the afternoon announcements, whether you're aware of it or not. So speak in Russian first until you're completely calm. I mean, it doesn't matter if you say the wrong word or stutter in Russian, since no one's going to understand anyway, right?"

Alisa secretly smiled to herself, relieved that it turned out exactly how Masachika said it would. Then after taking a deep breath, she faced the microphone once more and continued.

"Allow me to introduce myself again. I am the student council's accountant, Alisa Kujou, and I am planning on running for student council president next school year."

But even after taking a deep breath, it still took a lot of courage to say those next words. She was hesitant. She was still wondering if it was really okay to say this. But this was a greeting. This was an opportunity for everyone to get to know Alisa Mikhailovna Kujou.

Which means…I have to be honest. I can't stretch the truth. No bells and whistles. It's time for them to know the real me!

Alisa fired herself up, looked straight ahead, and began her story.

"I transferred to this school last year, and I still have not done enough to earn your praise. My work in the student council has only just begun, and I am not going to lie to you and tell you that I fully understand how difficult being the student council president is. In fact, there are probably many things I lack at the moment that prevent me from becoming the president."

I'm afraid of how they'll react. I'm terrified of revealing my imperfections. But I have someone who believes in me. I have a partner I can count on more than anyone else in the world—someone who knows my flaws and who still agreed to support me and cheer me on. And I believe those words, which is why I've done everything I can to weave my own.

"However, if there is one thing I am proud of..."

Alisa placed a hand on her chest, swept her eyes across the audience, and clearly declared:

"It is that I can work harder than anyone else."

This was one thing she could say with confidence. This was something she knew wasn't a lie.

"My entire life, I have always worked hard to achieve my ideal results. The fact that I have maintained my position as top student in my grade since my transfer should give you an idea of how hard I work."

That was when Alisa suddenly started to feel a bit out of breath, and she realized how awfully shallow her breathing was. Nevertheless, there was no time to worry about that. She couldn't pause. She had to keep talking to her audience.

"Furthermore, I was chosen as the ladies' MVP during field day last year, and I received first place for my class's shop during the school festival...! That was a team effort, of course."

I can hardly breathe! My legs are trembling. I'm having trouble hearing anything... Or perhaps I'm not allowing myself to hear.

"Yes, there are traits and experiences that I would lack as the student council president..."

Alisa suddenly had a flashback of what the audience said during the debate and of her performance during the afternoon announcements. The more she thought about how she *had* to keep talking, the more it felt like her throat was being ripped apart.

I knew I wouldn't be able to do it. Speaking my heart to the audience while looking them in the eyes? Me? The girl who always ran alone, never opening up to anyone? The world looks hazy. My legs are trembling, and I can hardly brea—

Keep your chin up
"Не вешай нос!"

As those Russian words suddenly slipped into her ear, Alisa could feel her five senses sharpen until she realized that she was looking straight down.

Did he just say that in…Russian? Don't tell me he practiced just for this moment?

The instant the thought popped into her mind, she felt the reassuring gaze of someone watching over her from the wing, and at that moment, everything seemed so ridiculous to her. She couldn't help but crack a smile because of how overprotective her partner was. Alisa lifted her head and saw a small commotion in the crowd along with the quizzical looks on their faces. She could…hear them, and at the very same time, she could remember her goal as she faced forward and confidently squared her shoulders.

"My apologies. There are still traits and experiences that I would lack as the student council president. For example, speaking in front of a crowd like this. I became painfully aware of this fault of mine after my somewhat poor performance during the afternoon announcements two days ago."

She honestly was heading in the same direction even now, and she would have continued to go down that path if it wasn't for her partner's help. However…

"However, I am talking to you now. I am speaking my mind to you all with my own words, and I plan to continue improving myself, one fault at a time."

Alisa could feel her words carve themselves into her mind as she spoke.

Oh… I'm not perfect. I was never perfect.

How arrogant I have been. I believed I was better than everyone

else based on my own set of values, and I looked down on those around me because of it. But in reality, there are countless things that other people can do and that I can't. And it isn't just my first actual rival, Yuki, or the first person I've respected, Masachika. Sayaka, Nonoa, Ayano—there are an endless number of people who can do something better than I can. But I never realized that until now. Even if I said I did, I hadn't truly felt that way deep down inside. But I understand now in my heart that there are plenty of people with praiseworthy skills and talents.

I just had to be pushed into a corner like this to finally realize it…

It's funny, but that is also part of what makes me who I am. I'm not good around other people, but my pride wouldn't allow me to admit that was a weakness. On the other hand, having so much pride drove me to overcome my weaknesses, and that is also what makes me Alisa Kujou.

Before Alisa realized it, she was no longer afraid to show her true self, no matter how imperfect. No longer was she thinking about the speech she wrote. Her expression conveyed relief as she faced the audience to open up her heart to them.

"What I can promise you is this: I will continue to work hard to become the ideal student council president, and if I feel like I am not fit to become the president before next year's election…then I will pull out of the race."

She smoothly lowered her head.

"Therefore, please watch over my progress and feel free to point out whatever you think it is I may lack. I will use your input to become the president you want. Thank you all for listening."

Her speech was followed by scattered applause after she removed herself from the podium. While it was far from enthusiastic, the applause was warm and encouraging. Alisa bowed deeply once more before exiting the main stage. Masachika breathed a sigh of relief as he watched and analyzed the situation.

It looks like they really liked her for the most part. She did very well, especially when you consider how Yuki instantly won over the crowd before Alya even got a chance. It looks like taking her speech in a completely different direction from Yuki's really paid off in the end.

"Oh, hey. You did really well out there." He praised Alisa when she returned.

"...You really think so?"

"Definitely. You were really cool," he added, gently patting her on the shoulder until the emotions in her eyes suddenly caught his attention.

"You seem relieved."

"I am… I feel a lot better now."

"…? Really? …Oh, it's my turn."

Masachika looked up as his name was called. He didn't immediately understand exactly what she meant, but the emcee called him to the podium before he could ask about it.

"I guess it's my turn. Be back soon."

"Good luck."

"Yeah, I've got this."

As he headed toward the podium, he glanced back once more at Alisa…and the other two behind her, and smugly declared:

"Time to win this show."

Once he stepped into view, every student locked onto him, seeing as he was the last member of the student council to go. He took his time, slowly walking to the podium, and when he finally reached it, he gazed out over the crowd with a confident grin.

"Hey. I'm student council member Masachika Kuze, and I plan on running with Alisa Kujou during next year's election. Oh, and one more thing…"

He paused, then dramatically swung his arms out and struck a pose. His left arm hovered under his chest with his left hand supporting his right elbow, and he held his right hand straight up in front of his face, closing his eyes. It was a pose only a narcissist with glittering eyes would make, and he was, in fact, sporting a leering grin like one before looking crookedly at the crowd.

"The vice president and true power behind the throne during Yuki Suou's reign in middle school...was me."

The crowd's reaction to the long theatrical pause between sentences and the overdone acting was...

"Pfft!"

"..."

"Okay...?"

...varied. Some laughed and some wondered what was wrong with him, but most people had had no idea. "Oh, he was the vice president?" they said. Masachika blinked a few times in what appeared to be confusion, tilting his head at the lukewarm responses, which he'd actually expected.

"Hmm? Did I just bomb?"

His bold statement made even more people start to laugh. He then cleared his throat, put his puzzled feelings behind him, and continued:

"Anyway, I was Yuki Suou's vice president in middle school and did a lot of work for her behind the scenes. Now, I know what you're thinking: 'Wait. Then why isn't he going to be running with Yuki for next year? Is he cheating on her? He must be cheating on her!'"

The laughter continued to travel like a wave across the crowd.

"'Why,' you ask?!" shouted Masachika, slamming his hands against the podium and silencing every last bit of laughter. He then sharply observed the crowd as they stared, eyes wide.

"Because I dumped her! I dumped Yuki's sorry butt, so it's not even cheating!" he declared with a completely straight face. The audience exploded with laughter once again, and some even jokingly hurled insults at the stage: "You're an asshole!" "Slow down there, man!" And just like that, the rising tension from moments ago had vanished. Masachika raised a hand to calm them, then lowered his voice into something more composed.

"Now, why did I dump Yuki and decide to go with Alya, you might ask? Well, before I answer that, I need to ask you all something first. My fellow students, what kind of person do you think deserves to be the president of the student council? The most gifted student? *I* don't think so. I think you have to be someone who, above all, attracts others… Yeah, I know what you want to say. 'That sounds like Yuki to me,' right? I know, I know. Just hear me out first, okay?"

His playful remark brought some laughter back into the crowd in addition to dispelling any doubts that arose.

"First, we need to talk about what specifically makes someone magnetic, and that is someone who is genuine, someone who listens to others' opinions, and someone who works hard. They're the kind of person you look at and say, 'Wow, they're working really hard, so I should work harder, too!' And most importantly, they have a pure heart. They will not hurt others to satisfy their own selfish desires. If anything, they will put others' wants before their own. People tend to gather around selfless individuals like that, and I think people who are able to get along with most of their peers deserve to become the student council president."

After offering a coherent explanation, Masachika slightly changed his tone and asked:

"With that in mind…how did you all feel about Alya's speech? I hardly had any say in it, by the way. Oh, except for the Russian bit in the beginning. I put her up to it because I honestly thought it'd be hilarious."

His confession was immediately followed by voices of surprise mixed with laughter in the crowd. "Was it really necessary to admit that?!" "That was your doing?!" Masachika waved his hand dismissively.

"There's no way Alya would have done something like that on

her own… Anyway, back on topic. When I heard Alya give her speech from the stage wing, I was honestly like, 'Wow, awkward…'"

The crowd began to buzz somewhat after he criticized his own partner's speech.

"But at the same time, I felt she was genuine and extremely straightforward. Wouldn't you all agree?"

After a good portion of the audience nodded in agreement, he approvingly nodded back and continued.

"Alya is an honest person. She's genuine. She isn't going to present herself as something she's not or claim she can do something she can't just to get people to like her and vote for her. And she's a hard worker, as she mentioned herself. She's extremely flexible and willing as well, to the point that she used the ridiculous hook I suggested to get the crowd laughing," he said in a joking manner, but his gaze narrowed seriously after that.

"Those are the traits that drew me to her and the reasons I want to support her. That is why I chose Alya over Yuki, and that is why I want you all to do the same as well."

He looked at the crowd before almost immediately adding:

"But, well, I guess it is pretty hard to put your trust into one guy's personal opinion. I'm sure some of you are thinking, 'Sounds like a matter of taste, if you ask me.'"

He shrugged and nodded at them as though these hypothetical skeptics had a point, then raised an index finger into the air.

"But let me tell you something. Not an opinion. A fact."

After pausing and waiting for everyone to focus on him…he played his trump card.

"Once Alya becomes student council president…Sayaka Taniyama and Nonoa Miyamae will be joining the student council as well."

The hard-to-believe announcement was followed by a brief moment of silence until a stir quickly rippled through the audience.

"We have already received their firm commitment. Can you all believe it? Once rivals during a fierce debate, and yet they are now talking about creating a new student council together. Alya has done something that Yuki and I couldn't back in middle school."

Masachika glanced over at Yuki in the wing as the audience sat in bewilderment and doubt.

"Yuki mentioned a few moments ago that she would be the only one who could change the school thanks to her experience over the years in the student council, but is that even true? In addition to Alya, you get Sayaka and Nonoa, two talented former members of the student council who were Yuki's most formidable opponents in middle school, and you get me—someone who has just as much experience in the student council as Yuki. So I ask you: Do you really believe she is the only person who can change this school?"

Students in the crowd exchanged glances as though he had a point, but Masachika wasn't done yet.

"Think back to what Yuki said during her speech: We don't have enough first-year students working in the student council this year, so we are severely limited to what we can do. But how does a lack of first-year students even limit us this much? The answer is simple: Any second-year student who could have helped already dropped out of the student council after losing in the election. Only one pair of talented individuals running for student council president and vice president ends up staying in the student council while first-year students, who lead the next generation, slowly drop out after each debate. This has been true every year there has been a student council as far as I know, and this is why the student council always suffers from short-staffing."

It was a hard truth known by all, but it was so normal to them that nobody actually thought deeply about it.

"But if we had more second-year students contributing in the student council, then surely we could stably manage it without being influenced by uncertain factors like first-years, right? And only a student council centered around Alya can do that. As student council president, she will be able to create a dream team of former presidential and vice-presidential candidates, and to me, that is the ideal student council."

Numerous students expressed excitement over his plan of having former rivals join and run the student council together. Their eyes sparkled at the dreamlike idea, which had never been done before. And yet Masachika still wasn't finished.

"Of course, Yuki and Ayano are no exception. When Alya becomes president, I am going to have them join us as well. After all, you heard Yuki. You saw how passionate she was about reforming the school. Even if Yuki did lose the race, I am sure she would be *thrilled* to help us if it meant making the school a better place!" he suggested with a smirk, bringing not only laughter but also assurance, since people now knew that no matter what happened, Yuki would be on their side. In the midst of their laughter, Masachika overdramatically bowed humorously one last time.

"I apologize for how long that was, but we need your help if we are going to make this the best student council you've ever seen. Thank you all for listening."

But the final surprise occurred the moment he stepped down from the podium. While he began his journey back to stage right, Alisa emerged from the wing…with Sayaka and Nonoa in tow.

"Hmm? Is that…? What the…?!"

"No way?!"

"Hey, look!"

"Whoa! Seriously?!"

The biggest surprise of all was proof of what Masachika had claimed. Alisa, Sayaka, and Nonoa stood together side by side before bowing once more to the crowd. They were instantly showered with explosive applause and cheering. The students had no idea what the agreement between Alisa and Sayaka actually had been like, but that didn't matter. Two candidates who they believed would never work in the student council had now joined hands with Alisa and Masachika, and that fact alone was enough to get people excited.

"Alya, you earned this applause," he said to Alisa by his side.

"…!"

He heard her breath catch in her throat and made a conscious decision not to look at her. The four of them began to return to the wing, but the applause and cheering did not end, and it was just as impressive as the reception their rivals received.

"Good work, guys."

"…Thanks."

"That was pretty dope, Kuze."

"…"

While most of them shared praise for one another, Sayaka, on the other hand, was wearing a complex expression and looking away. She resettled her glasses in silence, then stated in a flat voice:

"We're even now, right?"

"…Yes, we're even. Thank you," replied Alisa, bowing in gratitude as Sayaka's eyes wandered uncomfortably.

"As I told you all before, I have no intention of cheering either of you on, let alone supporting your campaign. While I will keep my promise of joining the student council if you become president, I will not help you during the election any more than this."

"I know. But I am going to continue to work hard…until I win you over as well."

"…You don't say," Sayaka bluntly replied before turning her back on Alisa and heading toward the side door in the rear. However, she suddenly stopped in her tracks.

"I'm looking forward to it," she muttered over her shoulder before promptly heading out the door.

"Good luck, you two. Like, I can't promise I'll vote for you, but I'll definitely help out if Lissa becomes the student council president," commented Nonoa cheekily, and she followed after Sayaka.

"Oh, cool. Thanks."

"'L-Lissa'?"

After watching in bewilderment as they left, Alisa's expression relaxed, and she looked over at the other stage wing, staring at Yuki with a fierce gaze. *This is why I want to become the student council president.* That was what her eyes were telling Yuki.

It might have started as a personal goal for only myself, but now I have to do it for Masachika, Sayaka, Nonoa—for the people who believe in me. That's why I can't lose, and I won't let your determination discourage me any longer.

Yuki confidently smiled back. *You can't afford to lose? Well, neither can I. That's the spirit. Now come at me.*

They stared each other down for another few seconds until Maria spoke up, snapping Alisa out of it. Yuki watched Alisa talk with Maria and Masachika with Touya as her lips twisted into a bitter smile.

"You got me," she muttered.

It was a battle she could have won. The disparity between their achievements and popularity alone was enough for Yuki to win, but she still went out of her way to crush Alisa in their skirmish during the afternoon announcements. It was only natural that she would win, and yet it somehow ended in a draw. No. While they received essentially the same amount of applause, Masachika's and Alisa's speeches had better hooks and were something people would be talking about the next day. So even if it sounded like a draw right now, Yuki, in reality, had just suffered a loss.

"Wow, I honestly wasn't expecting them to get those two to help out," muttered Chisaki in admiration.

"...Yes, that was definitely unexpected," agreed Yuki. It was completely unexpected...and it was most likely a consequence of Yuki's actions as well. The afternoon announcement—the battle she dragged Alisa into to break her mentally and hurt her chances in the election—ended up becoming what led Masachika and Alisa to asking those two for their help.

I went too far...and it ended up highlighting her integrity...

To make matters worse, her brother was now serious about this because of what she'd done. *So this is what they mean when they say, "Too much scheming will be the schemer's downfall," huh?* thought Yuki, grinding her teeth when Ayano suddenly bowed before her.

"You have my deepest apologies, Lady Yuki. If only I had done a better job of—"

"You didn't do a single thing wrong, Ayano. This is on me. I went overboard with my schemes and ended up misreading my brother."

She shook her head, cutting Ayano off.

Yes, I should have chosen to go after Alisa instead of reading too much into it. If I had done that, none of this would have happened. I assumed she would have passively gone for a draw. No... My overconfidence tricked me into believing that was her only option. I thought I would be able to win if we fought head-to-head, even if I was up against my brother. And my arrogance led me to believe his threats were merely bluffs, which made me confident I could easily crush them.

He saw right through me...and correctly predicted every single move I made.

He'd seen it all coming and still purposely made a big deal about threatening them. Yuki most likely would have been extremely wary of him if he hadn't had done that. "Strange. He's acting far too calm. What is he scheming?" she wondered.

It appears my dear brother was one step ahead of me the entire time... Ha-ha-ha. He really is amazing.

And yet, despite losing, Yuki felt oddly refreshed. Of course, she wanted to win, but at the same time, she didn't want him to lose. She wanted the brother she'd looked up to and respected since childhood to be just as amazing as she remembered him.

Ack. I can't be thinking like this.

She wanted to defeat her brother, but she didn't want him to be defeated, either. Though her feelings contradicted each other, this was how she truly felt. However, feeling this good about losing would surely cause her to lose again. That was why she had to seal those feelings away once and for all.

"You may have won this time, but you won't be so lucky next time." She grinned with confidence that she was going to win.

Chisaki's eyes wandered like those of someone who saw something they weren't supposed to as she quietly slipped away. Ayano watched the other girl leave out of the corner of her eye, then whispered to Yuki:

"Lady Yuki."

"Yes?"

"You really sounded like one badass last boss just now."

Ayano held her hands together in front of her chest, her eyes sparkling as if to say, "I finally get it!"

"You've got to be kidding me. The one time I wasn't even trying to…," mumbled Yuki, rolling her eyes at her partner.

Chin Up

"…It would have been a lot cooler if I'd accomplished my goal, too, though."

"It really would have been."

Masachika's and Alisa's voices echoed in the empty hallway. Following the closing ceremony, numerous students—mainly their classmates—teased them and complimented them on their speeches, effectively destroying the communication barrier between Alisa and her peers. Only after finishing homeroom and having their last student council meeting did they finally get to see the list of students who had the highest grades posted on the bulletin board in the hallway. Glittering in the top right corner was Alisa's name, to no one's surprise, and beside her name was Yuki's. A total of thirty names of the highest achievers were listed, but…Masachika's name was nowhere to be found.

"Number thirty-three… Not the most exciting result," uttered Masachika with a begrudging smile as he looked down at the report card in his hand. It was a major accomplishment when you consider the fact that he was ranked 202 out of 254 after their last midterms, but he was six points short of achieving his goal and making it into the top thirty.

"Well, I guess not everything always goes the way you want, huh?" he admitted.

"…You don't seem that disappointed." Alisa frowned.

"Eh. It is what it is." He nodded half-heartedly. It was true. He wasn't that disappointed. In fact, a part of him was actually pretty happy he didn't make it into the top thirty.

Because I hate to say this, but I'd be lying if I said I was completely focused on studying for the exams...

He was well aware that he hadn't put 100 percent of himself into studying during exam week. He'd lost concentration multiple times, which made him far less efficient. There was even a part of him that started to make compromises like, "Yeah, this should be enough." That was why he was happy he didn't achieve his goal, because if he had managed to half-ass his way into the top thirty, he would have probably stopped taking life seriously again.

"Heh! It looks like this genius does have his limitations, after all."

He brushed back his bangs in a suave manner.

"Please tell me you didn't just call yourself a genius."

Alisa stared at him scornfully with a chilling gaze.

"Eh. I just didn't work hard enough. That's all. I'm sorry I didn't do better." He shrugged with a less jovial expression.

"It's fine…"

"No, it's not. I need to do better. I'm going to take it more seriously next time," he declared, looking earnestly at the list on the wall.

"Do you have any regrets?" she asked briefly.

"No."

"Then there's nothing to worry about."

She turned around as though there was nothing left to discuss in regard to their grades.

"Let's go home. I'm kind of tired after everything that happened today."

"Yeah, let's go home…"

They walked side by side, but his eyes were wandering as if something were bothering him still.

"…Hey, Alya."

"Yes?"

"Uh… What are you going to do about that bet we made about my scores? You know, the thing about the loser granting the winner's wish. You need to make a wish."

Alisa stopped in her tracks…before almost immediately moving forward again and swiftly looking away from him.

"…I'll think about it."

"Didn't you say you already knew what you wanted me to do? I totally remember you saying something in Russian."

"Oh, that? …I was just talking to myself," mumbled Alisa, continuing to avoid his eyes.

"<Hmph. I honestly thought that you would…>"

She continued to mumble complaints to herself in Russian, and though vague, Masachika had a decent idea what she was angry about.

Now I get it… She didn't think she was going to win…

He was embarrassed that she'd had such high expectations for him, and he felt guilty that he'd let her down.

Uh… Oh, great. The only words I can vaguely remember are "<first name.>"

He was so uncomfortable that he started to think back to what she'd said, racking his brain to figure out what she could have meant until he reached a single conclusion.

In other words…that's what she wants? But…this is going to be stupidly embarrassing if I'm wrong. It'd make me look like a complete narcissist.

The internal conflict made him feel like his brain was being twisted…until he finally made up his mind. He justified it by deciding that this was also punishment for losing the bet and pocketed his pride.

"Hey…Alya?"

"…?"

"We were officially recognized as running mates for the upcoming election after finishing our speeches, right? So…I thought maybe we could both call each other by our first names now to show everyone how close we've gotten…"

Masachika internally cringed at how pathetic he sounded. He couldn't even face her. He kept his eyes straight ahead and quietly waited with bated breath. After a few seconds, which strangely felt like forever, Alisa responded softly:

"…Sure, why not."

"Huh? R-really?"

"Y-yeah, sure."

Not once did they look at each other during the exchange until Alisa suddenly cleared her throat, drawing his attention.

"Okay, so…"

She glanced at him out of the corner of her eye and hesitantly said:

"Masachika…"

"Y-yep…"

His entire body started to tingle. It wasn't just having her call him by his first name but her slightly bashful behavior as well.

"Th-that… That sounds natural. Let's do this," Masachika said only a bit reluctantly.

"R-really? Then I guess I'll start calling you by your first name from now on…," she mumbled, swiftly averting her gaze. The awkwardness was too much for a young teenage boy to bear, so when the front door finally came into view, he shouted in a needlessly loud voice:

"Oh yeah! We have to change out of our slippers!"

"O-oh, right."

Though it was something obvious that someone would usually get called out for, Alisa nodded as though it didn't bother her. They simultaneously reached for their shoes, which were side by side, before they began awkwardly chatting once more. Their conversation as they walked home together could only be described as neutral, but it was a sweet moment of youth—an uncomfortable moment that would make any lonely spectator jealous. Not once did their eyes meet. Not once did Alisa say Masachika's name, nor Masachika hers...until eventually they reached the fork in the road where their paths split, and they came to a stop.

"Well...this is my road."

"Yeah... See you later—"

That was when he suddenly realized something. The following day was the first day of summer break, which meant that "later" was going to be a long way away...at this rate, at least.

"See you..."

"Y-yeah..."

They still didn't make eye contact. Alisa had started walking toward the crosswalk, stepping onto the road, when...

"Alya!"

Masachika almost reflexively called out to her, but when he saw her turn around out of the corner of his eye, he nervously looked away.

"Like...I know it's summer break and all, but we still have a lot of work to do for the upcoming election. Considering the fact that Yuki and Ayano are together twenty-four hours a day, we should probably...," he stammered, staring off into the distance.

"We should probably...meet up a few times during summer break. Don't you think?"

And with that, he had reached his embarrassment threshold for the year. He could sense Alisa standing in front of him after coming back, but he was still unable to look her in the eye. In fact, it took everything he had not to just scream and run away.

"Masachika."

He heard Alisa say his name so close he could almost feel her breath.

"Hmm?" he replied, still staring at the ground. He could tell she was smiling at how pathetic he was being (he was well aware of it).

^{Keep your chin up}
"Не падай духом!"

Masachika looked up, discovering Alisa innocently smiling back at him.

Afterword

This will be our 3rd time meeting. Light novelist Sunsunsun here (aka the most loved man in Japan by the number 3).

I know you may be wondering what I'm rambling on about, but just give me a moment to explain. Kadokawa Sneaker Bunko, which published my debut novel (the first volume of this series), is celebrating its 33rd anniversary this year, and March (3rd month) of the 3rd year of Reiwa (2021) marked my 3rd year since I started writing web novels online. Plus, I was 3 to the 3rd power years old when I started, if we want to get technical. See what I mean? I wasn't exaggerating when I said I was loved by the number 3. Oh, and did you know if you write my name in Japanese (さん), it could also mean 3 as well? That's three 3s in a row! Anyway, before I forget, I wanted to mention that this series got 9th place in Takarajimasha Inc.'s 2022 light novel rankings (Kono Light Novel ga Sugoi! 2022). And what's 3 × 3? Plus, guess who got 6th place in "Favorite Female Character"? Alya. That's another multiple of 3 and— (The rest was omitted for your sake.)

Anyway, this is the third volume of *Alya Sometimes Hides Her Feelings in Russian*—another milestone. A lot of work went into this, and my editor seemed to have put a lot of work into it as well, because he asked a certain famous someone to recommend and promote my series. Who, you may wonder? Miki Yoshikawa, that's who. The extremely famous manga artist known for romantic comedies such as *Flunk Punk Rumble* and *Yamada-kun and the Seven Witches*, and she is currently working on *A Couple of Cuckoos*—a huge hit I'm sure you're aware of. I can't believe it. I have read all three of these series, so I'm sure you can guess how nervous I am. My favorite character is Hana Adachi, by the way. I love female characters who are fighters and very strong, despite not looking it... Hmm? Hold up. I never really thought about it, but was I influenced by Hana Adachi when I came up with the Sarashina family in my works? ...Hold up. Now that I think about it, I vaguely remember writing a web novel in which the heroine had the last name Adachi, and she studied under the Sarashina family... Hmm? And I had this strange rule where I would only use plant names to name these strong female martial artists... Was that also me being subconsciously influenced by Hana (*hana* = Japanese for *flower*) Adachi? ...The subconscious mind is an amazing thing. I'm sure a lot of it was coincidence, but I feel like this is, in a way, proof that people are influenced by experiences and things they've seen in the past when they create something new. Eh. Whatever. I guess it's not important.

Anyway, never in my wildest dreams did I imagine I would have someone who had been famous for her romantic comedies even before I ever started writing comment on and recommend my work. This is a web novelist's dream come true. Seriously, I'm in shock. All I have is love and appreciation for Miki Yoshikawa, who agreed to do it, and my editor, who set me up with her. Thank you very much.

Now you see why this novel ended up being so long at over 150,000 Japanese characters. I couldn't put out something half-assed when Miki Yoshikawa was going to be commenting on my work, so I put everything I had into this novel and then some. It ended up being one and a half times longer than the first novel. What is wrong with me? And this is after a lot was cut and edited, too. And after all that, it was still 150,000 Japanese characters long. The only reason the book doesn't look like a giant brick is because of the editor's magic. I feel really bad for him, to be honest. I'll make sure to take note of his struggles while I write the next volume. I'll probably just take note and do nothing about it, though.

The afterword this time ended up being four pages. Maybe this was a side effect of the editor's magic? And, well, I guess since it's going to be four pages long, I better start talking about the novel itself. I know I talked about the legal speed limit or something during the afterword in the first novel, but last time, I slammed on the gas and went way over the speed limit, and my editor didn't get mad at me, so I figured I'd go as far as I could this time. In fact, I came at this afterword with the mindset that I'd lose if I took it even remotely seriously...so I was never expecting to be asked to write more. Hmm... I don't have enough gasoline in the form of topics to speed my way through four pages, though...or so I thought. Wow. Would you look at that? I'm already out of pages. I wonder why... It was because I rambled about Miki Yoshikawa for way too long, wasn't it? I know. My bad.

Now let's talk about this novel... Oh, I know. Masha's homeroom teacher. While it wasn't touched upon in the story, Masha and her similarly bubbly mother met with her homeroom teacher for the student-parent-teacher conference...and, well, let's just say it must have been hell for that teacher. Yep. That should be enough about the novel itself.

Before we go, I would like to thank my editor, Natsuki Miyakawa, for all his help these past three novels...especially this time. In addition, I would like to also thank the following people:

Momoco for the godlike illustrations she did for me, even though she is extremely busy.

Sumire Uesaka for doing the voice of Alya again, Kouhei Amasaki for doing the voice of Masachika, and Fumihiko Tachiki for doing the narration for the commercial.

Kurone Mishima and Azuri Hyuga for doing guest illustrations.

Miki Yoshikawa for promoting my series, even though I'm still a novice.

(I have just realized what a dream team I've been blessed with after looking at all their names lined up like this. This is not something someone who just had their debut not too long ago deserves. The overpowered members continue to join the party until the rookie hero stops thinking for himself altogether. That's what this feels like.)

Ahem. And last but not least, everyone involved in creating this novel, and every one of you who read it.

I thank you all from the bottom of my heart. Thank you very much! I hope we can meet again in Volume 4. Until then.

Moving forward, I want to make Feelings in Russian even more exciting. ☺

momo